William Joseph Roberts

Presents:

What If...
Walls Could Talk

Three Ravens Publishing
Chickamauga, GA USA

MEN (ALMOST ALWAYS) IN BLACK by Jonathan Maberry, Copyright © 2025 by Jonathan Maberry

Credits:
Cover design by: J. F. Posthumus
Edited by: Jenny E. Wren & William Joseph Roberts
William Joseph Roberts Presents: What If… Walls Could Talk
by William Joseph Roberts /Three Ravens Publishing – 1st edition, 2025

Ebook ISBN: 978-1-966507-04-8
Trade Paperback ISBN: 978-1-966507-05-5

Table of Contents

What If…

By: William Joseph Roberts

Once upon a time, in the Gilbert Junior Highschool library I found a copy of Hawksbill Station by Robert Silverberg. This was same library where I found my first Conan collection hidden away behind other books and fell in love with Sword and Sorcery. I sought similar works, snagging and devouring whatever I could. I quickly expanded my reading list to authors such as Ben Bova, Isaac Asimov, Jody Lynn Nye, Mike Resnick, Robert Heinlein, etc after talking my mom into taking me to the big libraries in Williamson and Logan.

Speculative fiction has been one of my favorites for decades because it can leave you wondering **What If**… about so many scenarios and thinking through alternate possibilities. Those possibilities open a rabbit hole of ideas that you can explore and potentially learn something useful from.

And the possibilities that you can create yourself are virtually endless. From alternate history to paranormal or even far reaching into the future.

One specific story that comes to mind that has always stuck with me and left me wondering what else the character could have done is **"In the Walls of Eryx"** **by** H.P. Lovecraft and Kenneth J. Sterling in the late 1930s. It is a story about a prospector on the planet Venus who becomes trapped in an invisible maze while working for a mining company.

Just the fact that they came up with this concept in the 30s had my mind spinning. Yeah, I know there were others with far reaching concepts before, like **"The Time Machine"** by H.G. Wells in 1895, or the 1902 silent film **"A Trip to the Moon"**. But the concept of being trapped and helpless in an alien trap on Venus had me enraptured.

What is the maze made of, how deep into the soil does it extend, why couldn't you climb over, etc.

But that's the primary reason I love speculative fiction. It gets the gears spinning, thinking through other possibilities that the author may or may not have thought of, sending me on research tangents while adding fuel and fodder to my own writing slush pile.

Seneca Tower

By: Reggi Broach

Judge Sanderson raised his gavel. "I'm sorry Ms. Vanderhaven. The Johnsonville Historical Society has failed to produce sufficient grounds for halting the demolition of Seneca Tower. Extreme age is not sufficient grounds. This court finds in favor of the defendant, Myanmar Corporation. If you can come up with anything more, you may present it to me on Monday, otherwise, demolition can commence after midnight on Tuesday morning. Case dismissed."

The sound of the gavel banging on its base punctuated the finality of their case.

?

Late that Friday afternoon Ms. Vanderhaven met with Emmett and Katherine Lyles in the lobby of Seneca Tower. She went over the court case with them and sadly explained the situation.

"I'm sorry, Mr. and Mrs. Lyles, but this building just doesn't meet the requirements of the Historical Society. The only requirement it meets is that it's old. Nothing significant occurred here. We don't have any record of celebrities living here, no politicians, war heroes, nobody of any significance came from here." The older woman gave the couple an apologetic smile. She hugged a file folder and manila envelope against her chest. Most people would carry a laptop or other electronic device, but she preferred to make notes with pencil and paper.

"Ms. Vanderhaven, please, this building is over a hundred years old. We just need more time to check into everything," Mrs. Lyles pleaded. "This building, although it's horribly run-down, was beautiful in its earlier days. My brother and I grew up here. This place is special to us."

Ms. Vanderhaven glanced around the building's entry hall. It looked horrid now, but it was likely a very stylish building in its early days. The smell of excrement, mold, mildew, and perhaps decaying rodents stung her nose. "If you can get me something by Monday morning, I can get Judge Sanderson to issue an injunction against the Myanmar Corporation and stop the demolition."

"I'll keep looking. Thank you for your help." Mrs. Lyles dabbed her moist eyes with a tissue. Her husband pressed his hand against her back to encourage her to leave.

Ms. Vanderhaven was glad to leave the horrible smells and the dangerous building behind. She swung the front door open and stepped carefully down the front steps. With every step her shoes ground and crunched on the broken concrete. She slipped a pair of sunglasses on to protect her eyes from the late afternoon sun.

Mr. Lyles held the door open and again encouraged his wife to leave the building. He didn't have the same ties to this building that his wife had, but he was doing what he could to indulge her. He followed her from the building in time to see a limousine pull up in front.

The sleek black car seemed out of place in the surrounding slums. They stopped to watch the car. The chauffeur jumped from the car and opened the rear door for his passenger. An expensive, shiny black men's shoe landed on the sidewalk in front of the little group who had just exited Seneca Tower. A tall, thin man with tan skin and salt-and-pepper hair stood in front of them. He fastened the buttons of his double-breasted black suit. "Excuse me, do you represent the Myanmar Corporation?" The man's accent revealed his Hispanic background.

Ms. Vanderhaven answered first. "Um, no, I'm sorry. My name is Ms. Vanderhaven and I'm with the Johnsonville Historical Society. The Lyles were trying to stop this building from being destroyed. I'm afraid I've been unable to offer any help on the matter."

"I too would like to stop the destruction of this… beautiful old building. My name is Espinoza Castillo. I specialize in acquiring and restoring old buildings, among other ventures."

"Espinoza? I think I remember you. Didn't you live on the fifth floor of Seneca Tower?" Mrs. Lyles asked.

"Why, yes, I did. Forgive me, Senora, but what is your name?"

"My name is—was Katie Lee. I go by Katherine Lyles now. This is my husband, Emmett Lyles."

Espinoza stuck out his hand to Emmett. "It is a pleasure to meet you. May I ask what you've done so far to stop the destruction of such a… fine piece of architecture?" he asked as he glanced at the dilapidated structure.

Ms. Vanderhaven answered. "I've been looking for a reason to turn this building into a historical monument. Was the building built by a renowned architect? Did some historically relevant event happen here, or did some important person live here? So far, we haven't been able to find any such qualification."

"Let me see what I can do. Do you have a card, Ms. Vanderhaven?"

"Oh, of course." Ms. Vanderhaven scrounged in her purse, pulled out a card, and handed it to him. "As I told the Lyles, we have until Monday morning to get a judge to stop the demolition from going forward. I'll keep looking on my end, but please call me if you come up with anything."

Espinoza pulled a shiny card holder from his pocket. He removed two business cards from it and tucked Ms. Vanderhaven's card into it. He handed one of his cards to the Lyles. "Katie, it is good to see you again. Please call me if you can find anything that would help. If you need help to look into this, I will do all that I can to help. This building is my top priority now." He handed the second card to Ms. Vanderhaven. "Thank you both for caring enough about this monument to our history. I hope to hear from you soon or I hope I will find something to help." In a quick yet elegant motion, Mr. Castillo was back in his car and on his way.

The Lyles and Ms. Vanderhaven left the neighborhood in sullen moods. There had to be some way to restore the building to life.

"Hey, did you guys hear that?" One yelled.

"Hear what?" Six yelled down from nearly the top of the building.

Two whimpered. "We're going to die. I'm too young to die. The paint on my walls is barely dry, and the carpet on my floors is still plush and thick."

"Oh, shut up, Two. Your last coat of paint is twelve years old and so is your carpet. My paint is only nine years old, and we pulled out the carpet on all the floors except yours ten years ago. It was harboring fleas." One retorted.

"Hear what?" Six yelled again. "All I can hear is Two whining. I did see that fancy-schmancy dude in the limo, but I couldn't make out what they were saying."

"We are going to meet the great architect in the sky next week." Four spoke in his bold preacher's voice.

A string of high-pitched Spanish echoed through the building.

"English, Five, English. For crying out loud. Ever since those Hispanic families moved onto the fifth floor, she can't seem to remember to speak English." Six yelled.

"I saw that man, the one in the car. His name was Espinoza. That one was so sweet as a boy, but he was a mean one once he got into his teens. Maybe he made good for himself if he's trying to save us." Her voice spoke in Spanish-flavored English.

A soft voice came from three. "I remember that woman who was in here, Katie. She was a hard worker, and so were her parents. I'm glad they made it out of this neighborhood. Katie was valedictorian when she graduated from high school and went on to college. Her parents were so proud of her and her brother. I remember hearing them say that her little brother is some big-time lawyer across town now. He does corporate law or something. I really don't know why she cares what happens to us. We're falling apart. Whatever Myanmar Corp is going to build in our place will be new and fresh, not old, and smelly."

"Who are you calling old and smelly?" One snarked.

"We are! All of us. You stink too. You just can't smell it anymore. The building superintendent lived on your floor and kept all those air fresheners in the building so people would think the building was being cleaned and kept up." Six rebutted.

Two whimpered again. "What are we going to do? That corporation is trying to kill us."

"There is a time to live and a time to die. This would seem to be our time to die. We must prepare our hearts to meet our maker and confess all our sins." Four stated somberly.

"What hearts? What sins? We're a building, not people. Four, you're just as bad as Five speaking Spanish. Just because that street preacher lived up there doesn't make you a preacher too." Six snarked.

Two whimpered again, "We're all about to die and you're yelling at us."

"Six is just trying to give us the honest truth, albeit a bit bluntly." Three commented. "By the way, is Seven okay? I haven't heard anything from him."

"Muh muff-fuh nd muh errs er tpdp.—kt tick er err wut yrr syn."

"What was that? What did he say?" One asked.

"I don't know. He hasn't said much of anything in years. I think he forgot how to talk," Six grumbled.

"It's all those drugs, that vile loud sinful music, and the booze his tenants kept in there. They were dealing out of those apartments, you know. It's no wonder Seven can't talk anymore. Those drug dealers were hiding drugs under the floor, in the walls, the air vents, and in the ceiling joists. I think there were times they hid stuff on the roof." Four's voice resounded in a mournful tone.

"Yeah, I'll bet you know all about that, don't you Preacher Four." Six snarked again.

Three 's framework creaked in the wind. "Six, leave him alone. That poor street preacher was trying to warn people about those drugs. He was a great influence on the children in this building."

"All the children except his own. His boy was the worst," Six retorted.

"His father tried to teach him, reason with him and spent many long hours praying for him. You could hear that man's prayers echoing through the halls and air vents in the wee hours of the morning." Four responded sadly.

"The super tried to shut him up many times, but he just kept right on praying. But that preacher was no better than his son. He skipped out on three months' rent," One added.

"I really don't know what happened to the preacher. He just up and disappeared one day. I remember he was filled with righteous indignation the day he disappeared. I never saw his son again either."

Seven mumbled excitedly.

"If you can't talk normally, Seven, just shut it," Six yelled.

"Oo—oo, remember that little old lady, Miss Maggie? She used to watch those murder mysteries all the time, like Matlock, Murder She Wrote, Columbo—" Two began.

"Yeah, yeah, we got the point. What about her?" Six interrupted.

"Maybe we could solve the mystery of what happened to the Street Preacher and his son."

The arches in Three's door frames raised. "We're a building that's about to be torn down. Why should we care? Our former tenants, except for little Miss Katie, don't care about us. Why care about them?"

Four groaned as his floor and ceiling joists sagged. "The Street Preacher cared about this building and the tenants. He fixed Miss Maggie's cable when the super couldn't be bothered. He read Bible stories to the kids on Five and helped them with their homework. That man was always cleaning stuff up around the building and even did some painting."

"That's because he was a little short on his rent. The building super gave him some odd jobs here and there, but I guess he got too old and just couldn't handle it anymore so he up and disappeared." One remarked.

Two whimpered again. "Please can't we re-enact the crime of the street preacher's disappearance? I don't know what else to do except worry about… the end."

Four creaked in anticipation. "I for one would like to know what happened to them. I'll go along, Two."

Three joined in. "I've got nothing better to do."

"Si, Si, I will help."

One groaned, "I suppose I have more knowledge on the matter than most so I guess I will help."

"Six? Please say you'll help too." Two pleaded.

"I'm just going to sit here and laugh at all of you."

Seven groaned, creaked, and muttered a long line of unintelligible words.

Two creaked slightly. "I think he's in too."

True to his word Six laughed. "Like he's going to be a lot of help." Something above him shifted and popped. "Ow, Seven, watch what you're doing. Your floor ends where my ceiling begins, mister."

Another string of words erupted from Seven.

Two's paint peeled slightly. "I think it's a good thing I couldn't understand what he said this time." Moving on she asked, "Who remembers the day the preacher disappeared?"

Four sighed. "I do, but it started with his son. Every week that no good kid would go up to visit Seven. I can't say for certain what he was doing up there. I wouldn't want to gossip and start rumors, but when he would come back down, he was in a really good mood, and he'd be singing some song about Heaven on the Seventh Floor."

One laughed heartily. "He was up there seeing Pretty Penny. I bet that was costing him a pretty penny. That kid didn't have a dime to his name."

"What are you saying?" Four demanded.

"Penny was a prostitute. She was closely associated with those drug dealers across the hall."

Four's floors creaked and groaned. "Oh, my, that explains so much. That preacher's kid was all the time running errands right after his trips up to Seven, always switching bags and making more trips up to Seven. I knew he was up to no good. His daddy found one of those bags one day. I think it was the day he left. He opened the bag and then he turned white as a sheet. He grabbed that bag and stormed out of here. That was the last time I saw him."

"MM—mm ruh rappin. MM—mm ruh rappin." Seven squeaked and creaked excitedly.

"Ah, ow, Seven, I said cut it out. Your floor joists are poking me again." Six snapped.

Two squealed with glee. "Oh, goody, I think we're getting somewhere. One, did you see him come back?"

"Yeah, his kid met him on the street. Oh, were they yelling at each other? I have never seen that kid so beside himself. He punched his old man in the face and knocked him onto the sidewalk. When he saw his old man on the ground, he just took off running. I never saw that kid again."

"What happened to the Preacher?"

"He came back inside, but— everybody be quiet, the security officers are coming."

"Why should we be quiet? They're just going to tear us down in a few days. I say we keep talking all we want." Six snidely commented.

"I thought you didn't want to help solve this mystery." Two retorted.

"I don't care about solving your mystery. I just don't want anybody telling me what to do."

"Shut up, or they'll have ghost hunters or something poking and prodding us all over the place." One ordered.

"Oh!" Two's paint peeled a little more.

Three whispered quickly, "Ghost hunters might spare our lives a while longer."

?

A couple of security guards approached the chain-link fence put up by the demolition company. "Joe, are you sure you want to stay inside there tonight?"

"Yeah, Trey, it's fine. It's not like it's haunted or anything." The two men laughed. "You know how it is when a building gets this close to demolition. You get some bleeding heart wanting to come in and chain themselves to the building so it can't be destroyed or treasure hunters looking for whatever might bring them a buck."

Trey shook his head. "I'm sorry, they don't pay me enough to deal with that stuff. I say just lock it up and let them deal with it in the morning."

Joe grinned. "You never know, I might find some of that treasure while I'm keeping other people out."

"Good luck with that. If somebody wants that crap bad enough to climb an eight-foot fence, I say, let 'em have it."

Joe tapped his sidearm. "If they're that determined, I can let 'em have it."

"It's your funeral, man. Be careful."

"Ah, I'll be fine. Just let me know if you decide to order food." Joe closed the gate and padlocked it shut.

"We probably will order from Milly's Diner. Is midnight good for you?"

"Yeah, here's a twenty. Get me one of her Philly Cheesesteak sandwiches, fries, and a large coffee. I'll see you around midnight."

"Alright see you at midnight."

Joe went inside and locked the door. He dusted off the reception desk before he sat down. "Oh, man this place is a nasty mess. I better get paid some serious bucks for this."

Joe's phone rang. "Yeah?" He answered.

"Is the coast clear?" A voice on the phone asked.

"Wait ten minutes then I'll meet you at the front gate."

"Why the delay?"

"My partner just left. He needs time to get back to the office. If he's still around, he might see you. I also need time to turn the breakers back on."

"Fine. Ten minutes. Don't be late."

Joe turned his flashlight on and headed down to the basement. He flipped the main power switch on, and several lights immediately came on. Several bulbs were burnt out but there was enough light to move around without tripping over something. The sudden appearance of light sent several rodents scampering for cover. Joe just shook his head and walked back toward the first floor. He went outside and unlocked the gate.

One whispered. "What's going on? I think this guy is up to something."

Two snickered. "Another mystery to solve."

"Shh, they're coming back," One hissed.

A box truck drove inside the gate and Joe waved it around to the back. He locked the gate and went around to greet his visitors. He led them in through the service entrance. "Okay, Frankie, Vince, I got the power on, but a lot of the lights are burned out. My buddy's bringing me food at midnight so you need to be out of sight by 11:30 and if you aren't done you can start back around 1:00. Where's my money?"

"Here's half now. You'll get the other half once we're done. Where's the elevator?"

"Elevator? That thing hasn't worked in several years. Sorry, you gotta walk it up. Which floor are you going to?"

"That isn't your concern. You just stay on the first floor and keep watch." Frankie answered as he picked up his gear and started up the stairs.

Vince shook his head and followed Frankie. "No elevator," he muttered.

As they headed past the second floor, Two whispered, "Where are they going?"

"Shut up," Six hissed.

The two men stopped. "Did you hear that?" Frankie asked.

"I can't hear nothing but my own wheezing going up these stairs," Vince muttered.

Reaching the top floor, they dropped their bags on the ground and sat down to catch their breath. Having no chairs, the two sat on the top step.

Vince shook his head. "Man, I'll be glad when we're done with this job. This place smells like puke."

"It's not like you've never smelled puke before. I've seen you hung over… lots of times."

"I like drinking, and other less than reputable habits, but I don't like the after-effects or smells that remind me of them. C'mon, let's get this over with. We're already going to have to take multiple trips up and down those blasted stairs. The man better be paying us good for this job."

"Don't worry. He is."

"Let's get the merchandise first, where did he say he stashed it?"

"All over the place. He stuck some in the air vents, some behind the sink under the cabinet, and he had bookcases installed with false backs that go into the walls. This floor is going to be a goldmine of drug money and smack. I've got a map. Let's start here." Frankie pulls out a floor plan of the seventh floor and points to one of the apartments. The two went into the apartment and in a few minutes had it cleaned out.

They moved to what used to be Pretty Penny's apartment. The dealer who lived on the seventh floor before the building was closed down and condemned, had leases on every apartment on that floor. Penny was one of his employees, offering special favors to certain customers. She conducted business of her own on the side.

By 10:30 PM, they had cleaned out every apartment except the one used as the dealer's main headquarters. Frankie pulled a sledgehammer from one of the bags.

"What's that for?" Vince asked.

"We have to take out one of the walls."

"One of the walls? Why?"

Frankie smirked. He picked up a second sledgehammer. "Hurry up, we need to get this done and get out of here before that other guard comes by. Start here." Frankie pointed at an internal wall.

The two pounded at the wall making deep indentations and cracks. Dust sprayed into the air, then drywall began falling onto the ground. Vince coughed and wheezed. With each blow, the old wiring in the building shorted, making the few remaining lights flicker and blink.

Seven moaned and groaned. The dust tickled whatever it was he had that equated to a human's nose. One final blow was all he could take. He sneezed and a blast of air blew drywall and a skeleton out of the wall onto the floor. A cold wind whipped through the broken windows. Seven inhaled deeply and spoke clearly for the first time in years. "Free, I'm finally free," his hoarse voice groaned. "I can speak again."

Frankie knew about the skeleton and was looking for it but hearing the voice of Seven sent chills down his spine. He jumped back and his face paled.

Vince yelled, "YAH!

The two looked at the grinning skeleton whose hollow eyes stared back at them. Their hearts raced. "Is this some kind of joke? Who said that?" Frankie yelled.

Seven laughed with glee.

Six hissed from below them, "Be quiet, they'll hear you."

"I won't be quiet anymore. I have a tale to tell. These two are evil men and they are up to no good. I'll speak to whoever I please. It's not like they can stop me, and no one will believe them anyway."

"Who are you?" Frankie demanded as he pulled a gun from under his waistband. "Show yourself!"

Seven laughed maniacally. "My name is Seven and I'm the floor beneath your feet, the ceiling over your head, and the walls that surround you. I've had my fill of you and your kind. You stuffed my every orifice with your drugs, money, and now this poor fellow. Then you whacked away at my walls with your hammers. I've had enough of you."

The lights flickered and went out. The floor trembled and shook, more drywall crumbled and fell. The plaster from the ceiling was already sagging but now it began to give way.

Six yelled. "Seven, stop before you bring us all down!"

Five squealed, "Aye yai yai."

"Heaven help us," Four cried out.

Three worried silently and Two whimpered and cried. One eyed the security guard whose attention was no longer on the small television he had hooked up at his desk.

The security guard muted the TV, put his hand on his handgun, and moved cautiously toward the stairs. It was hard to walk silently on the creaky floorboards littered with broken glass and debris. He started up the stairs. The sounds of running steps coming down the steps gave him reason to pause. He looked up between the rails and saw Frankie and Vince barreling down the stairwell. "Hey, what's going on up there?"

Frankie paused long enough to lean over the rail and yell. "Don't come up here!"

Joe backed away from the stairs. The two men blasted into the lobby.

"What happened? Did part of the structure collapse or something? What was all that yelling about?"

Frankie grabbed Joe by the throat and pushed him against a wall. "Were you pulling pranks on us?"

Joe's eyes darted back and forth nervously. "What are you talking about? I've been down here watching my shows until you guys started taking this building down. What was going on up there? Who was doing all that yelling and screaming?"

Deciding Joe wasn't behind whatever happened to them up there, Frankie eased off the man.

Vince glanced at the stairs again. "Frankie, we didn't grab our bags. We need that stuff."

"You want to go back up there? I'm not going back up there. I need to talk to the boss."

"Tonight? It's already 11 o'clock."

Frankie looked back at Joe. "We'll be back tomorrow to get that stuff during the day. Don't you let anyone up there, and you don't go up there either. Got it?"

"Got it. What—What happened up there?"

"None of your business." Frankie snapped. "Remember nobody goes up there."

Joe gave Frankie a nervous nod. "Yeah, I got it. Nobody goes up there."

Frankie shoved Vince toward the door and the two scurried into their truck. Joe headed for the gate to let them out. He secured the gate again behind them. Looking back at the building, he heard what sounded like frightened whispers coming from the building. Frankie and Vince were clearly scared out of their minds, but by what? Were there squatters in the building somewhere? Maybe he should check it out despite Frankie's warning. No, not yet he decided. If someone was in there, it might be best that they think everyone was gone first and then they would drop their guard.

?

Joe went back to his desk and turned the television back up and waited for his dinner to arrive. Forty-five minutes later, his partner brought his food. The two ate dinner together then Trey left Joe and went back to his office.

An hour later, Joe needed to get up and walk around so he decided to check the building for vagrants. He went through all the rooms on the first floor and found nothing. The upper floors groaned and creaked. They seemed to beg him to climb higher. He moved cautiously to the second floor, which was devoid of anything questionable.

"Don't stop searching," Two whispered, pushing him onward and upward.

Three was just as empty. Four, Five, and Six showed no signs of anyone hiding or living in there either. The higher he got; the less Joe expected to find anything. After searching the sixth floor, he was ready to head back downstairs.

Seven groaned audibly.

The noise drew Joe to ascend the last flight of stairs. He reached the seventh floor and found two duffel bags sitting on the floor in the hall. He glanced around. The lighting was dim from the lack of working bulbs in the fixtures, and they flickered occasionally as a circuit was interrupted by the movements of vermin or breezes blowing exposed wires. Joe opened the first bag and found dozens of unopened packages of heroin. He whistled under his breath. "Oh, man, that's a lot of smack, and worth a lot of dough, too." He glanced at the second bag, "And what are you hiding?" Joe's eyes widened. "Jackpot!" He said to himself. The second bag was packed full of money.

Reason slipped in and gripped him. Frankie and Vince ran out of there and left this behind. Those guys were no-nonsense tough guys. What had frightened them so badly that they left a fortune in cash and drugs behind?

Joe pulled his gun out of its holster and slipped the safety off. He searched the floor methodically. Nothing seemed amiss until he reached the apartment where the two had broken the wall. Joe's heart skipped a beat when he spied the skeleton on the floor. He stumbled backward against another wall. His gun hand shook.

This was not good. If Frankie and Vince knew he had seen this, they would probably kill him. He could take the money and run, but Frankie knew Joe's family and where they lived. Joe's wife had primary custody of their kids. There's no way he could convince her to uproot them and disappear for any amount of money. Frankie would certainly use them to get Joe to bring the money back.

The walls seemed to whisper, "What are you going to do?"

"Call the police."

"The next dead body could be yours."

Joe pulled himself together. "Alright, Alright, I'll go to the police."

The whispers went silent, and the building itself seemed to relax.

Joe called Trey to pick him up. He told his friend what he found and the two drove to the nearest police precinct.

A detective walked them into a private office where they could talk. "My name is Detective Bryan Robinson. How can I help you?"

Joe shifted nervously in his seat. He glanced at Trey knowing he could lose his job for what he was about to say. "My name is Joe Fielding. I'm a security guard at Seneca Tower. These two guys said they had some personal stuff in an apartment they used to live in and asked if I would let them come in and get it. I let them in, and they went up to the seventh floor. I didn't figure there was anything they could hurt or anything really worth much up there. I let them go up, but there was some major noise coming from up there and those guys took off like scared rabbits. I went up there to see what all the noise was, and I found some stuff that you need to know about. I'm pretty sure they're going to come back for the stuff they left up there."

Detective Robinson scowled. The mention of Seneca Tower caused a chill to run up his spine. "What stuff did you find?"

Joe pulled a pen from his pocket and clicked it repeatedly. "There— There were three things of interest. One was a bag of what looked like some kind of drugs and there was a lot of it. The second thing was money. There was a lot of that too."

"Did you disturb any of it?" The detective asked suspiciously.

"No…well, I opened the bags then closed them right back. The third thing scared the life out of me though."

"What was it?"

"A dead body, a skeleton. Whoever it was, they've been in the walls of that building for years."

"In the walls?" the detective asked.

"Those guys apparently carried a couple of sledgehammers in their bags. There was a fresh hole in the wall and drywall all over the floor around that skeleton. I don't know where they got the drugs and the money because nothing else looked messed up. They were looking for something because they had another bag, besides the mess they made when they tore down the wall. That bag was big enough to carry the skeleton out of there."

"You think the skeleton scared them?"

"I don't know, Detective. I just know something scared them. They came barreling down those stairs like they'd seen a ghost. They shoved me against a wall and threatened me. Told me not to let anybody upstairs. It sounded to me like they were going to come back sometime after daylight. If you come over there with tons of police cars, they'll know I told you about it. Detective, I have a family. I don't want to put them in danger, but I'm not covering up for them."

Detective Robinson scowled at Joe. "I suspect you were a little more involved than you're saying, but I'm not interested in a minor miscalculation on your part. Tell me who these men were, and we'll let your part in this go."

"One of them's name is Frankie and the other is Vince. I've seen them around, but I don't normally have any dealings with them. I'm pretty sure they work for a local dealer, but I have no idea who. I don't have anything to do with that, I swear. They just asked me for a little favor, and I let them come inside a condemned building. That's all."

"I'm just curious. Why didn't you take the money and run?"

"These aren't the kind of guys you can run from. They'll find you or they'll find somebody you care about and… I didn't want them to hurt my family. I hate my ex-wife, but I didn't want them to hurt her either. I may not like her but she's still my kids' mother."

Detective Robinson leaned back in his seat and laced his fingers together across his stomach. He swiveled back and forth as he thought for a moment. Deciding on a plan, he sat up straight again. "Alright Mr. Fielding, we'll come in tomorrow, but we'll make it look like a building inspection and not a police action. We need to catch these men with the drugs and the body in order to arrest them. We'll do this in a way that keeps you and your family safe. You go back to doing your job as security and leave the rest to me."

Joe nodded nervously. He hoped the Detective was right. As Joe and Trey left the police station Trey quietly said, "Joe, you know you could get fired over this."

"Yeah, I know, but at least I'll still be alive… I hope."

?

With the building empty again, the floors discussed the recent events and talked to Seven.

"Seven, are you crazy? Talking in front of the humans like that?" Six demanded.

"What happened up there? Tell us!" Two asked eagerly.

"Oh, they found that dead guy and…" Seven laughed heartily. "Oh, it feels so good to be able to talk and laugh and take deep breaths again."

"Dead guy and what? Finish your sentence before that security guard comes back." One insisted.

"Oh, the drug dealers killed some guy years ago and they tore the wall out, shoved him in there, and covered him with lime to cover the smell."

"What guy? Who was it? Was it the Street Preacher?" Two pummeled him with questions.

"I don't know who he was. I never saw him before the day they killed him."

"Maybe it was the street preacher. Four said he was upset about his son running drugs for the dealers. Maybe he went up there and confronted the dealers. Tell us exactly what happened." Three responded.

"Oh dear, that was nearly twenty years ago. Let me think." Seven coughed and sputtered. "Not used to talking anymore, my voice is a little hoarse."

Four jumped in. "Well, start slow. What did the man look like?"

"He was a scrawny-looking little fellow. He was wearing a black suit and tie. He was waving around this big, black, leather book with gilded page edges. As a matter of fact, when those two goons got him out of the wall, that big book fell out with him. It's laying here on the floor beside him." Seven replied.

"It sounds like the street preacher," Four said.

Two gasped. "Did we solve the mystery of the missing street preacher? It was really a murder mystery, after all. Tell us why the dealers killed him."

"Mm—I don't really remember. With all this powder in my system, things are really fuzzy. I remember them yelling at each other and that guy waving his big black book around. He tried opening it and showing that drug dealer something in it. He kept yelling about sins and paying for sins."

"Yes, that's my street preacher all right." Four's voice was somber.

"What good did it do to solve the mystery of the missing preacher? We're still going to be demolished next week," Six snidely added.

"Hey, button it up. The guards are coming back." One yelled.

"Pay attention to what they say. I want to know what the cops told them," Seven hastily yelled.

?

Joe and Trey walked into the lobby. "Joe, I'm staying here with you for the rest of the shift."

"Thanks, man. I could use the company. I know that detective said he would protect me, but these guys are drug dealers and apparently murderers. I'm kind of worried."

"He said he would beef up the patrols for tonight. He'll get a team in here under the guise of looking for asbestos in the morning. You'll be fine and so will your family."

"I hope so. Thanks for sticking around tonight."

?

Two white vans pulled up in front of Seneca Tower right after sunrise. Men came in and out of the building carrying equipment and wearing white hazmat suits and respirator masks.

Sweat rolled down Joe's back and beads of perspiration dotted his forehead. He wasn't sure if he was sweating because of the summer heat, or from the fear of getting caught ratting out Frankie and Vince. His own perspiration added to the foul odors of the dilapidated building.

Joe's phone rang as Detective Robinson was standing in front of him. His mouth ran dry as he gave Detective Robinson a guilty look when he saw the name pop up on his phone. "It's Frankie. What do I do?"

"You answer it, sound busy, and tell him we're checking the first floor for asbestos in preparation for the demolition. Make sure he knows we're just on the first floor and that we'll begin asbestos removal on Monday. If he asks why you're still here, Trey asked you to pull a double. Now answer it." Detective Robinson said quickly.

"Yeah, this is Joe."

"What's going on in there, Joe? Did you go upstairs last night? Who are those guys?"

"No, I'm not walking up those stairs. The floors are half rotted out and I'm getting too old to take the stairs. There's a bunch of guys checking the building for asbestos. They said they were only checking the first floor because they weren't sure if it was safe to be upstairs either. I think they're going to start tearing it out on Monday. Listen if you guys got more to do here, I suggest you get it done quick. These guys will be done here in a bit. I'm pulling a double, so I'll be able to let you in, around lunchtime."

There was silence on the other end of the phone as Frankie reported to someone. Joe could hear an angry voice, but couldn't make out who Frankie was talking to. He heard Frankie, "No, I'm not going back in that place. It's haunted I tell you. That guy's ghost is in there."

The second voice argued back.

Frankie answered. "I can't. Vince got high and drunk last night. He's totally wasted. He was scared out of his mind too. I'm not going back in there."

The two came to an understanding and Frankie spoke to Joe again. "We'll be over there in an hour or two. Keep everyone off those top floors and we'll pay you a little extra for your trouble."

"I'm always glad to earn a little extra money. I'll see you shortly. I gotta go these guys got some questions." Joe got off the phone and breathed a sigh of relief. He looked up at Detective Robinson. "You got to keep me out of this. If those guys think I ratted them out…"

"I'll do my best. If I have to, I'll put you in witness protection and I can push your family into it too. Hopefully, that won't be an issue."

"Do your best? Hopefully?"

"Trust me." The detective offered a reassuring smile then headed up the stairs to finish securing the crime scene.

Two shiny black shoes stepped next to the smiling skeleton. As a bag of drugs and the bag of drug money dropped on the floor, Espinoza Castillo knelt next to the skeleton. "So, preacher man, you thought you would strike back at me from the grave, scaring my people away like that. You aren't going to beat me. This is my territory, not yours."

"Boss, can we just do this and get out of here? Who was this guy anyway?" Frankie asked.

"He was a street preacher who lived on the fourth floor. He found out I was using his son to run drugs for me and tried to run me out of here. He found a load of my drugs and dumped them in the river, so I killed him for it. I was going to kill his kid for losing the drugs, but the old guy made me a deal. He offered his own life to save his son's life. I took him up on it—sort of. I still planned to kill that stupid kid, but he disappeared. If he shows his face in this neighborhood, I'm still going to kill him."

"I'm right here, Espinoza," came a voice from the door of the apartment.

Mr. Castillo stood up and turned around. He and Frankie reached for their guns.

"Uh—Uh, don't move. The two of you are under arrest." Detective Robinson stepped clear of the doorway. "So, you *killed* my old man."

"I was just reminiscing in the old neighborhood and found this body. Frankie and I were just about to report it to the authorities."

Detective Robinson pulled a remote control from his left pocket. He pointed the control at the various cameras tucked into the shadows of the room. "That's not what you said on camera."

Espinoza's face flushed. He maintained his calm and asked, "So the wild preacher's kid turned into a cop? You used to like my drugs and my fringe benefits. How did you end up as a cop?"

"When Dad got rid of the drugs, I was scared out of my mind. When he disappeared, I got more scared. I entered a rehab program and got clean. I decided I wanted to stop guys like you. I just transferred back here four months ago. You are going to be the first big bust I've had since moving back to the old neighborhood."

"I could use a man like you on the police force. I got a big bag of cash right here and I could throw in some smack too. Just don't get caught using and get thrown off the police force. What do you say? You can make all of this go away and earn a fortune to boot."

The power flickered and went out as a sudden breeze slammed the apartment door shut. A whisper traveled with the breeze, "Make them pay…"

Frankie's eyes widened and his heart pounded. It was just a breeze, and the whisper had to be his own guilty conscience… or maybe the preacher's kid was playing tricks on them. If he had installed a camera, maybe he put up speakers too. It was his way of making them confess—he hoped.

Det. Robinson glanced at the cameras. The technicians had wired them to the building's power supply so obviously they were not still recording. The rapid footsteps of his fellow officers came toward them in the hall. Espinoza stood slowly thinking he might have a chance to pay back the stupid kid who lost his drug money and stood before him as the cop who was getting him arrested. He would still go to jail, but he would get a certain amount of satisfaction along with it.

Seven whispered again, "He killed your father. No one will see…"

Det. Robinson shook his head. "No. It's like my daddy used to say, 'Be sure your sins will find you out.' He gave up his life to try to save mine. I won't dishonor his sacrifice, and I certainly wouldn't work for the man who killed my own father. Espinoza Castillo, you are under arrest. Guys, come on in here."

The room filled with police officers. In a moment, Frankie and Espinoza were cuffed and ready to be hustled from the room. Frankie was griping wildly. "I told you we shouldn't have come back here this building is haunted and that preacher's ghost has it in for us."

Detective Robinson smiled as he listened to Frankie's wild claims. One of the arresting officers approached the detective. "Sir, Mr. Castillo wants to talk to you."

The Detective pulled himself away from securing the crime scene. "What is it, Espinoza?"

"That security guard ratted me out, didn't he? How did you find me?"

Detective Robinson smiled and played on Frankie's fears. "Nah, Daddy told me."

Frankie's eyes widened and he began to rant again about Seneca Tower being haunted. Espinoza yelled at his subordinate, "Shut up before I shut you up!"

The officers started to escort the two men away when Detective Robinson added. "Hey Espinoza, it's just like Daddy always said…"

"Yeah, I know, 'Be sure your sins will find you out.' It's the last thing he said to me."

?

That night the building, devoid of people, discussed the day's events.

"Seven, why would you encourage that preacher's kid to kill those two men?" Four asked.

"Ah… they deserved it. I was just giving the kid a chance to even the score."

"I'm proud of him. He straightened his life out, honored his father's memory, and obeyed the teachings from the big black book." Four's joists stretched as he puffed up.

"I'm proud of us." Two giggled. "We solved a mystery, just like—"

"Oh, don't start with your murder mystery reruns again. What good did it do? We're still going to die." Six creaked and groaned.

Three sighed. "He's right. They are still going to destroy us, even if Seven stopped Espinoza from getting away with murder."

Two whimpered. "We solved a murder. That should count for something."

"It doesn't count for anything," Six replied sullenly.

"Dios tenga piedad de nosotros," Five whispered softly.

"I don't think I even need a translation for that one," Four responded.

"Hey, perk up everybody. This is a crime scene. They can't demolish us yet." One tried to give them a little hope.

"How long?" Three asked.

"Uh…" One stalled hoping the others might get distracted.

Six picked up on the delay. "How long, One?"

"A week… give or take…"

"Give, don't take. Our time is short enough." Two squealed.

"Well, that's more than we had," Three responded pragmatically.

Four sighed. "A week isn't likely to change much, but I can at least die satisfied that my street preacher made a difference, and his son got his life straightened out."

"Satisfied or not, dead is still dead," Six added. His comment silenced the conversation.

?

Days, then weeks went by with people coming and going, crime scene investigators, real asbestos inspectors, and hazmat teams. The identification of the late Reverend Charlie Robinson got the attention of all those he had helped years ago.

"Can you believe it? We're going to be refurbished. We aren't going to die after all and it's because we solved a murder," Two chattered happily.

"We didn't solve anything. The police did that." One corrected.

"I would say Seven had a great deal to do with that though. If he hadn't broken the cardinal rule of never speaking in the presence of humans, we would be long gone by now." Three explained.

Four spoke up, his voice cracking, "I can't believe they're going to change the name of this building to honor our beloved street preacher. We'll be known as Robinson Tower. He helped so many people. He deserves to be honored."

Five wept loudly and threw out a string of Spanish.

"Speak English if you want us to understand you, Five." Six groaned.

"Espinoza Castillo was one of the little boys who grew up on my floor. He started out as such a good little boy. I can't believe he turned out so bad. If I get my hands on him—" she railed on in Spanish again.

"Seven, you're being awfully quiet. Are you alright?" One asked.

"They may give us a makeover like they said, but is anybody going to want to stay on the seventh floor? Because I couldn't keep quiet and they found the preacher's body up here, everybody thinks I'm haunted."

Four answered him, "No, they will know that the preacher is at rest because his murderer was caught, and his body has been properly laid to rest."

Five sniffled again. "I'm so excited to know there will be people living here again. I've missed the pitter-patter of little feet, the laughter of families and children."

"So have I," said Four.

"Eh—kids just break stuff," One gruffed.

"And they're noisy," Six added.

"Oh, they make me smile." Two was already smiling at the thought.

"Well, I wonder what adventures are coming next," Three said.

"I don't know, but I'm glad the preacher's kid got himself straightened out. I know his daddy's got to be crying tears of joy in heaven now," came Four's tremoring voice.

?

A year later, the building was restored to its original beauty. Mr. and Mrs. Lyles, Ms. Vanderhaven, and Detective Bryan Robinson stood in the lobby of Robinson Tower for the dedication of the newly remodeled building.

Mrs. Lyles wiped happy tears away. "Ms. Vanderhaven, I'm so glad you got the Historical Society to petition to have this building declared a historical monument."

Ms. Vanderhaven smiled. "This was all because of Detective Robinson's father. His newfound fame and notoriety made the building qualify. I still remember the newspaper headlines, *Street Preacher Stops Drug Dealers from Beyond the Grave.*"

Mrs. Lyles laid her hand on Detective Robinson's arm. "Bryan, I am so sorry for the loss of your father. I'm glad we could turn this place into a monument to him."

"Thank you, ma'am. I was lost back then, and I suppose I'm most grateful that his sacrifice saved me." Bryan looked around at the large portrait of his father mounted in a large gold frame with a brass light to keep the picture always illuminated. A few feet away was a memory board where visitors could write down meaningful encounters with his father and post them for others to see. There were already several notes, and the building hadn't officially opened for business yet.

The party headed outside to meet the press, and the mayor for the official dedication. Bryan hung back a moment looking at his father's face. He had a thousand regrets for his younger days, but his gratitude healed the pain. Bryan looked around the room one more time. "Thank you," he said aloud.

"You're welcome," Seven whispered.

The Haunting of Brilliant, Ohio

By: Alyssa Casto

"I can't go on without you." The warm summer breeze wrapped around Lory's whispered words and carried them through the dark green leaves of the giant oak trees along the sheer hillside that overlooked the Ohio River. Nothing eased the dull ache penetrating her soul from that fateful night just over a year ago. Not the heat of the midday sun that sliced across her front porch and kissed her exposed arms, or the heavy humidity that clung to the air and sent little trails of sweat down her back while she stood watching the dark blue ripples.

Another small breeze stirred through the valley and wafted the rich scent of fertile soil and the sharp-sweet aroma of the small cherry tomato bush that flourished just around the corner. A smell that would always remind her of what she had lost. What they all had lost. Dark thoughts swirled and settled over her like a heavy cloak. *We can't afford to lose anything else.*

Lory didn't need to check to know that the tiny yellow flowers had fallen away and were now replaced with little oval fruits dangling from the thin branches, ripe and ready to be plucked from the vine. She would allow nature to take its course. Time ripening the fruits until they went to mush and dropped to the ground. Seeds burrowing with the rains and ensuring it sprouted next year—not that she expected to be there to see it. As soon as she was able, she moved her family to the other side of the county.

She was left wondering for the billionth time since the accident, *what if… What if things could have been different?*

Lory closed her eyes and tilted her head back, stepping further into the sun, trying to allow the warmth to penetrate deeper. It didn't. Instead, she felt the constant cool of a numbness that pervaded her daily life.

Another gust of air, this one a little stronger than before, stirred up more scents of nature and lifted strands of her waist-length dark hair to wrap around her. The light brushing reminded her of the ghost of a long-lost embrace. She swayed gently with the wind, losing herself in the faint memory.

"Beautiful day, isn't it?" A masculine voice called out, jarring her from her wandering thoughts.

Her next-door neighbor, Benjamin, stopped at a spot on the corner of her house, tucked just beyond her line of sight. He straightened, jiggled a handful of tiny, bright red tomatoes in one hand, chose one, and plopped it into his mouth. Lory felt her mouth go dry at the satisfied smile spread across his face as he strode forward along the narrow well-worn trail that connected their houses, tossing another one in his mouth without swallowing the first.

"You know," he said, rolling the carcass and juice of the fruit around his words as he stepped up on the landing next to her. She resisted the urge to back up onto the porch to put a little more distance between them. His dark brown eyes loomed over her as his body partially blocked the sun. "These really came in great this year."

"Thanks." Lory spun away and moved onto the porch to readjust the furniture, brush away errant pieces of debris that wandered onto the cement slab, and pick up any toys she found. There weren't many these days, but each one she found tucked away squeezed at her heart, making her wish they could go back to the happier days of the past when they would relax with the kids playing as they watched the barges float by.

Benjamin joined her on the porch, leaning against the pillar, crossing his arms and legs. She could feel his gaze raking over her with each movement she made, but she refused to acknowledge the unwanted attention.

"You know, ever since the car accident–" Benjamin's words trailed off.

They heard it first. The fluttering of birds taking to the skies seconds before a deep rumbling sound traveled from somewhere high up behind their big hill and moved toward them within the span of a breath.

The solid platform beneath her feet did little to keep her stable as the tremble grew stronger with each passing second as it traveled through the valley. Lory reached out for the back of the patio chair just as Benjamin pulled her flush against his body, using the same chair for leverage. She could feel every inch of him hunched over her and she struggled to calm her upset stomach.

Lory tried to push him away, but he tightened his grip and whispered in her ear, "Wait till it passes."

She waited until she felt his muscles slacken, and she spun away just as the final shift beneath them abated. "I'm good, thanks."

It hadn't been a full earthquake, more of a shifting rumble, but the whole experience left her feeling off-balance. Ever since they started blasting high up on the hill to 'reinforce the hillside', the quakes began. Sometimes the blasts could be heard in the distance, but other times the quakes seemed to come without any detonation. It had set the entire town on edge and all of them looked forward to when the project was completed.

Benjamin groaned loudly just as his phone started ringing, sauntering around Lory and back to the tomato bush so he could peer through the ten-foot gap between their houses to study the wood line.

"Yeah, I felt it." Benjamin shook his head. "What'd they do this time?"

Lory couldn't hear the response from the person on the other line.

"They weren't supposed to do that yet."

Curious, Lory leaned over the chair to watch him as he plucked more tomatoes from the vine and tossed them back one at a time. Benjamin turned, catching her looking at him, and gave a wink as he chewed. Lory straightened and continued to tidy up the porch—pretending she wasn't listening, even though everything was set straight, trying to glean any information from the phone call she could.

"Yeah, I'm on my way. Tell them not to go on until I get there." Benjamin took another handful and waved them in the air to say goodbye as he walked back to his house. The noisy metal screen door squealed on its hinges and then slammed shut as he stepped inside.

Lory breathed deeply, expanding her lungs as far as they would go, and tried to expel all of the emotions evoked from the exchange as she let her eyes roam beyond his pink two-story porch and onto the next house down the hill. A small blip of red against a vibrant green lawn surrounded by a chain link fence. Even at this distance, she could see the small blur of white on the front of the cap hovering over narrow shoulders sitting cross-legged in the grass—a silhouette she'd recognize anywhere.

She studied her middle son as he played by himself on the lawn of the babysitter's house. Kevin lifted his face to the warmth of the sun, just like she had done moments before Benjamin's unwanted interruption. The scene reminded her of the gentle innocence of childhood causing a softness to bloom inside of her chest. It seemed like only the love for her children was able to break through the walls she had erected around her heart.

Her gaze wandered away from his cap as she studied his shoulders, the red t-shirt, and jeans, which appeared to now have dark patches that could only be dirt. She smiled and shook her head as her gaze flicked back up to his face as he turned away from the sun. She realized, even at this distance, that his lips were moving. As she continued watching, he picked up something long and curved with odd erratic bumps all along the object. Uncertain what the item was, her eyes flicked up to his still-moving lips as held it up, as if presenting it to someone.

Lory's heart chilled once again.

$$?$$

"I'm worried about Kevin," Darla said, as she cut the sandwiches in half and stacked them high on the plate before taking them and the bag of chips to the table. Once done, she poured three glasses of milk and took two sodas out of the refrigerator, handing one to Lory. "He's still not making friends with the other kids."

They both glanced out of the front door where a little ghost was holding a sign that read 'Welcome Home, Bootiful!' suction-cupped to the window. On the far side of the concrete and wrought iron porch, Kevin sat still playing in the grass. Red cap pulled low over his brow, the sun reflecting off of the faded white logo that used to be an arrow but had flaked away until all that remained was a small sliver that now looked just like a mermaid. Yet another eccentricity he was teased for, but Lory would never force him to take it off. Not when it was the last old, yet beloved item Tom had passed down to him before his accident.

"I worry about him too. His doctors say he's doing okay, everything considered." Lory had taken him to every doctor imaginable since the accident, including his weekly appointments with the child psychologist. "They all said there wasn't much that could be done. Just be supportive as he works through this rocky bit."

"I hope he snaps out of it soon," Darla said, calling the gang to come eat. The kids rushed over. All but one. "It's been over a year." Even though there was no malicious intent, and Darla was Lory's closest friend, agony ricocheted through her as if she'd been caught in a blast. She swallowed hard and pushed the pain into the dark well deep inside of her. It consumed the emotion and numbed the sting enough so she could release a breath she hadn't realized she held.

Darla started to head in the direction of the front door, but Lory held her hand out to stop her with a quick, "I'll do it," as she popped the top of the can and took a drink, enjoying the distraction of the fizzy bubbles tickling her tongue coating her mouth with its rich, syrupy-sweet flavor. Kevin didn't glance up as the glass door closed with a quiet click on the gasket hinges.

"I feel it too," Kevin's words traveled to Lory over the breeze. He looked down at something on the ground, picked it up, and raised it in the air. It was the same item she saw him holding while standing on her porch earlier. When she entered through the gate, she'd gone straight inside to speak with Darla. It was about half the size of her forearm, caked with clumps of dirt along its slightly curved shaft that ended in points at both ends. "They used to dig underground with these?"

At first, Lory thought he was asking her. She opened her mouth to respond but realized he was studying at the same vacant spot as he did before—once again caught in a one-sided conversation.

"Kevin?" Lory's voice cracked around the tightness in her throat as he jerked and looked up at her. His bright green eyes sparkled in the sun under the brim of the ball cap. The logo, much easier to see now up close, and the mermaid image was even more pronounced.

"Can I see that?" Lory held out her hand, waiting patiently while she watched a series of emotions pass behind her son's eyes. Finally, he handed it over, tiny particles of dirt crumbling off and raining down into the grass and onto her palm.

"It looks like an old pickaxe head." Lory turned it over in hand and brushed more globs of damp soil from the tool. "Did you just find it?"

Kevin nodded and looked away. Curious about his avoidance, Lory pressed on.

"Where'd you get it?"

"Around back. Before the last quake."

Instantly, Lory was on alert. She was pretty sure Darla hadn't given him permission to leave the gate. She opened her mouth to reprimand him but saw his arms wrap around himself as he started rocking back and forth. As much as she wanted to correct his misbehavior, he'd already been through too much, and she knew right now what he needed was comfort. Not to be told he'd done another thing wrong.

She lowered herself onto the grass next to him and pulled him toward her.

"Are you okay, honey? Did the quake scare you?"

"No, I'm not scared of them anymore." Kevin leaned into the embrace but didn't wind his arms around her like he used to. "I was told that it's all happening just as it should."

"As it should? Who told you that?" Lory jerked at his words and felt him stiffen. Her brain circled a bunch of different scenarios about who could have told him such nonsense, every single one of them made her grow more concerned than the last. Kevin was still acting so strange, and it seemed to be getting worse by the day. She would call his doctor on her way to work and see if she could get him seen first thing tomorrow.

Instead of answering her question, he asked, "Am I in trouble?"

"No, sweetie. I just want to know who told you about the quakes."

Kevin glanced up at her and then quickly away. He held so silent she wondered if he would even respond, but Lory was willing to wait as long as needed, even if it meant being late for work. She was determined to get to the bottom of this.

"You don't want me to tell you," he finally whispered.

"Sure, I do."

"No, you don't." Kevin looked up at the same spot he had been showing the toy to earlier. Lory followed his gaze and saw nothing other than the chain link fence, houses, and trees beyond. Even though there was nothing there that she could see, something about the way he studied the spot gave her chills.

She pushed the sensation to the back of her mind and continued. "It's okay. I won't get mad at you. I promise."

"Yes, you will," Kevin replied, fidgeting in place. Lory saw eyes flick in the same direction as before. A tiny shake of his head and then he suddenly popped up. "I'm hungry."

Lory debated if she should continue to push. They needed to have a heart-to-heart about this soon, but he was obviously going to continue to avoid the conversation. She checked her watch to see that she only had ten minutes before she had to leave for work if she wanted to make it on time. She debated what was best, but finally relented, knowing if she left a few minutes early she could have more time to wait if the doctor's office put her on hold like they usually did.

"Go on without me. I'll be there in a minute." Lory watched as he readjusted his cap, making it look as if the mermaid tail was waving goodbye, and then ran inside the house.

?

"What if all of this activity is stirring up the ghosts of this town?" Darla whispered the following morning when Lory arrived to pick up the kids. Her cute ghost and bat nightgown doing nothing to ease the tension hanging in the air. Normally, she didn't believe in stuff like that, but between the delay of not being able to get a hold of the doctor's office yesterday, and being caught off-guard with this latest quake, she was still recovering from the nerves that lingered.

Lory knew she shouldn't be surprised to hear something like that come out of her neighbor's mouth. The ghost decor suction-cupped to the front door at Lory's shoulder was just the beginning of Darla's penchant for all things spooky and supernatural. She watched all the paranormal shows, and the same silly-scary ghost decor bled into the house year round.

"Did you feel it?" Darla asked, ushering Lory inside.

"Yes," Lory replied, not ready to talk about it. It had been a long, hard shift and she'd been so distracted with racing thoughts of being the first person to call into the doctor's office the moment it opened, that she almost fell face-first into the reinforcement wall in front of her house when it hit. Luckily, her hands connected with the cement wall—which held back the nearly vertical hill—before the rest of her body followed, and she was able to use it as support instead.

It was more than that though. As soon as the tremor passed, Tara, the neighbor across the street, straightened herself and closed the mailbox with a fresh newspaper in her hand. Lory raised her hand in a small wave, but her neighbor didn't wave back. Instead, she flinched, and her eyes narrowed as she studied Lory warily. Even though they hardly ever talked, Tara had never acted so rude.

"People are saying it picks up after the evening fire station sirens go off. Something about the high-pitched sounds calling them in."

Lory tried to tamp down the chill that raced through her. Instead of allowing herself to consider such a thought, she chose to blame it on the damp dewy air clinging to her face. Even though it was well past dawn, it took much longer for the sun to ascend high enough in the sky to warm the ground inside the valley.

"Have you heard the ferry whistles?" Darla asked.

Lory shook her head.

"I swear I can hear them almost every night." Darla pointed to a spot behind Lory. "Did you know they used to transport people back and forth between Brilliant and Wellsburg back in the day? There were docks right there by the American Legion."

Lory glanced over her shoulder toward the river at the tiny sister town in question. Even though it was just on the other side of the river, it was actually a different state. The only thing that separated Ohio from West Virginia was the fast-moving slice of water that ran between.

Not wanting to go into it first thing, Lory opted to change the subject. "Did the quake wake them?"

Luckily, Darla took the bait and peered inside.

"Only Samantha. The boys are still out."

"Alright, let me go wake them up," Lory pushed forward into the house as Darla stepped out of the way.

"Hi, Mom," Samantha greeted her sleepily from the couch where she sat munching on cereal while watching one of the shows that she was addicted to. The screen showed four pre-teens trying to convince a giant green parrot to get into a service elevator.

"Hi, honey," Lory said, bending down to press a kiss to the top of her daughter's head. A quick peek at her bowl showed she only had a few bites left. "Go ahead and finish up here and then grab your stuff. I'm going to get the boys moving."

She found both boys in their usual spots. Cole on the top bunk in the upstairs bedroom, leg thrown over the edge of the bar. He was easy enough to wake up and shuffle off toward the stairs, but when Lory tried to rouse Kevin, he was unresponsive. Exhausted, but not wanting to scare him, she called out again and gently shook his shoulder.

"No, no. I don't want to go," he whined and stirred in the spaceship blankets.

Lory brushed the hair back from his forehead and made soothing sounds, knowing he was caught in the foggy dreamscape between sleep and wake, and she didn't want to startle him further.

"Come on. It's time, love," She whispered as she rubbed his shoulder with a little more pressure, trying to coax him awake.

"Mom. Mom!" He cried out, lurching upright, immediately reaching out for her.

She sat on the edge of the bed, slowly rocking him as he sobbed quietly in her arms. A few long moments later, he relaxed in her arms and exhaled loudly. She used the blanket to brush away the remaining tear streaks and kissed the top of his head.

"Come on, honey. Let's go home."

"I don't want to go."

Lory continued to make soothing noises as she helped him get out of bed and slowly led him down the stairs.

?

"Mom!" A high-pitched voice called as she felt herself being yanked from the clutches of unconsciousness to realize Samantha was standing above her while shaking her shoulder. Instantly, she came to full awareness, heart-stuttering as she sat up in bed and grabbed Samantha by both shoulders.

"What is it? What's wrong?" Lory looked around but didn't see anyone else in the room with them. "Are the boys, okay?"

Samantha nodded her head as she shook Lory's hands loose and raced for her slippers.

"Here," She said, throwing them on the floor in front of Lory's feet. "Put them on. The suits are here."

The words filtered in sluggishly as Lory's mind struggled to place what exactly the phrase meant, but once it caught up, she shoved both feet into the slippers and threw a discarded jacket from the chair around her shoulders. She raced down the wooden stairs just behind her daughter and pushed out onto the porch.

"How long was I asleep?" Lory shielded her eyes from the bright afternoon sun and stared off in the same direction as her daughter. There were clusters of people standing around along their hilly street. She recognized each one of the faces, though she didn't usually interact with any of them because of her work schedule, they had all been nice enough after Tom's car accident. Bringing covered dishes and offering their condolences.

"About three hours," Samantha answered,

That meant she had awoken about an hour before her usual time. She didn't feel as tired as she usually would after Darla had given her the extra time to catch up on rest the previous day—a gift she was eternally grateful for now that the suits were making their rounds. Glad she would be out and ready for their stop at her house. She felt absolutely certain they would be picked this time. She began silently praying, just to be safe.

A dark object on top of the small circular table caught her attention. It was caked with dirt which had spilled over the surface of the table and trailed down to the cement slab. She tried to ignore the zing of frustration at just having cleaned the space.

"What is that?" Lory asked. It was difficult to tell. She could make out the tall, slender lines with a bulbous middle that thickened toward the bottom, and something dangled at the top.

"I think it's a lantern," Samantha said. "Kevin found it."

Lory straightened, instantly alarmed. Her mind jumped to the pickaxe from yesterday. "Where did he find it?" She demanded.

Samantha shrugged and leaned over the railing to look down the hill again, drawing Lory's attention back to why she'd been awoken in the first place. She made a mental note to ask Kevin as soon as they wrapped up things here.

"Where are they?" Lory wondered aloud. She tried to watch where her neighbors were looking to determine which house, but everyone kept shifting and looking in all different directions.

"They're at the Hadsell's," Samantha said, leaning far over the rail, long brown hair swinging low toward the ground. "They already went to the Renforth's and Motto's."

"So, they're skipping around again." They had experienced the erratic movements of the suits over the last year. Only really focusing on this side of town, the people in suits wove from one house to another, offering each homeowner the opportunity to buy them out. There were rumors that if they wanted the property bad enough, they would pay above market value, but Lory wasn't sure how accurate that information was. She was happy to accept market value without complaint if that meant getting out of here even a single moment faster—as long as it was enough to buy a decent place far away from here.

"Do you think they'll come here this time?" Samantha asked.

"I think so," Lory said, eyes flicking to all the houses that sat empty along both their street and the ones on the adjacent street below. The neighbor to their right had gone with the first wave, and the ones diagonal to them had with the last.

"I hope not," Samantha said, folding her arms on the banister and resting her chin on top. "I have basketball camp next week and then Vacation Bible School."

"Don't worry. Even if they did make an offer, you've seen that it takes a while for the families to actually move out. Things like this take time."

"I know, but I don't want to leave my friends either."

"I know, sweetheart. But it will be for the best for all of us—especially for Kevin." Just thinking about her son made her straighten and look around. "Where are the boys anyways?"

"Probably around back." Samantha didn't even have to turn around to see Lory's concerned face before she added, "They're fine. Just playing at the edge of the woods."

"Samantha, you know you're supposed to all stay in the house when I'm sleeping."

"We were!" Samantha exclaimed, throwing both hands into the air and waving them around. "We only came out when we heard people talking outside and then saw the suits. I told the boys to stay on the porch." She rolled her eyes. "They didn't listen."

"Can you go check on them, please?"

Samantha sighed but nodded and walked along the narrow path that led around the tomato bush and up toward the woods between Benjamin and their house.

A small group of neighbors a few houses up from theirs were looking in her direction and pointing at her, all wearing the same look of suspicion. Lory tried to decipher why they were all acting strange towards her. She pulled the edges of her jacket tighter around her body and noticed the fluttering of her nightgown blowing in the gentle breeze. Heat rose up her neck and burned her cheekbones, but she refused to allow them to chase her off the porch simply to get dressed. They all knew she worked nights, and she didn't want to miss hearing the knock just to change because it's what they would prefer. They could all deal with it.

Two suits emerged from the Hadsell's house, drawing Lory's attention away from the stares. She held her breath as they stood outside for a moment, both bent over a document one was holding out and talking between themselves. Once they were done, the person holding the paper put it in their case and snapped it closed. They walked down the curved driveway and trod slowly up the hill, ignoring their audience as they made their way toward Lory's house.

She held her breath.

Waiting.

Hoping.

Feverishly praying that they would make their way toward her.

They both shifted in closer, right behind Benjamin's car, and she bounced on the balls of her feet, a tiny sound of excitement broke free from her throat. She felt a wide smile spread across her face as her heart soared, ecstatic to greet them and accept their offer. Finally, their luck had turned.

Lory waited for them to turn in and head for her stairs.

They didn't. Instead, they walked right on by her stairs and her car, pressed so close to it that she would swear they brushed up against it as a white car slowly crept down the hill. The driver leaning so far forward over the steering wheel that it looked like he was driving with his chin. Lory saw his eyes jump to the suits and a look of understanding dawned on his face as he passed. Once he was through the thickest cluster of bodies, he accelerated the car the rest of the way down the hill and out of sight.

Lory wound her arms around her torso, trying to tamp down the pain of overwhelming emotions rising from her core. Once again, they had missed out on the opportunity to get out of the place that held so much agony. How long would it be until the suits returned? Would their name be next on the list, or would they skip their home altogether, leaving her family to be the only inhabitants on this side of what was quickly turning into a ghost town?

Her mind raced as fast as her tumultuous emotions were, as she set out for the rear of the house, steering clear of the bush full of fat, red tomato tear drops, reminding her of the hot ones spilling down her cheeks.

"We'll go soon," Lory sighed to herself under her breath, not feeling the pressure of her nails digging deep crescents into the palms of her hands.

"That's weird," Lory said, staring at the phone in her hand. Four rejected calls. Each one going straight to voicemail.

Lory hadn't been feeling very well after everything that had happened before her shift and requested to leave work early. She'd been lucky that, for once, they had been fully staffed—something that never happened—and her request had been approved. She tried calling Darla to send the kids home as soon as she arrived, but Darla hadn't answered her phone. Her neighbor's van was parked out front when she arrived, however, when Lory peered through the glass of the front door and windows, there was no movement beyond the television screen inside. The interior door stood open, and the outer glass door was unlocked, so she let herself in and wandered around the house calling out.

The house was lit up as if it had been prepared for a funky Halloween party, yet stood completely empty.

She circled around the back of the house, still calling out.

No answer. Nothing stirred beyond the gentle rustling of the darkened leaves on swaying branches. Fear crept in as her feet carried her down the road, guided by the warm yellow glow of the street lights that illuminated the blanket of darkness that had settled over the valley.

A tiny orange glint flickered to life from the porch across the road. Lory called out to Tara, remembering her neighbor's nightly routine of smoking her half a pack of cigarettes while people-watching under the dark cover of evening. At the sound of her name, Tara's cigarette twirled in a great arc and landed in the yard, the front door banging closed behind her as it landed.

Confused and growing more concerned by the moment, Lory continued down the center of the road, calling for Darla and the kids by name, until she came to the four-way split halfway down the hill. Headlights zoomed toward her. She barely made it to the curb as it passed by, only to hear brakes squeal as the car came to a shuttering stop while she struggled to calm her galloping heart.

"You're home early," Benjamin called out after he reversed to catch up with her and put his car in park in the middle of the road.

"Yes. Have you seen Darla or the kids by any chance?" Lory's stomach churned at his lack of concern about blocking traffic, an uncomfortable reminder of why she was home so early in the first place. She was glad to see no other headlights were approaching, but his lack of consideration for the other drivers wasn't any of her concern.

"No, I'm just getting off of work myself," he replied.

Even with the streetlights, it was still too hard to see what was happening at the other end of the road. She thought she spotted movement and set out to investigate.

"Hey!" She heard Benjamin call out from behind her. "Let me park my car and I'll help you look for them."

Lory waved her hand and called out a quick, "Thank you," as she continued on. She would have turned down his assistance altogether if it had been for anything less important. The only thing that mattered was that she found her children and got them home safely before it got any later. For them, she would accept even his help.

A long, loud noise tore through the air as a howling horn roared to life, echoing an eerie reverberation through the valley and straight down Lory's spine.

Once.

Twice.

The third and final blare of the fire station curfew siren finally went silent. The stillness hung heavy in the air as the dense fog slowly crept down over the trees like a white blanket used for a ghost costume, swallowing everything that it touched. The image of the ghostly trees reminded Lory of Darla's claims that real ghosts would now be free to roam the streets.

Shaking off the silly thought, Lory continued, heart leaping when she heard a familiar voice calling out for Kevin. She took off at a sprint and easily caught up with Darla, who was surrounded by a rowdy group of people gathered just outside of the fire station.

"What is going on?" Lory asked, as she searched the crowd, but only spotted Samantha and Cole. Kevin was nowhere to be seen. "And where's Kevin?"

At the mention of his name, all eyes turned on her, each with either a look of suspicion or anger. She ignored all of them and refocused on looking for his ball cap among the throng.

"They found more old mining equipment," Darla said, shaking her head. Her tone implied something much more serious going on, but Lory didn't understand what that had to do with her son and why Darla didn't just tell her where her kid was.

Lory's already racing heart rate spiked even higher. She tried to keep that fear out of her voice as she replied with a simple, "Okay?" as she glanced back to see Samantha call out for Kevin while she dragged Cole along through the townspeople, none of whom she recognized.

It was strange to see no one else helping them look for her child. Frustrated, she caught up with Darla and demanded, "Why is no one else helping look for him? They're just standing around watching."

Darla stopped and stared at Lory for a long moment as if she should know exactly what Darla was thinking, but Lory didn't understand the unspoken message.

Finally, Darla took a deep breath and responded, "They're blaming it on Kevin."

"What are you talking about? Blaming what on Kevin?"

"The mining tools." Darla waved her hands in the air. "They think he's communicating with the ghosts that are being stirred up with the blasts. More items appear every day. They started chucking them into a pile at the park on this side of town. Today, there was enough to fill the bed of a truck."

"That's ridiculous! Why would they think that?" Lory did not mention how he had found the two mud-caked items in the woods earlier, but there was no way he could have unearthed a truckload's worth in only a couple of hours.

"Because everyone sees him talking to nothing but air and he's always nearby whenever a new piece is discovered."

"Did they ever think maybe he just has an over-active imagination as he tries to process the grief of the loss of his father? Seriously, he's a little boy. There's no way he could have had anything to do with all of this!" Lory waved her hand around, astounded that these grown adults were so superstitious they had lost all rational thought and were projecting all of their fears onto an eleven-year-old little boy. "Besides, these hills are riddled with old mining tunnels. All the blasts are just shaking things around enough for them to rise to the surface."

"There's more going on with that boy than even you realize." Darla pointed a finger at Lory. "I know you've been busy with work, but I'm here with him day in and day out. I also know a lot about paranormal activity. That boy definitely has a connection to the other side and people are starting to notice. It's scaring the pants off of them."

Lory wanted to defend her kid. Even Darla seemed to be against him. Why did no one understand he was just dealing with grief in his own way— just like the doctors said? Why was everyone trying to single him out? Her mind spiraled, but she slammed the door shut on her errant thoughts. Stressing over the fears of others wouldn't help them find Kevin. That was the most important thing.

She swallowed her retort and led with what really mattered. "So, where is he then? What happened?"

"After they found the latest pile, they came to the house and started yelling at him through the fence. I came out as soon as I heard the noise, but he had already run off through the back gate."

"What did they say to him? Did they follow him?" The questions spilled out of Lory's mouth as fast as they entered her mind. Then a terrible thought filtered in, chilling her to the bone. "Did they do anything to hurt him?"

Darla shook her head. "From what I understand, they only yelled at him, and no one has seen him since. Trust me, they're looking for him too. Just for different reasons than we are." Darla's lip curled in disgust, and she spat in their direction as she raised her voice to add, "They're riled from the quakes and demanding answers. As if a little boy would know!"

"I don't care how scared they are. How could they treat a child like that?" Lory shot a look of fury in their direction. Some of them shifted on their feet, but the most senior members raised their chins and stared right back.

"I don't know. They shouldn't have, and I'm sure they will all feel terrible about it in the morning, but it's dark out and their fears are making them irrational."

"Which direction did he run? Where could he have gone?"

"Samantha caught up with him at one point, by the church," Darla said, pointing toward the building just across the tracks perched on a big hill. Lory started that way, but Darla grabbed her arm to stop her. "We've looked all over that part of town and couldn't find him. He could be anywhere at this point. Samantha said he yelled at her, "Go on without me," but he slipped away, and we have no idea which direction he went after that."

"How long ago?"

"About thirty minutes ago, just as the streetlights were kicking on."

"Alright, you take the kids back to your house and call the cops. We'll get some help and find him before it gets any later." Lory started to walk away and then spun around again. "And make sure you check your phone. My calls wouldn't go through."

Darla jerked in surprise, pulled her phone out of her pocket, and pushed the button to activate her phone screen. "Strange. It's showing full signal and plenty of battery." Lory saw a tremor race through Darla's whole body. "There's something in the air tonight… It's a heavy feeling." When she met Lory's eyes again, she quickly added, "Or maybe it's just something to do with the fog."

Confused, Lory looked up to see the fog was now only one street above them as she pulled out her phone and pushed to redial. Darla's screen lit up a second later as the familiar ringtone of ghoulish sounds filled the air.

"Shit." Darla quickly silenced the phone before lifting her shoulders in an apologetic shrug. The crowd glared at them even more ferociously than before. "Sorry."

"Just make sure you keep it on you." Up ahead, Samantha was still pulling Cole along by the hand. "Get them home. I need to find Kevin before he gets lost in the fog."

She watched long enough for Darla to catch up with her kids and pull them up the hill before she set out, walking right by the large group, not even stopping as Lory stared into the eyes of each person who was brave enough to meet her gaze. "You should all be ashamed of yourselves."

Then she stormed away, allowing her instincts to guide her feet as she called out for her son.

The fog covered the bottom portion of the valley within moments. The entire town was encased in a thick wall of wispy white clouds, only illuminated by the small balls of light from the streetlights overhead and the occasional light left on inside of one of the few remaining occupied houses. The narrow beam of light from her phone did nothing but help make sure she stayed on the sidewalk and didn't trip into one of the many huge missing chunks of uneven cement.

Lory stepped down off of one sidewalk and crossed a small street with stubbles of grass growing up through the cracks to get to the other side, nearly running straight into a thigh-high wooden post. She held onto it, trying to get her bearings in the near-complete darkness looming ahead. To the right, through the thick veil of fog, there was a blinking red light and further down another street light that switched from green to red.

"Wait—what?" Lory said to herself out loud. "Where am I?"

When Tom was alive, they had often taken the kids to the playground closest to their house. Lory knew by the direction she'd navigated from the firehouse and the familiar post, that she was at the far edge of the park;

however, there were no traffic lights on this end of town. No need for traffic lights now after the township had raised the highway and walled off the northern portion of town to prevent the worst of the river swells from the spring rains. This had all taken place decades before their family moved into their current home. The only remnant was a short strip of an old road that led to a dead end at the barrier—right where the streetlight continued to flip through its colorful sequence.

A gust of cool air stirred her hair forward, long tendrils blocked the lights from view. Lory ran her fingers through the front of her scalp, gathered the heavy mass with one hand, and held it back out of the way to reveal that the fog had parted, a wispy curtain pushed aside by the strength of the breeze.

Backlit by the sudden appearance of the large crescent moon, she watched as the road continued on much further than she remembered, until finally, the breeze died down at the edge of an exposed riverbank. Movement inside the thick cloud drew her gaze and she squinted to get a better look. After a long moment, she realized there was a group of people shrouded in shadows and smoke that stood in small clusters above the surface, almost as if floating in mid-air.

Are the ghost stories true?

Lory grappled to understand why the barrier was gone and how the people had gotten up there when a deep, sorrowful timbre of a sole fog horn blared to life. The sound startled her and caused goosebumps to race along every inch of her body as the long ominous tone enveloped the shrouded valley.

Through the wisps of fog at the other end of the cleared path, Lory noticed new movement. A massive dark shape appeared floating above the water. There were no lights, but the motion of the people and what must be a vessel they stood on, swayed in time with what could only be waves of the river below.

A ship. One without any electricity.

One of the taller shapes onboard stepped forward. A slender, shadowed form with a large round miner's hat on his head stepped forward and touched two extended fingers of his right hand to his temple and then brought them to his lips to blow her a slow kiss.

Lory's heart skipped a beat. Without thought, she moved, compelled toward him as if an invisible and overpowering gravitational force drew her forward.

"Tom?" Lory called out. The past and present collided into a single, pivotal moment. Time stood still as she glided toward the love of her life. Cloaked in darkness and mist, she couldn't see his face, but she knew the outline of her husband in his work uniform, and the gesture he had always used when he left for work.

Another strong breeze blew, as a smaller figure stepped forward and stood in front of Tom. Her husband reached down and put his hand on the tiny shadow's shoulder, as the fog once again parted enough to allow moonlight to shine down on them to illuminate the white mermaid symbol above the bill of the dark cap.

Sirens and loud whistles sounded from somewhere behind the clouds, but Lory ignored the noise as she leaped into action, calling out to her son.

"*Kevin?*" Lory rushed forward, only to come to a sudden halt as a car horn blasted as bright white headlights slashed through the fog. She stepped backward just in time to avoid being run over. Dazed, she watched as a car zoomed by, bright red, white, and blue lights whirled, momentarily blinding her. Even though she struggled with the disco of lights burned into her retinas, Lory put her arms out on either side of her body to regain her balance, as she chuckled at the irony of the situation. The cops had finally shown up, but she'd already found her child.

Her vision started to clear as the shrill sound of brakes screeched to a stop not too far down the street. She squinted to peer along the tunnel through the clouds created in the wake of the vehicle. A figure leaped out of the driver's side door and rushed to the right side of another vehicle that was stopped in the middle of the road.

The fog had been so thick she hadn't even realized there had been a car sitting idle in the street.

Lory shook her head and looked away, knowing how dangerous it was. How lucky they were that the cops had managed to spot them and stop in time to not rear-end them.

"Come on, Kevin" Lory yelled and started forward again. Another horn blared, even louder and closer than the first. She stumbled backward and fell hard onto the cement, as two fire trucks and an ambulance raced by. Brakes pierced through the noise of the sirens as they took positions around the idling cars. Doors opened and slammed shut as people in reflective uniforms grabbed their gear and raced over to where the cop was hunched over in front of his car. Two men wheeled in a stretcher.

Her heart lurched, realizing someone must have gotten hurt. She said a silent prayer for the person, as the other part of her sighed with relief that at least she knew Kevin was safe.

With Kevin on her mind, she glanced back toward the ship and waved them forward. "Come on, it's time to go home." She crossed the street and stepped onto the adjacent sidewalk.

The breeze settled and the fog thickened, but not before she saw Tom shake his head and point toward the accident. Confused, Lory glanced at the scene again. Her new vantage point allowed her to see between the shifting bodies of the first responders to where a single figure rested on the ground.

A second long, low blast of a ship's fog horn sliced through the air.

Lory's gaze swept back to Tom, to see a wall of mist. She took off, racing along the side street toward the river, only to encounter the reinforcement barrier of the highway.

"Tom?" she called out as she stumbled backward, looking for a break in the divider, but finding none. "Kevin?"

No ship.

No response.

"Help!" She cried as she spun and ran for the police, knowing they would be able to help reach her family. The faces of uniformed strangers all turned toward her, some of them rose, while others remained working on the person still lying on the ground, sneakers shifting as they worked on the prostrate figure. Something about the sneakers tickled at her memory, but she shoved it aside. Nothing was more important than finding her child and husband again.

She pushed on, rushing toward the outstretched arms that reached out for her. A large man in a police uniform caught her first and pulled her to the side.

"Ma'am?" he asked, in a calm, authoritative voice. "Ma'am, you can't be here."

"I need—help. My family—" she said between gasps, trying to slow her galloping heart and draw in enough breath to explain what happened.

"Let's go over here." The officer dragged her away from the scene.

"I know—" Lory pointed to the scene, surprised to see that the body was much smaller than it had first appeared. "But—wait!"

She dug her heels into the pavement as he continued to shove her out of the way, but her eyes were glued to a pool of dark liquid spread out around the body. With each second the pool expanded further to surround a dark object lying on the ground.

One of the responders shifted, making the fog swirl and dance away, as the beam of one of the headlights illuminated the small circular object.

A ball cap with a mermaid swimming through a sea of red.

Lory somehow shook loose of the iron grip holding her back and raced forward screaming Kevin's name. Her thoughts ricocheted as she grappled to understand what was happening.

The hat. The mermaid. The blood. Her son?

He had to be okay.

She ignored the voices that called out to her as she crumpled next to him and touched his shoulder, careful not to jostle him, or get in the way of the paramedics.

"Please, please. Don't go." A loud ringing noise filled her ears and blocked out the cacophony of sounds around her. She ignored the ringing and the hands that tried to tug her backward, refusing to leave his side. "I can't go on without you."

Then, just as suddenly as it started, the ringing stopped. Everything around her seemed to halt, almost as if suspended in time.

Through that silence, she heard a soft whisper brush against her mind, so gentle and in a child's voice so achingly familiar.

Two words that shattered her soul into a thousand tiny pieces.

"Go on."

?

Lory wandered through most of the next few hours in a state of cold confusion, as the sun rose above the hills and sliced through the row of windows lining the reception room at the hospital she knew like the back of her hand. Sobs no longer tore from her throat, as they had when they first arrived, and the achingly familiar nurses told her she had to remain on the outside of the Emergency Room's double doors. Now, there was just a constant flow of tears as pieces of her broken spirit leaked out of her eyes, blinding her from seeing the tops of the houses and trees lining each side of the valley.

Darla showed up moments or hours later and pulled her for a tight hug, but Lory's system didn't even register the embrace. Lory's internal clock was completely destroyed, and she had no concept of how long it had been before the doctor came out, wringing his teal surgeon's cap in his hands. The look in his eyes told her everything she needed to know.

Kyle hadn't made it. Deep down, she had known he was gone long before the doctor delivered the terrible news. Knew what Kevin had whispered to her through the darkness of the fog, but a mother's hope never wanes.

One of the nurses whom Lory knew, but couldn't recall the name of, came by to hand her a packet of information with a bunch of "Important numbers", but her brain wasn't processing anything beyond the nurse telling Lory that his body would be placed in the Morgue until she decided where to have it sent. She didn't even notice when Darla took the packet from her lifeless fingers and thanked her, before guiding Lory out to her car, and then snapped her seatbelt across her lap.

Benjamin was waiting outside when Darla parked in front of her house.

"Lory, I'm so sor—" Lory thrust her hand out, cutting off his words.

"No." Halting whatever condolences he intended to offer. There was nothing anyone could say or do to ease even an ounce of the pain created by the nightmare that was now the reality of her life.

"But I can help..."

Lory stared at him until he shifted uncomfortably and finally looked away.

"Not now, Ben," Darla said as she ushered Lory up the stairs and through the chain-linked fence.

The spot where she had last seen Kevin alive and talking to the wind under the brim of his mermaid cap mocked her. She lost control. She dropped to her knees as a scream tore from her throat while she ripped at the contemptuous blades of grass.

Front doors slammed closed behind curious onlookers still in their pajamas. Tara stood across the street, hand slapped across her mouth, eyes as wide as saucers.

"*You!* You did this to him!" Lory screamed, pointing an angry finger in Tara's direction and then swinging it wide to point at anyone who dared to look in her direction. "All of *you!*"

At Darla's firm touch, she collapsed onto the smaller woman and allowed herself to be guided inside where the two tiny, scared faces of what remained of her tiny family stood next to a graying lady with features remarkably similar to Darla.

?

Darla would not allow them to return to the house alone, but Lory and the kids needed to be home. Needed the security of something familiar in the chaos of such an earth-shattering loss. Darla followed them to their house, set up a place to sleep on the couch, and guided the sobbing children downstairs to make a meal for everyone.

Lory headed straight for Kevin and Cole's shared bedroom and threw herself down on the tiny twin bed filled with his favorite stuffed animals. She pulled each one to her and hugged them tight to her chest as she wailed, wishing there was something—anything she could do to bring her son and husband back.

At some point, she must have cried herself to sleep, because the next thing she knew, she was being shaken awake. Lory fought the hands and voice calling out to her, not wanting to leave the blissful darkness that surrounded her, but even as she did, her mind instantly leaped to the harsh reality of what happened as the reel of events replayed in her mind.

"You need to come downstairs. People are at the door."

"Tell them to go away," Lory said, even though she was already rising out of the bed. "I don't want to see anybody."

"You need to come down for this."

Darla helped her into her bathrobe and followed her down the stairs. Samantha and Cole clung to one another, fresh tears flowing from their red, puffy eyes. Lory rushed forward to see two men, in pristine, navy suits standing in front of a cheery Benjamin on the other side of their glass door.

"Hello, we're with the County and we'd like to make an offer on your house," the man with the clipboard tilted his head as he spoke, eyes flickering between Lory's face and the children. The second man fidgeted with his tie. "Uh, may we come in?"

Lory stared at them for a long, silent moment before dark, chaotic laughter bubbled up from some dark place deep inside her belly.

"*Now?* You show up *now?*" Lory shook her head as fresh tears burned hot trails down her cheeks. The unrestrained laughter continued on even after she slammed the door closed on the wish fulfilled hours too late.

Blackberry Kisses

By: William Joseph Roberts

"You heading back out already Rufus," Ammon Young, owner and operator of the Stone Bridge Saloon asked as I pushed my way through the swinging front doors. I glanced about the place before slowly making my way over to the bar.

"Yeah," I started to say, then looked over my shoulder at others in the room. "I've had my fill of civilization for a while."

Ammon smiled wide and nodded, the motion bounced the tips of his heavily waxed mustache. "I can't blame you. There's been plenty of times I wished I could pack it up and ride off into the sunset myself." He chuckled then leaned over, propping himself up with his elbows on the bar. "You sticking around the area, heading out to prospect a bit more, or are you heading for greener pastures?"

I glanced back over my shoulder and noticed a few folks staring in my direction like they were trying to listen in on our conversation. It wouldn't have been a problem if I hadn't recently come into town with a load of gold. I'd deposited it with the local banker for its current raw market value per ounce, which was fine by me. I didn't have the time or inkling to refine the raw gold ore any further than I had.

I also didn't have any doubts that one of these rustlers was just waiting to follow me out of town, hoping they could find where my claim was.

"There's a few other spots I wouldn't mind checking out just to see if anything was around," I replied, trying to sound as hopeful as possible. Stone Bridge was a small village at best, and the locals always talked, especially about new money coming into town. I'd like to say that every wrangler and rustler in the area knew what I'd brought in by now. There was a better-than-likely chance somebody had already found out, but what could you do? I'd just have to take my chances, taking a roundabout route back to my claim to throw off anyone trying to follow me.

"Well, you didn't come in here to have me jaw your ear off. What can I do for you, Rufus?"

"I'll take a bottle of whiskey if you have one to spare."

Ammon nodded and grabbed a bottle of whiskey from beneath the bar. "The whiskey I've got," he said. "That'll be a dollar."

"No, not that whiskey," I said, shaking my head. "I want one of those bottles from the top shelf." I pointed at one of the dark green bottles on the top shelf of the back bar.

Ammon turned, looking at where I pointed, then turned back to me. "That's a bottle of Old Monongahela rye whiskey carried here on the backs of traders all the way from Pennsylvania. It's eight dollars even a bottle, and that one's already been opened. Are you sure, Rufus?"

I nodded, set in my decision. "I'll take that one," I said, then reaching into my pocket dropped eight gold dollars on the bartop, each one clinking on the others with the distinctive sound of gold coins.

Ammon looked taken aback, then turning slowly he grabbed the bottle from the top shelf. "I can't rightfully argue with a customer that knows what they want." He gently placed the bottle in front of me. "It's supposed to be one of the best whiskeys made back east."

I pulled the cork and breathed deeply of the intoxicating fumes. "That'll do nicely," I said, then returned the cork, driving it deep to lessen the chance it would spill in my saddlebags.

"If you're in a mood for the rare and expensive out here, I got a little something extra that you might be interested in," Ammon said.

"You don't say? And what might that rarity be?"

"Fresh blackberries I grew myself. I had the vines shipped out here special from back east. I've been tending them for the last two years and they finally produced. Berries as thick as a cowhand's thumb. And as juicy as anything you've ever tasted."

I hadn't had a blackberry or anything close to it since I'd left Pennsylvania five years ago. And that last time was a blackberry cobbler made by Miss Jones, owner of the little hostel outside of Pittsburgh I'd stayed in before heading west for Saint Louis Missouri. I'd have much rather had strawberries, but beggars really couldn't be choosers out here in the wilderness.

I felt around in my pocket for the other coins I still had on me. Coins wouldn't do me any good in the wilderness. Spending them on something worthwhile before I could lose them made a lot more sense. I fished another gold dollar out of my pocket and dropped it on the bar. "Give me whatever that'll get me," I said.

Ammon reached under the bar, producing a wooden bowl with berries as big as he'd said and handed me one.

"Good as I promised. And the sample is on the house."

I took the offered berry and chewed slowly. The sweet tart juice bursting with flavor flowed across my tongue. Ammon wasn't lying. They were probably the best blackberries I'd ever had. I nodded and smiled. "Those are wonderful. You've outdone yourself, Ammon."

He bundled most of the bowl into a piece of baker's cloth and handed it to me.

"You make sure to let me know what you think of that bottle when you come back this way."

"Not sure exactly where I'm going next, but if I pass back through, I promise I will," I replied. He smiled with a nod as I grabbed the bottle and hurried for the entrance.

"What's your rush, Rufus," a voice I knew all too well spoke up before I could make it out the door. I turned toward the voice and sure enough, there was Dutch McGee and his buddy Bartholomew Jones, whom most folks just called Bart, or bad breath Bart, since his breath stank of putrid rot.

"Places to be, gents." I tipped my hat at them and then continued toward the door. I hadn't made it two steps toward the door before I heard the scraping of chair legs against the floor.

"What's the rush, friend?" Dutch said. I heard the slow jingle of spurred boots heading in my direction before I could turn back toward him.

"A man buys a bottle of whiskey and not share it among friends ain't so personable a man, is he Bart?" He flashed a yellow, crooked toothed grin my way. Everything about the man was as crooked as his smile. He was the type of feller who would sell his own grandmother for the right price. I smiled back as cordially as I could without letting the disdain I had for the man show through.

"A man buys a bottle of whiskey and it's a matter of his own business," I replied snarkily, then continued out the doors.

Mollie, my mule let out a guffawing whimper when she saw me step through the saloon doors.

"I'm sorry, I know," I replied to her grumping. "I promise, this is the last thing. I'm as ready as you are to get out of town." Mollie brayed at me. Lucy, my little lovebird chirped in response to Mollie. There used to be two of them, Lawrence and Lucy. It was rough on Lucy when Lawrence got sick and passed away. Lovebirds mate for life, and even after he'd passed, she wouldn't leave his side. She'd attack me when I tried to pull him out of the cage. It took me two days to bury him, and even then, I had to distract her. Since then, she'd sorta bonded to me. Lovebirds normally sit side by side most of the time when not hunting and such, so she gets a bit riled up whenever I'm gone for long. I know I can never replace Lawrence, but she at least seems content when she sits on my shoulder and nuzzles up against the side of my face.

"I didn't forget about you, young lady," I said, removing the cover from the wire cage mounted to Mollie's pack saddle.

Lucy chirped and bounced excitedly around the cage.

"Look, Lucy. I haven't forgotten you. I got you something special," I said taking the knot out of the bundle of berries. I dug one of the largest berries from the satchel and handed it to her through the cage door.

She chirped and sang a happy tune as she bit into the juicy berry then devoured it.

"That little squab wouldn't be more than a snack," I heard Dutch say from behind me. I almost reached for the flintlock pistol tucked into my belt, but instead, I pulled the cover back over the cage and hurriedly tucked the satchel of berries into the saddlebags.

"She ain't for eating," I replied, unlashing Mollies lead from the hitching post.

"I would hope not. Seems a waste of time, you ask me." Dutch spit a thick mouthful of tobacco juice onto the ground in front of me.

"No one asked you, Dutch. Now if'n you don't mind, I've places to be."

"Naw," he said around the wad of tobacco as he moved it from one cheek to the other. "I don't mind at all. We'll be seein' you around, *Rufus*." Dutch and his hired man Bartholomew both chuckled as they watched me, and Mollie walk on out of town.

The way he said my name sent a chill up my spine. Stone Bridge was a great little town to restock at, and it had a bank so I could deposit my haul and not risk carrying around a load of gold ore with me out in the backcountry. I had no plans to return to Stone Bridge anytime soon. Cause when I was done, I planned to head back to Salt Lake City. There was this pretty little widower gal who seemed to take a fancy with me on the trip out from St. Louis.

I hadn't been looking to make friends on the trip out west. I'd just planned to go about my business and more or less get away from civilization. I had had my fill of people while working in the steel mills back in Pittsburgh, but there was something about her that I didn't mind at all. She enjoyed my company, and I enjoyed hers, without any expectation of anything else. Maybe she just needed someone to talk to, or just somebody to listen to her.

Anne-Marie was an interesting sort. She loved everything about nature. She told me things about animal husbandry I would have never in my life thought to consider. From my understanding, she and her late husband had a nice spread of land and a healthy herd of Durham shorthorn cattle, but all that came to an end when Governor Boggs signed the Missouri Executive Order 44, known as the Execution Order to the Mormons living in Missouri at the time. Her late husband was one of the first gunned down in cold blood, but she escaped and fled the state with the other Mormons of the area to head west where they hoped they would be safe.

During the trek west, we'd talk about what we saw, the threat of natives, what we might find when we arrived at the Great Salt Lake, and our hopes for the future.

We even talked quite a bit about God and their holy book. There's was a bit different from what I remembered my mama reading to me, but that didn't bother me none. I never was much of a religious man, so it wasn't like I was leaving something important behind if I did decide to convert to their ways.

I figured I'd already made plenty on this vein of gold ore. And besides, it didn't look to have much more left to it anyway. I might be able to buy something nice for Anne-Marie. Might even see about settling down. The land up that way wasn't too bad. I'd heard it was decent enough for cattle and grapes. Maybe that's what we'd raise if she wasn't already married, and she'd have me. It had been a few years, but you never know.

If lady luck was on my side, I wouldn't cross paths with Dutch or any of his cronies again. It would be a blessing to work my claim and to be on my way. I'd just have to wait and see what fates had in store.

"Nothing to do for it now," I said to myself then scratched the side of Mollie's jaw. "We just keep trekking, following our feet, and we'll eventually get where we're going, won't we old girl?" Mollie snorted at me and continued walking.

We settled it down for the night, making camp in a small arroyo, backing up to some sandstone boulders that made for a good spot to get out of the wind. After starting a small cook fire, I fed Mollie a decent meal of dry fodder after her long trudge through the desert and gave Lucy some special seed I'd saved back for her.

"High on the mountain top, a banner is unfurled…." I sang low, not wanting to give away our hiding spot. The likelihood of coming across someone in the backcountry was slim, but one could never be too careful. There were too many people out there who would take advantage of anyone if they had a chance.

Lucy had heard me sing that tune so many times she jumped right in to provide the rhythm to the hymnal. Anne-Marie had taught me that song during our trek across the country. It was one of her favorites, and it had been written by one of her family members. For the life of me, I couldn't remember the songwriter's name. John? Joe? Joel? Something like that, but I just couldn't recall. I shrugged away the thought. It really didn't matter anyway, it was still a pretty song.

We continued through several more tunes, me singing to Lucy's accompaniment, low enough to not attract attention but just loud enough to run off any possible predators like coyotes. We finished our dinners and turned in for the night, blanketed by the bright shining lights that hung in the heavens above.

It was only another half-day walk to reach the claim, even with the roundabout route. I couldn't have gotten any luckier on its location. It was tucked away in a canyon so narrow that Mollie barely fit through the opening. I had to remove the gear then bring her through so she'd be out of sight and safe in camp.

The luckiest part of this claim was the freshwater spring that trickled through the sandstone and fed onto a small rocky pool at the back of the canyon.

Everything was still there, exactly where I had left it when we left the claim. I got things settled into place, stowing our gear in small alcoves I'd carved into the back wall near the pool. Mollie settled in for a long drink at the pool. No sooner had I removed the cage from Mollie's back than Lucy started chirping, wanting out of her confinement.

I waited to let her out of the cage until I'd gotten everything moved around so she wouldn't happen to be in the wrong place at the wrong time. Once that was done, I removed the cover from the cage and opened the door so she could flit about. She never really went too far. I figured if she ever wanted to leave, she'd leave on her own, but until then, I'd make sure she had what she needed. Following suit with Mollie, she headed to the water and began bathing in it, cooling herself. She sang her happy song between each beakful of water from the pool.

She was so happy to be out of her confinement that she sang a chortling song then flew over and landed on my shoulder. Chirping excitedly, nuzzling her beak against the side of my face she made kissing sounds then said 'thank you'.

"You're welcome, Lucy. I just didn't want you to get hurt on the trip or lost. Anytime I can let you out of that cage, I will. Just doesn't seem right to keep someone caged up all the time, but sometimes it's safer."

Once she was done singing her happy tunes, I went right back into my regular routine as if I'd never left. Getting myself a drink first, I washed off the dust of the trip from my face and neck before I went back to crushing the quartz I had previously mined. It wasn't hard work, really. Just time-consuming.

The sandstone ground down just as well as the quartz, but with the good granite rock I'd found and brought with me, it made easy work of crushing and grinding the quartz to get to the gold.

The rest of the evening I sat there, grinding, crushing, and pounding away at the dirty clear crystal. Placing the dust I made into a pan, I sifted and swirled it through the pool to wash away the debris and retrieve the gold. There weren't any large chunks like anyone would wish for, only tiny flakes, some of them nearly too small to see in some cases. By using a hollow piece of strawgrass, I siphoned those pieces out without too much trouble and put them into a little bottle. The next morning, I was up before dawn and made a good hearty breakfast. A fatty hunk of bacon, a couple of fried eggs, fried potatoes, and a few biscuits. What I didn't eat for breakfast I'd have for dinner when I came out of the hole later that evening.

That's when it was *really* time to get to work. The worst part of it all was getting into the opening that I'd carved into the stone. I should have dug the opening wider a while ago, but since the vein was nearly worked out it didn't make much sense to put that much work into it. If there ain't no more quartz to dig out, there ain't no more gold to get. It would be a lot of work for nothing just to open the hole up a little bit.

The hours tended to pass quickly when you're down in the cool quiet of a mine. But it made it much more bearable when you had company. Mollie stayed out at the campsite, guarding everything. I wasn't too worried about her wandering away either. I left enough grains for her to munch on over the course of the day, so she'd stay close.

Lucy, on the other hand, was my partner in crime when it came to mining this hole. She was my cave canary, even though she wasn't a canary. But I figured the principle was the same. That was the whole reason I bought her and her mate. They'd let me know if I got into some bad air, and I could have time to get out. I'd even made her a smaller cage, so it was easier to carry her into the tunnel. It wasn't anything special. Just a wooden box with wide openings, but it did its job.

We scooted our way into the hole to where it widened out. The candles I left behind were still in place, and I quickly lit my lantern, then lit a small taper from that which I used to light each of the candles I'd placed, carving a small shelf for them in the wall of the seam. It wasn't a lot of light, but it was enough for me to work by and not so much that it would get too hot in the mine. I crawled from there, pushing my pick and other things ahead of me. The seam wasn't so big that I could stand, but that didn't bother me much. Kneeling was fine enough to work the claim. We continued, scooting our way to the end where I'd last been digging.

Once I reached the end where I'd left off digging, I placed Lucy and her little wooden cage back on the shelf I'd carved into the wall above me so she was out of the way and less likely to get hit on accident.

This part of the seam was easier to work with my little handpick than the regular-sized one. It was easier to swing and control in the tight space. I had to decide if it was worth carving out all of the surrounding rock for this little bit of quartz and possibly gold ore.

I chipped at the stone and started to hum, keeping time as I worked. Lucy joined in, her song a beautiful melody that echoed through the mine. We'd sing songs like Amazing Grace, De Camptown Ladies, or High on the Mountain Top, entertaining ourselves and keeping each other company.

I worked and toiled in the dusty underground until I had filled several buckets and sacks. Once that was done it was time to carry it all back out and to start extracting the ore.

I always carried Lucy out first, and then I collected the bags and buckets afterwards, snuffing the candles as I made my way out of the hole. Once again settled back in camp I'd set Lucy free so she could fly about and do as she wished, then I'd settle myself down at my grinding stone. As I worked the quartz with the grinder, it carved a bowl-like divot into the sandstone. It meant there was more debris to wash away in the end, but the divot kept everything more or less together, and I didn't have to go chasing pieces of quartz too often.

It wasn't hard work, just quiet tedium, accompanied by song as I ground down the raw chunks to dust that could be sifted.

There was something to be said about the sound of wind blowing through a canyon, the trickle of water, and a happy songbird singing her happy song. She dove and fluttered and splashed away in the pool.

That's when I remembered the blackberries that I'd gotten from Ammon. "What do you say about one of those nice big blackberries to go with lunch? But you aren't getting so much that you'll make yourself sick," I said, dusting myself then fished around in the packs until I found the bundle of berries

I got a blackberry for me, a blackberry for Lucy, and a carrot for Mollie just cause I couldn't rightly give a treat to one and not to the other one. Mollie did her happy snort, and Lucy sang away as happy as a lark.

Day after day, week after week, till almost a month had gone by, I'd dug the seam nearly clean, to the point where it was no wider than my pinky finger. It was going to take a whole lot of work to go much further. I scooped up the leavings, then brought one of the candles close to the seam. There was still a thread of gold in there, I could see it amid the dirty quartz.

"Maybe if I'm lucky it'll widen out a little further in," I said, turning back to Lucy. "What do you think? Should we keep going?" She chirped and sang. At least it was sandstone. It was fairly easy digging. Just tight, and sometimes hard to breathe once the dust got all stirred up.

Using my small hand pick, I marked lines on both sides of the seam as a guide, then got back to digging. It wasn't looking too good. Most of the day was spent widening that hole with little other results to show for it. I scooped up what quartz I did have, which was only about half a bucket's worth. The rest was nothing but stones, gravel, and dust.

Before I reached the entrance, I could hear Mollie making a fuss like a rattlesnake had come up into the sanctuary of our little campsite. Maybe a coyote had wandered in. If it had, I felt bad for the poor thing. It wasn't a nice end for the last one she'd gotten hold of.

Cautiously, I made my way up to the opening, sliding out of the hole.

"Can't be much further," a voice said from somewhere in the canyon.

I froze.

"That ain't no good," I whispered to myself. Hurrying, I slid out of the opening, leaving all my gear behind, and made a beeline straight for my packs. My shotgun was already loaded with powder and shot. I fumble around for my cap case. I slung the leather strap of the cap case, cartridge pouch, and powder horn over my neck then fumbled in the case for the priming caps.

Just after I'd bought the gun, an old timer told me about a fella he knew who managed to shoot himself in the foot with a revolver that used priming caps when his hand was nowhere near the trigger. The shot took off at least two of the man's toes on his right foot. Most folks said the guy was just stupid, got his trigger hung and a few others said it was dumb luck. The old timer who'd been out in the world awhile and had seen a thing or two said it was the heat of the desert that did it. He said the caps were like nitro, that they were unstable in the right conditions, and if they got too hot, they'd blow off just like they'd been struck.

What he said made a whole lot of sense, so from then on, I followed his words of advice. I kept a bit of wax on hand to put over the nipple so the powder couldn't fall out and to keep moisture from getting to it. Whenever it came to shooting something for dinner, I'd been plenty fast enough getting the cap on there.

But damn if it didn't make things slower now. Grabbing a couple of caps from the case, I half-cocked the hammers of the double-barreled shotgun, removed the wax, and placed the caps over the nipples. Both barrels were already loaded with lead shot. That was good enough for killing most small game for dinner or for scaring away the larger critters.

I cocked both hammers back and hurried to the far side of the canyon where Mollie was.

"Shhhh, it's okay, Mollie," I said, rubbing her side, trying to calm her. Leaning up against the canyon wall, I waited for whoever was wandering up on my claim to come around the edge of the canyon. Whoever they were, they were not in any sort of hurry. And they weren't worried in the slightest about being heard. They were taking their sweet time, jabbering on and on about nothing in particular, then I heard one of the last names I wanted to hear.

Dutch.

And sure enough, it was Bart that had said it. Their voices carried and began to echo off the walls the closer they got. I could tell when they were about to come around the corner of the canyon, their gun belts scraping along the rock through the narrow section.

"I really don't care what you wanna do with that old sum bitch, Bart. You do whatever makes you happy. The *main* thing I want is his gold. Terrence Johnson, the banker, said he brought in over $50 worth of gold the last time he came to town. There's a whole lot of money. And I want in on it."

"So, we don't have to kill them right off?" Bart asked.

"No, Bart, we don't have to kill him right off. But I don't want to spend too awful long out here. I'd like to get back to town where it's nice and comfy. And I got a sweet soft thing waiting for me back there who sure is a hell of a lot prettier to look at than your sorry ass."

I know it was dirty to shoot a man in the back. But the fact that they were going to kill me, and probably Mollie and Lucy to boot, I didn't see a problem shooting them unawares before they had the chance to do anything else.

As soon as I saw Bart round the end of that corner, I let loose with both barrels at the same time. That 10 gauge kicked something like a mule, bearing down, tearing into my shoulder.

I hurried and pulled two more cartridges from the case, dropping in the powder and the shot with the wad right behind. I slid the rod out and packed them home till they made that distinctive 'tink'. It wasn't quite as good as the sound a ball made when it seated, but it was good enough.

"That some bitch shot me!" Bart wailed and screamed.

"Why'd you stick your head out there before you looked around." I heard Dutch berating him. "And why are you screaming? He didn't hardly even break the skin. Look at you."

I heard Dutch let out a curious chuckle.

"Is that the best that you got, Rufus? You ain't going to do nothing but pepper poor Bart here with that scatter gun."

"Yeah, is that all you got, old timer?" Bart shouted at me.

That got me thinking for a moment. We weren't much different in age. It's a mileage that made the difference in a man. I had to laugh at him calling me an old timer when I was barely in my thirties.

But he did have a good point. This scattergun was only going to be good to pepper them with buckshot. We were probably thirty to forty yards apart. Quickly I pulled two cartridges from the back of my case I'd set up special and removed the ball, then twisted the end so I didn't lose any of the powder. I pressed one of the lead balls into each of the barrels and drawing the rod once more, packed them into place before I pressed a cap over the nipples and fully cocked each barrel.

By this point Mollie had retreated to the back of the Canyon, squalling for bloody murder.

"Why don't you two go on home? Ain't nothing here for you."

"I beg to differ," Dutch replied "You got a *whole* lot of reasons for us to be here. Any amount of gold makes it worthwhile in my book."

"Then I reckon we have ourselves a problem," I replied.

"I reckon we do," Bart interjected.

"Let's be peaceful about this, Rufus," Dutch said. "You hand over all the gold, cash, anything valuable like watches, rings, guns, things of that nature. We'll call it even and let you live. We'll even let you keep that flea-bitten mongrel of yours so you might not die out here all alone in this godforsaken desert.

Anyway this went, I knew they weren't letting me walk out of there alive. The sheriff would have no choice but to lock Dutch up if I were to go back to Stone Bridge after Dutch and claimed he'd robbed me. Especially if he'd tried to sell my gear. Most of the folks in town knew me, and Dutch wasn't the type who wanted to spend his days in jail, so that left only one other option.

I knelt close to the wall and aimed, ready to take another shot. "Alright, Dutch. You got yourself a deal. Let me walk out of here, and I'll give you what I got."

"That is mighty kind to you, Rufus," said Dutch. "I'm glad to see you come to your senses. I promise you, this is a mutually beneficial agreement for both of us."

Bart was the first to jump out from the corner with his pistols at the ready. He must have expected to jump out and surprise me. Gun me down where I stood.

I pulled the first trigger before Bart even knew what had happened. That shotgun kicked twice as hard as before, shoving me backward. It nearly knocked me off my feet.

I recovered as fast as I could and placed the bead right on Dutch who popped out from the corner a split second later and hadn't had time to react to the first shotgun blast. Before he could turn tail and run, I pulled the second trigger, and my entire world turned into a cacophony of fire and smoke.

The blast sent me flying backward, skidding across the sandy floor of the canyon. My face felt like it was on fire. Several spots felt like something had struck me. The stink of burnt hair and flesh overwhelmed the smell of spent powder. Several slivers of steel stuck out from my cheek, and one spot felt like several pieces of buckshot had lodged themselves under the skin. I plucked one of the slivers out of my face, and the world spun around me once more.

The echo of Dutch's screaming sounded distorted, and his words as he cussed me sounded oddly wrong.

"You son of a bitch! You'll pay for my eye!" He cried, his wails echoing through the canyon.

I rolled to my side, getting to my knees as quickly as I could. The world spun again, and the ringing in my ears grew to a nauseating level. Next to me on the dusty ground was what was left of my William Moore shotgun. The second barrel had split and curled back to one side. I shuffled back to my packs and retrieved my gun belt and my flintlock pistols. Quickly I primed the pans, set the frizzens, and readied them before sliding them back into their holsters.

Forcing myself to my feet I fought back the dizziness and disorientation, shuffling my way over to the corner where the canyon path turned. There on the ground, Bart lay motionless in a pool of drying blood that soaked into the dusty canyon floor. I peeked around the corner and found Dutch lying on the ground. He kicked at the sand, whimpering and his hand against the side of his head attempting to staunch the flow of blood.

I hadn't been sure I'd hit him, but apparently, the shot had removed his left eye and quite a chunk of meat from that side of his face. His cries almost sounded like the whining of a spoiled brat that had gotten his ass whooped for something he most certainly deserved.

"Listen real good, Dutch," I said as loudly and firmly as I could. "I, for one, do not condone cold-blooded killing. You and your man planned to kill me. I say your current situation is an open advantage for me. Take a second and say your piece to get right with the All-Mighty because you're fixing to meet him."

I gave him the span of a few moments before I pulled the trigger. The little .54 caliber pistol kicked, rising with the shot. The ball buried itself deep into Dutch's chest. Blood pooled beneath him, seeping from the wound and soaking his shirt a dark crimson red.

His entire body went limp.

Slowly, I took my time reloading the pistol. I was pretty sure that Bart was dead. I watched closely, seeing no sign that he was still kicking, but one more shot to be sure wouldn't hurt. Lowering the pistol to aim at his chest, I pulled the trigger one more time just to make sure Bart was no longer a threat.

Shuffling my way back into camp, I knelt beside the small spring pool and washed the sweat and dust from my arms, face, and neck. Slowly I plucked at the slivers of shrapnel still embedded in my face and arm, urging buckshot from under the skin, and back out the holes they had made.

"What do you two think?" I shouted toward Mollie, then realized I'd left Lucy in the hole. I hurried, scrambling to my feet to make sure she was okay.

She chirped and made one hell of a racket. I knew that tone. She was not happy with me at all. Probably because I'd abandoned her in the hole by herself and she couldn't tell what was happening outside.

I opened the cage, letting her out and she flew right up to my shoulder and nuzzled the side of my face.

"It's okay darling. I'm alright."

Her twittering got even louder at the sound of my voice. And she must have been able to tell that I was hurt with the way she pecked and inspected the wounds on my face and arm, bouncing around here and there.

"I think we've been out here long enough, don't you? Maybe it's time to head north. I don't think we'll have to worry about those two anymore, at least not until the afterlife. Let's finish out this seam in the morning and see if it doesn't fan out again like I think it might. If it doesn't, we'll go on and head for Salt Lake and see about visiting Anne Marie. I believe you're going to like her. And I know she's going to absolutely adore you." Lucy kept chittering at me, nuzzling in against my cheek again.

Even after all of the commotion, we were back to our evening routine like nothing had transpired. Singing along with Lucy's twittering chirps, I set the rhythm by grinding down the quartz I'd already dug out of the seam.

The next morning we were up early before daylight again and sliding into the hole as hints of morning started to creep across the top of the canyon.

Like so many other mornings before, Lucy and I slid our way into the claim, lit our candles, and made our way up to the work spot.

I set Lucy's cage on the little shelf I had carved out on the side of the wall. This time I took up the big pickaxe and swung with everything I had.

The quicker I could carve out the raw stone, the quicker I could get down to the quartz. I carved my path wide, hoping that the vein would widen out again.

Three heavy strikes and the hole opened up into another chamber. Cold, stale air flowed out from the opening, chilling my sweat drenched face.

"Well, we might just be in luck, Lucy. Might be bad, too though. You never know till you look closer," I said, trying to see anything beyond the darkness. I continued, widening the opening large enough that I could reach in with a candle and take a look around.

Lucy acted perfectly fine, and the candles were fine, other than a slight flicker from the flow of air, so I figured there wasn't any bad air in the place. Leaning through the opening with a candle in hand, I wriggled my head and shoulders into the next chamber.

It wasn't just a cavern, it was a room with hand worked stone that I was looking into from just below floor level. I wasn't sure how far back into the canyon wall I had actually dug. My tunnel had been a twisty sort, going up and down and off to the side like. I reckon I could have been deeper into one of the nearby hillsides. Maybe it was some kind of Indian burial mound nobody knew about, and I just happened to stumble on it.

Sliding back out, I widened the hole enough that I could easily slip my whole body through. Grabbing Lucy, I pushed her ahead of me just to be on the safe side and shimmied my way through with a candle in hand.

"I'll be damned," slipped out of my mouth before I even knew my mouth was saying words.

The walls of the room were carved and painted in the same kind of symbols that Anne-Marie had shown me in her people's version of the Bible. What she had shown me was supposed to be some kind of embossed golden disc that John Smith had found buried back east. They always did remind me of the ancient Egyptian artifacts I'd seen in a museum in New York City when I'd visited with my parents decades ago.

I turned slowly, careful not to move so fast that the candle flame snuffed itself. Each wall of the chamber was carved in the same imagery. Clay jugs, bowls, and other pottery that contained rounded stones, and the desiccated remains of something unidentifiable that sat stacked in one corner.

Maybe this was some kind of storeroom? I thought to myself, but why would they go to so much trouble with the decorations on the walls if it was a storeroom?

It was something for sure that I needed to go tell Anne-Marie's people about. I was sure it was something they'd be interested in.

Maybe.

There was nothing in the room that I could take to prove what I was saying except maybe one of the small stones, but they were just rounded stones. I pocketed one then a thought hit me.

I hurried out of the hole and back to camp, grabbing the cleanest piece of canvas that I could find and charcoal from the cookfire. The canvas was the heavier type, great for keeping the rain off, but it might be difficult to do a rubbing. I think I had any other options, then I remembered the cotton sacks for flour and sugar. I transferred what was left in the flour sack to another container and hurried back into the claim.

I was determined if there wasn't anything for me to take, I'd make something to take.

Sliding back into the chamber, I cut the sack down each side and laid it out flat against the wall over a section of wall with the most interesting group of symbols. I had no idea what it might have meant, but it would be perfect to prove what I said was true.

Carefully I rubbed the charcoal across the sackcloth, successfully transferring the impression of the carvings. Satisfied with the results, I rolled the cloth into a small bundle and tucked it into my shirt, hoping it wouldn't smudge or smear. Grabbing Lucy, I made my way back out, gathering my gear along the way.

"Anne-Marie is going to be so excited when I show her this," I said to Lucy, setting her free once we were back out in the open. I hurried to pack up camp then stopped, looking overhead. "Hell, it's too late to get started today. We'll have to leave at first light. But we can make the most of it now and get everything we can ready to go.

I set back into my daily routine, grinding away at the remaining quartz so nothing was left behind. I'd need the coin the gold would earn once I made it back to Salt Lake.

This was just the thing to get in good graces with Anne-Marie and her people. I know they don't care much for outsiders, and I can't say I blamed them considering the way they were treated, but she knows I'm a good person. It's not like I plan to take advantage of her.

And if she just happens to be married already, then I'll let it be and go on my merry way. But I'll still let her people know what I found.

The evening seemed to pass as slow as molasses in winter. I was excited to get on the road. The camp was all but packed and ready to go by the time the sun had set, and the fire had started to burn low.

I lay there looking up at the stars in the sky through the top of the canyon, like looking through the crack in a door to a whole other world beyond. That's when a shooting star soared the length of the canyon and disappeared beyond the edge to the south.

"Did you see that, Lucy? A shooting star is good luck. You're suppose to make a wish on a shooting star."

She chirped and sang at me I thought in reply to my words. I'd barely heard the scuffle of boost on the sandy bottom of the canyon floor. I turned toward the sound and watched a shadowy figure emerge from the darkness into the dim firelight

Dutch hovered over me, staring down with one bloodshot orb and a bloody vacant socket. He looked as pale as any corpse I'd ever laid eyes on. Like something from the great pit returned to this world to exact its revenge on me for killing him.

"By the power of the All Mighty, I cast you out, demon!" His entire body shook and quavered as he struggled to shuffle forward, one foot slowly in front of the other.

"You will pay," he said in a raspy tone, forced through dry chattering lips. He forced a dry swallow and took another breath. "You dirty… son of a bitch."

His arm rose and I rolled before he could pull the trigger. I threw the first thing my hand landed on and threw the stone in his direction. He fumbled, dodged, and fell sideways, crumpling to the ground.

He weakly brought the weapon up once more, but I grabbed a chunk of wood from the fire and threw it at him. He flinched in a feeble attempt to dodge. Kicking at the ash and hot coals in the fire pit in his direction, I dove to the side, easily dodging his shot that aimlessly ricocheted off the canyon walls.

I hurried over to where my packs and gear were stacked and ready to load onto Mollie, retrieving my pick. Feebly, Dutch tried turning himself in my direction.

I dashed to the side, expecting another shot, but only saw Dutch sitting there, each gasp for breath was accompanied by a wet sucking gurgle

"Were you too damned dirty and corrupt that the devil decided to spit you back out?" I asked.

Dutch flashed a weak smile and let out a grunt. "I believe the old demon left me alive long enough to drag your sorry ass with me," he said, slowly raising his pistol once more.

My pickaxe came up faster than his pistol as I charged forward, side stepping him and sunk the dulled tip into his back. He coughed, gasping worse than any miner I'd ever heard. Placing my foot on Dutch's back, I wrenched the tool free and struck at him over and over again.

Before I realized it, Dutch was an unrecognizable mass soaking into the canyon floor.

My stomach churned from the stench of blood and the excitement of the fight. Cursing Dutch's eternal soul for the stink of blood sure to be stuck in my nose for days, I dropped the pickaxe and dragged myself over to the pool where I washed away the dust and gore as best as I could in the dim fire light.

"That's not exactly a good way to end an evening, is it Lucy?" I said. Lucy took flight and landed on my shoulder, chirping and chiding at me again. She nuzzled her beak against the side of my face and buried her face into my thick matting of whiskers.

"Yeah. I think we're safe, darlin. Dutch won't be coming back to bother us any more. What do you say about a little something too calm our nerves before we try to turn in again?" She chirped and sang as I fished out the cloth with what remained of the blackberries, a carrot for Mollie, and the bottle of whiskey from the packs. After calming Mollie, I sat beside the fire, opposite from Dutch and began to rekindle the flames. It wasn't so much to keep off the cold. It was a comfortably warm evening for the desert. It was more to keep the demons of my mind at bay. I raked together what coals remained, adding a bit more fuel to stoke the flames, then I unwrapped the bundle.

Lucy sang one of her happy songs, and I hummed along with her for a moment before handing her one of the berries.

I uncorked the bottle and took a long drink. "Yep…" I looked at the pretty printing on the label, tracing the scrolling letters with my thumb. "I think I'm over being a miner and ready to head north." I took another long swing from the bottle. "Maybe it's high time to look into some other profession." I smiled at the thought of Anne-Marie. "Maybe it's time I gave farming a shot. Raise some cattle, maybe some kids." I shrugged and took another drink then ate one of the berries myself. They were slightly shriveled by this point, but just as flavorful as the day I bought them from Ammon. "You never know, I might be good at running a farm."

Lucy chattered and pecked at my hand then flew back up to my shoulder where she nuzzled against my cheek.

"You want another one?" She sang her happy tune once more. I held up another berry and she ravenously dug into it, nipping my fingers in the process and covering her orange beak in the dark purple juice.

I took one more long pull from the bottle then lay back on the ground, staring up at the star-filled sky. Lucy perched herself on my chest, and I handed her one more berry. Another flash of light and a shooting star blazed across the sky overhead. The vastness of the heavens was almost overwhelming, especially out in the darkness of the backcountry.

Lucy sang her happy tune, and I looked back at her, prancing about my chest. "I really like those berries too. We'll have to thank Ammon if we ever see him again." She nuzzled the tip of my nose, leaving behind a wet juicy blackberry kiss.

"I love you too, Lucy," I said and kissed her on the top of her head. Even with all the trouble, I knew we'd be all right.

Inconceivable

By: Lorraine Sharma Nelson

July 20th. 1969

He stared at the footprints — for what else could they be? — in front of him.

A dream.

No. *A nightmare.*

In that instant, American Astronaut, Neal Armstrong — the first *man* to step foot on the moon — knew that nothing on earth would ever be the same again.

He blinked, taking a deep breath of the oxygen being piped into his helmet. *This can't be what it looks like. It's not possible.*

Inconceivable

"Neal?" Astronaut Edwin *Buzz* Aldrin's thin, crackly voice piped into his helmet. "Why didn't you answer me? I said —" Buzz stopped somewhat ungainly beside his colleague, following Neal's line-of-sight. "What's that?"

Silence.

Neal continued staring at the strange, oddly-shaped prints, outlined in vivid detail on the lunar soil, leading away into the horizon.

"Neal? What the hell is that?"

"What does it look like to you?" Neal's voice was eerily calm, but Buzz could sense the tension behind it.

"It … it looks like some kind of footprints. Only, it's all wrong. And, impossible." He glanced at Neal, whose gaze was riveted on the anomaly. "What … uhh …?"

"We need pictures. And, we need to contact Mission Control."

Buzz's breathing accelerated, sounding unnaturally loud in the confines of his helmet. "This changes everything, doesn't it?"

Neal Armstrong turned toward his colleague, his movements clumsy on the alien surface. "Everything, Buzz. It changes everything, moving forward. For all mankind."

TRANQUILITY MILITARY BASE
October 23rd. 1975

"At ease, Mitchell. Relieving you."

Travis Mitchell looked up, a trace of annoyance on his weathered face. "About time, D'Angelo. You're twenty minutes late." Mitchell rose to his feet, stretching broadly. "Man, I'm bushed."

D'Angelo took the vacated seat, his gaze scanning the computer screen in front of him. "No unwelcome visitors yet, I see."

Mitchell glanced at him. "You say that every time. If there were, you think we'd be standing here, rapping?" Mitchell grabbed his book and lunch bag. "However, if you ask me, I'd say it's unlikely we'll know when they come back. And, when we do find out, it'll be too late. "

D'Angelo smiled. "Paranoid much? We've got the entire moon and earth under surveillance, Mitch. If they're anywhere near, we'll know."

"Carmine, they landed on the moon who knows how long before us. They came from *outside* our solar system. *Outside*, man." Mitchell shook his head. "Six years later, and I still can't wrap my head around it. Does it not occur to you — to anyone in the International Space Alliance — that they may have dampening devices to hide their approach?"

"Cloaking devices, you mean?" D'Angelo said, with a grin. "No, it hasn't occurred to me. That kind of technology would be almost impossible."

"*Star Trek* references notwithstanding, I want to stress my point, again, that *that* kind of technology is nonexistent for *us*. They most probably already have it. And, who knows what else, besides. Hell, they're probably already here, watching us."

"You're saying they're Klingons?" D'Angelo's grin widened.

Mitchell rolled his eyes, spun on his heels, and strode away. "When we're under attack," he shot back over his shoulder, "I'm going to be yelling *I told you so*. Not that it'll do much good when we're all busy being vaporized."

"Phasered, you mean?" D'Angelo couldn't resist one last *Star Trek* reference, then laughed when he heard Mitchell's disgusted snort. He turned to Julie McCormick, hunched over the console nearest to him. The glare of her computer screen bouncing off her glasses made her look even more robotic than usual. "How about going for some coffees, Jules? I'm buying."

"Get your own coffee," she snapped, reaching to the printer to tear off the latest results. "Some of us actually have a job to do."

D'Angelo sighed, settling down at his console. Ever since Armstrong and Aldrin detected the first signs of the existence of extraterrestrial life six years ago, the world had literally changed. Gone were the plans for the rest of the Apollo program. Proof of alien life changed the course of the Space Race. Instead, within a year, the United Nations Security Council formed the International Space Alliance, universally referred to as the ISA. Six short years after the discovery, a military base was established on the Sea of Tranquility, manned by crew from all twenty-seven member countries.

Amazing, D'Angelo thought, *that just a few years ago, many of these countries were at war with each other, over borders and religion. Now, earthly grievances seem petty in comparison to the threat of extraterrestrial invasion.* He reflected on how wars between nations ground to a halt in the wake of the revelation that humans are not alone in the universe.

It was deemed illogical for men to fight amongst themselves when facing God-knows-what from superior alien creatures zooming around the cosmos. Funds that were previously used for military purposes were diverted to the ISA's military base on Tranquility, with a second base planned for Mars.

Still, despite man's new humanity to man, a pall of paranoia hovered over the earth. The general consensus was that it may be invaded by aliens at any moment in time. The ISA was created to protect the earth from alien invasion. Its presence was supposed to reassure its citizens that an attack was never going to happen.

Instead, it had the opposite effect.

The speed by which it was created convinced everyone that doomsday was imminent.

Still, despite the fear gripping the world, it was the first time in human history where all of mankind was on board with one common goal: to protect life on earth at all cost.

But, was the ISA and the military bases a solution?

More importantly, were they enough?

?

Idilé Idibara hummed to himself as he swept the outer edge of the Sea of Serenity in his rover. As always, the complete lack of noise served to calm, to relax him. God, he loved this job. He still couldn't believe that he got paid to scout this entire section of the lunar surface. He'd been at it for seven months now, and each time he ventured outside the base, and started up the rover, a thrill swept through him. A tremor of excitement.

It never got old.

Yet, as he glanced at the stunning blue marble on the horizon, hovering in the blackness of space, he couldn't help but think how alone, how vulnerable, his home planet looked. *Does it even occur to people*, he wondered, as he turned the rover to the far side of Serenity, *how extremely exposed we are? If there really was an invasion, who would come to our defense? It's not as if we had our own version of Star Trek's Federation, consisting of numerous alien races, ready to defend our own world.*

We would be entirely alone.

Idilé's humming faltered when he made a wide curve around a particularly large boulder. He slammed on the brakes, his heart starting to thud in his chest.

What the actual hell?

What *was* that?

He stared at the small silvery orb, half embedded in the soil, already reaching for his radio. "Tranquility, this is Idibara. I've come across something. Over."

"Tranquility here. Go ahead, Idilé."

"Carmine, there's something half buried in the soil on Serenity. Something round and silvery. Request orders. Over."

"Jesus," D'Angelo said. "Hold the phone, buddy. I'll patch Colonel Yamada in. Over."

Idibara sat still in the rover, listening to the sounds of his own breathing, which was definitely not calm and controlled right now. He didn't dare take his eyes off the orb.

It didn't make sense.

Either an alien astronaut was careless and dropped it at some point.

Or …

They wanted it to be found.

?

Colonel Kenji Yamada, and Major Rafe O'Connor stared at the orb, now securely encased in a thick transparent dome in a clean room, free of all contaminants. O'Connor brought his face closer to the round window through which they observed the sphere.

"Thoughts?" he murmured, fingers clenched by his side.

Yamada slowly shook his head. "Too many to count, but the one question I want answered, I probably won't know the answer to until it's too late." He glanced at O'Connor. "Was it left behind by accident, or left there for us to find?"

"Has Acharya's team been able to make any sense of it?"

"Not yet. They're still working on identifying the material." Yamada squinted as he pressed his face up against the window. "Remarkable stuff though. They tried to scrape some shavings off the surface, but weren't even able to manage that."

"Couldn't they slice a piece off with a laser?"

"They considered it, but dismissed the suggestion. We don't know if it's a bomb set to activate when tampered with. At this point, all we can do is sit tight."

"Be sitting ducks, you mean?"

Yamada's gaze snapped to his colleague. "Yes, Rafe. That's what we are. If anyone thinks otherwise, they're kidding themselves."

O'Connor shifted his stance, a scowl clouding his face. "But, there must be something —"

"We can do?" Yamada shrugged. "Fine. Tell me what, and I'll do it. But, before you spout off, be very sure that anything you suggest will not cause any harm to either the station, or the earth. Can you give me your word on that?"

O'Connor opened his mouth, then shut it, his teeth clashing together.

"That's what I thought." Yamada put a hand on O'Connor's shoulder. "Come on. Let's leave our very competent scientists to do their job. I'll buy you a cup of coffee in the Mess."

As the men strode off, O'Connor wondered if they were sitting on a ticking time bomb.

?

Yamada was in his office, reading through the report that Acharya had sent him. Pages and pages of nothing. A throbbing began behind his eyes, just as his phone rang. Grateful for the disturbance, he grabbed the receiver. "Yamada."

"Sir, you'd better come down to the labs right away," Acharya's voice, brimming with excitement, leapt out at him.

"You've made a breakthrough." Yamada was already on his feet, reaching for his uniform coat.

"No, sir, Colonel. But something is definitely happening."

?

Yamada stood with the group of scientists in the clean room, each of them encased in a pristine clean suit. "What does it mean?" Yamada finally said, after staring at the markings that had suddenly appeared on one side of the orb.

"We don't know, sir. At least not yet." Acharya looked at Yamada. "The people in this room are the best linguistics and language specialists in the world, not to mention physicists and chemists. If they can't crack the code, no one can. But, you have to understand that it won't be easy. We have no reference point to start from. It's not like we're deciphering ancient Egyptian scrolls. This is something literally alien to us."

Yamada turned and strode toward the sealed door. "I don't want excuses," he shot back. "I want answers Call me when you have them."

The scientists watched as Yamada exited the room, before the inner door sealed with a hiss behind him.

"I'll take first shift," Suraya Shastri said, turning to Acharya.

"I'll join you," Maria Cordova said.

"And me." Keith Brodie stepped forward.

Acharya nodded. "Fine. We'll continue to work in shifts of three. I'll have a new schedule sent out, so everyone be sure to check it for your shift."

There was a murmur of consent, before most of the group exited the inner chamber. Suraya, Maria, and Keith stayed behind to begin the long, laborious process of deciphering the enigmatic, alien symbols.

"Where do we begin?" Maria said. "I mean, it's …"

"Don't say *hopeless*," Suraya added, busy with a camera.

"Well, it is," Maria muttered, then forced a smile. "But, never let it be said that we shy away from a challenge."

"This is a wee bit of a challenge," Keith said, jotting down notes. "It'd be easier to sprout wings and fly back to earth."

"Enough with the negativity." Suraya put the camera down. "We're going to crack this code."

"Whatever you say," Maria said, snapping her notebook shut, and following her toward the door.

"We just have to think like aliens," Suraya said, smiling. "Think outside the box. Forget everything we know about language and linguistics,"

"Is that all?" Keith said, grinning. "In that case, easy peasy, lemon squeezy."

"It's a terra-former of some kind," Suraya explained, "to adapt the moon to the alien atmosphere."

"Excellent work, Dr. Shastri," Yamada said, beaming at her. "You three cracked the code. And, it only took you two weeks."

"Actually, sir, much as we'd love to take credit for it, we didn't crack anything." She looked at Acharya, who gave her a slight nod. "At precisely nineteen hundred hours, lunar time, the orb started vibrating. At first slowly, then faster, until it shattered its dome —"

"At which point we scampered out of there faster'n you can say Robbie Burns," Keith jumped in.

Yamada barely glanced at him. "Continue," he said, his jaw tight as he looked at Suraya.

"It rose into the air, then hovered halfway up. Then the vibrating stopped. And then it started spinning."

"Really fast," Maria said. "It became a blur."

"How about we let Dr. Shastri tell us what happened?" Yamada said, slicing a quick glance at Maria and Keith.

"Yes, sir," they said, in unison, and turned to Suraya.

With all eyes on her, Suraya cleared her throat and continued. "Maria's correct. The orb became a blur. Then, a gaseous substance sprayed out of it, filling the room." She looked at Yamada, her face grave. "Thank God the clean room is sealed, or else we wouldn't be standing here right now."

"God had nothing to do with it," O'Connor said. He had been standing quietly by, arms folded. Until now. "Did you manage to analyze the gas?"

"We found elements of sulphur and carbon, and trace elements of hydrogen," Suraya responded.

"What kind of creatures would breathe that?" O" Connor asked.

Suraya looked at him. "That, Major, is the sixty-four thousand dollar question."

"Never mind that. Is it safe to assume that there are more orbs out there that are starting to terra-form?" Yamada asked Suraya.

"Sir, I think that is a very safe assumption," Suraya answered, face drawn.

Yamada looked at O'Connor. "I think it's time to alert ISA that we need the goddamn cavalry."

Suraya walked down the hallway that linked the labs to the research domes. It was hard not to acknowledge that the population of Tranquility Base had more than tripled in the last month. Already the sanitation and water departments were complaining about resources being stretched to the limit. The lunar base was not made to house this many people.

And, yet, the additional forces were necessary. They were here to protect mankind's very existence. And, most probably will risk their lives doing so.

"Hey? Dr. Shastri? Tongue-twister? Wait up."

Suraya quickened her pace, and heard the person behind her do the same.

"Suraya, stop."

She turned as Rafe O'Connor caught up to her. "Call me Tongue-twister again, and I'll forget I know you."

Rafe grinned. "You know your name isn't easy to pronounce. How long did it take for me to learn how to say it?"

"Long enough for me to lose interest."

"I deserved that. Look," he said, running a hand through his dark brown hair. "Can we call a truce? Things are about to get messy."

"About to?" Suraya gestured around her, at the people scampering back and forth, faces grim, fearful. "Look around you, Rafe. Things are already messy."

"Well, they're about to get worse." He glanced around, then grabbed Suraya by the elbow, ushering her into a utility room off to the side. "They're on their way."

Suraya stared at him, her brows drawing together. "Who's on their way?"

Rafe made an impatient sound. "Come on, Suraya. Who do you think?"

She stared at him, her stomach turning into a ball of lead. "No," she whispered. "It can't be happening already."

"Already? Suraya, honey, this has been years in the making. You know as well as I do that they could pop up anytime. Well, here they are."

Suraya's heart-rate intensified once she realized that Rafe was scared too. She could see it in his eyes. Whenever he experienced deep emotion, his blue eyes darkened to a shade away from black. As a scientist, she found the process fascinating. But, as a woman who had been involved with him, she had found it endearing. Despite the cool, aloof exterior he portrayed to the rest of the world, she knew that he felt things on a deep and vulnerable level.

That was then.

This is now.

They were no longer involved. Hadn't been for almost six months now. Rafe had broken it off with no explanation, other than stating that it was the right thing to do, given the circumstances. When pressed, he refused to say any more.

Suraya's world had tilted at the rejection. He didn't know it, because she hadn't told him, but she had fallen hard for him during their year together. Getting over him was one of the hardest things she'd ever had to do. Work had been her salvation. She threw herself into it. Taking double shifts when she could. Barely eating, barely sleeping, She worked relentlessly. Until the time came when she could think of him without her insides twisting into knots.

Now, here he was again, staring at her as if she had the answers to the universe. "Tell me the truth, Rafe. Do we stand a chance against them?"

"Yamada thinks —"

"I don't care what Yamada thinks. What do *you* think? And, the truth this time."

Rafe's eyes narrowed at her words. "All right. Here's my take. I think we're going to be decimated. Wiped out. Every last one of us."

Suraya swayed, and would have dropped like a log, if Rafe hadn't grabbed her.

"Hey, take it easy. Sorry. I shouldn't have said —"

"Yes, you should. I'm okay. Just … just give me a minute." She took a deep breath, thinking of all the people she loved on that beautiful blue world that hovered just out of reach. Mom, Papa, her kid sister, Suvendri. All her relatives and friends.

Everyone.

Everyone she knew.

Everyone she didn't.

In that moment, they were all precious to her. She wanted to reach out. Wrap her arms around her world. Embrace all of humanity. Protect them. Shield them.

But how?

"What can we do?" Her voice was little more than a gruff whisper.

Rafe stared back at her. "Fight like hell to save the human race," he said, quietly. "We won't give an inch. To our last breath, we'll defend our people."

Suraya nodded. "How long before the announcement is made. About their imminent arrival?"

"Eighteen hundred hours."

Suraya glanced at her wristwatch. "Two hours from now." She looked at Rafe, eyes burning with unshed tears. "Two hours before everyone realizes that Doomsday has finally arrived."

"Suraya, listen —"

"Don't say it," she snapped.

Rafe frowned. "Don't say what?"

"Anything about … us."

"I have to. You need to know why I broke it off." He cleared his throat. "It had nothing to do with you. I —"

Suraya held her hands up, palms out. "Oh, please. Spare me the 'it's not you, it's me' speech." She turned toward the door. "I've got work to do, alien invasion notwithstanding. And so do you."

"I love you, Suraya."

"Go to hell." She slammed the door behind her.

?

When the announcement came, Suraya was at her desk, working systematically to finish the translation of the latest symbols to appear on the orb. They had to find something, anything, to give them an edge. The markings had to provide some clue they could use to their advantage. Some sign that could give them a fighting chance.

All she had to do was find it.

And yet, what chance did she have to find it, when the world's greatest scientists had already taken a stab at it? Granted, she was included in that category. But, still…

Her office door being jerked open, without even a knock, made her raise her head in irritation. "What is —?"

"Did you know?" Maria stood at the door, eyes wide, face flushed, breathing erratic.

"Maria, why don't you sit —"

"Tell me. Did you know?"

Suraya rose to her feet. "I found out only a little while before you." The image of Rafe telling her he loved her flashed before her, and she pushed it away. Now was not the time to analyze that particular can of worms.

Maria hiccuped, hands pressed to her mouth. "What are we going to do?" she whispered, in muffled tones.

Suraya shrugged. "Keep working. It's the only thing we can do. The only thing left to us."

Maria stared at her. "How can you think of work at a time like this? What does it matter? What does any of it matter?" She gestured at the piles of notes and files, piled on Suraya's desk.

"It matters," Suraya said quietly. "What else are we supposed to do? Lay down and wait for death?" She shuddered. "Not me. No, sir. I refuse to die without any dignity. I'll fight until the end."

"So, you think there will be an end?" Maria whispered.

Suraya looked at her, blinking back sudden tears. "They're an alien race that has mastered space travel. Technologically hundreds of years ahead of us. There's the hope that, because they're an advanced race, they may be benign. Compassionate. But …"

"But?" Maria asked. "Suraya, for God's sake, spit it out."

"Okay, look. The reasoning is that if they were benign — you know — a space-faring race exploring new worlds, then why did they not reveal themselves to us at their initial landing? Why hide on the dark side of the moon?"

"Maybe they're just observing us? Or, maybe they've seen how brutal the human race is, with all the wars and greed, and hatred, and racism and —"

"Or, maybe they're waiting for the right, strategic moment to strike," Suraya added. Maria shot her a horrified glance. Suraya held up her hands. "Hey, ISA words, not mine."

"But, you agree with them?"

"Let's just say I'm keeping an open mind, but the deck is stacked against us."

"But, what if —?"

A piercing alarm sounded, making them both jump. Simultaneously, red lights in Suraya's office, and the outer office began flashing.

Maria's eyes widened. "You … you don't think they're already here, do you?"

"Come on." Suraya grabbed her by the arm, ushering her out the door. "Everyone out. You know the drill."

"Are we being invaded," Mary Jane, the secretary, asked, jumping up from her desk, and hurrying to join the women.

"Well, considering that the alarms were installed for just that purpose, I'd say that's a pretty good possibility." Suraya hurried down the corridor, with both women on her heels. Around them, men and women were rushing in every direction, all heading for their assigned bunkers.

Just as the women reached their bunker, Acharya appeared, his face a sickly grey. "Dr. Shastri, come with me."

"Dr. Acharya? What are you doing here? Shouldn't you be in the Command Center?"

"Yes, and so should you. Let's go."

"Me?"

"Yes, you. Is there another doctor here with your name? Hurry now."

Suraya turned to the two women staring at her, faces pinched with fear. "Get down there, and don't move."

Maria clutched her arm. "Don't go. You'll be killed. Come with us."

"I'll be fine. Go on down. I'll join you as soon as I can." She forced a smile she hoped was reassuring, but neither of the women were buying it.

"I'll come with you," Maria said. "You'll need my help."

"Me too," Mary Jane whispered.

"We don't have time for this," Acharya barked. He turned to a lab technician hurrying toward the bunker. "You there. Escort these ladies down to safety."

"Please go," Suraya said, knowing they would protest. "Every minute counts." She waited long enough to see the elevator doors close, with her colleagues safely inside, then turned to Acharya. "Let's go."

"Acharya, where in blazes have you —?" Rafe stiffened when he saw Suraya hurry into the Command Center on Acharya's heels. "What the hell is *she* doing here?"

"My job," Suraya snapped. She looked at Acharya. "Where do you want me?"

"Colonel Yamada wants you at the science station, with the other key personnel," he said, nodding toward the man in the crisp military suit who was watching the big screen in the front of the room. Suraya glanced at it. And felt her blood gel in her veins.

It wasn't the dozen or so ships she'd been expecting to see.

It was an armada.

"You should be in your assigned bunker with your colleagues," Rafe said, beside her. He stared at the screen, hands clasped behind his back. Despite his seemingly unruffled exterior, Suraya could sense the tension rolling off him.

"I'm exactly where I should be," she said, wondering if he could hear her above the hammering in her chest. Watching the screen, she felt light-headed. These kinds of things didn't happen in real life, did they? They were reserved for blockbuster movies, like *2001: A Space Odyssey*. Or TV shows like *Star Trek*.

But, there they were, an entire fleet of ships, rapidly approaching the moon. No movie. No dream. This was real life. This was really happening.

"We don't fire until we see their intention," Yamada said. He turned to Suraya. "Take your post, Doctor."

"Yes, sir." She moved past Rafe, studiously avoiding his gaze. If they lived through this, they had to talk. But for now …

Well, there was a war to be fought, and her job was to make sure the Tri-compound her crew had been working on was ready to be launched. Whether it would work was another story entirely.

"Will it work?" Rafe asked, from behind, as if reading her mind. She turned to see him standing behind her chair.

"Stop stalking me," she hissed. "Don't you have a job to do?"

"My job is to see that you do yours, so I can do mine. So, will it work?"

"How the hell should I know? It's not like we have an alien in captivity to try it out."

"But you said —"

"I said that there's a possibility that dangerously high levels of sulphur and carbon, in a disulphide solution, creating a heterogeneous colloid, can —"

Rafe raised his hands, a small smile tugging at the corner of his mouth. "Enough. I'm sorry I asked."

Suraya sighed. "Our reasoning is that since high levels of oxygen can cause oxygen toxicity in humans, maybe a similar effect is true of them and the gases they breathe."

"Very clever," Rafe said, one eyebrow raised appraisingly as he looked at her.

"Why aren't they doing anything?" Acharya burst out, standing a little behind Yamada. "What are they waiting for?"

"They're toying with us," Rafe said. "They know as well as we do that we're outmatched in every way."

Acharya turned to him. "They don't know that," he snapped. "They don't —"

When the initial blast hit the base, it was so sudden and unexpected, so swift, that it rendered everyone at the Command Center, speechless. The room stilled. For a long moment no one spoke.

Then everyone moved. Suraya watched as the international team spun into action, like the proverbial well-oiled machine. Her gaze darted to the screen that showed the entire base, and she stifled a scream.

The front end of the base was gone. Demolished. Thank God for the protocols put into place for just such a scenario. By now, steel doors would have slid into place, effectively sealing off the areas exposed to the moon's exosphere. She had to believe that everyone in every sector of the military base had been ushered into their assigned bunkers, below the lunar surface, like the Command Center.

Because, if anyone had been left behind in that sector, there would have been no chance of survival.

Yamada gave the order to fire all weapons. "Take no quarter," he bellowed. "Take the bastards down."

The base rumbled with the release of firepower. Suraya watched, along with everyone in the room, as the charges hit their targets.

With no effect.

"Keep blasting," Yamada said.

"The earth bases are retaliating, as ordered, sir," someone remarked to him, as around them rockets carrying enough bombs to annihilate the world, sped toward their mark.

And failed spectacularly.

"We're not going to win, are we?" Suraya whispered, watching as the alien ships sustained nothing from the powerful blasts making contact.

"Doesn't look good," Rafe said. His hand found her shoulder, squeezing gently.

"Keep firing, dammit," Yamada yelled. "Unleash everything we've got. Those inhuman bastards *can't* reach our world."

"Sir, they're already there," Keith Brodie said, his voice laced with terror.

Yamada turned to Suraya. "We fired your gas bombs too. What happened? Why didn't they work?"

"Colonel, in order for them to work, they have to penetrate the hull of the ships and gain access to the interior. They have to taint the atmosphere *inside* the ships. Since nothing's been able to penetrate the hull of any of their ships, those gas bombs are as effective as shooting peas with a slingshot."

"Then what use are they?" he roared, pointing at the big screen. "Look at them. They're attacking our world. Our people. And we're sitting here, twiddling our thumbs."

"Sir," Suraya said, "the whole world is fighting back. The aliens can be killed —"

"How do you know?"

"Because, all organic life can be killed. It's a fundamental law of nature. We just need to get close enough to —"

"Close enough?" he bellowed. "Close enough? How much closer can we get? They're right there? Military bases all over the world are firing at them. Do you see any effect? No. You and your team were our last hope to disable them. You and your useless gas bombs." Yamada was purple in the face now, breathing heavily.

"Time for Plan B," Rafe muttered to himself. And, before Suraya could ask him what Plan B was, he stepped forward, addressing Yamada. "Sir, if I can gain access to their mother ship —"

"Mother ship? This isn't a sci-fi movie, Major. This is —"

"With all due respect, Colonel," Rafe's fingers curled into fists by his side. Suraya could sense the effort it took not to lash out at Yamada. "I have no doubt that Dr. Shastri's gas bombs will work. I suggest gaining access to the biggest ship — the one that's holding back — which I suspect is the mother ship, and releasing the gas bombs in there. Maybe the other ships are controlled by it, and —"

"That's a big 'maybe,' Major."

"Yessir, but we're running out of options."

"And, how do you expect to gain access, Major?"

"Have you noticed that some ships are dropping down from it, on the underside? One of our capsule rockets can easily enter through there."

Yamada looked at Rafe. "So, you deposit the gas bombs in there. Then what?"

Rafe shrugged, a wry smile tugging at his mouth. "Not just the gas bombs. I crash the capsule inside. *Kaboom.*"

Yamada cleared his throat. "There's no coming back from that, Rafe."

"No, sir."

"I'll go with you," Suraya said, rising from her chair.

"No," Rafe snapped.

"My team is the only one that knows how to deploy the gas bombs. I can't send any of them. I won't. So, it has to be me."

"Suraya," Rafe said, taking a step toward her, "this is a one-way mission."

She smiled at him. "I know that, silly. Let's go. No time to waste."

Rafe stared at her for a long moment, then turned to Yamada. "All their ships are focused on fighting. The mother ship is alone at the back. Keep their attention diverted long enough for us to gain access."

"You got it," Yamada said. He stood to attention, and saluted, his gaze shifting from Rafe to Suraya. "God speed, you two."

?

It took twenty minutes to get Rafe and Suraya prepped, and ready for action. Then, everything seemed to happen at once, and before she knew it, the two of them were speeding toward their intended target in a capsule-sized rocket.

Suraya, strapped down, turned her head to look at Rafe. His gaze was on her, eyes glistening.

"So much wasted time, sweetheart —"

"Rafe —"

"Let me finish. We don't have much time, and I need to come clean. I broke up with you because I got scared. You'd become the most important thing in my life, and I was losing my focus. I told myself that I had a job to do. A duty to the world. I convinced myself that the only thing to do was to make a clean break of it with you. Get back on track …" he sighed, shutting his eyes. "Only …"

"Only what?" she asked, struggling to be heard above the roar of the engines.

"Only I didn't realize that without you *my* world lost focus. The more I tried to forget you, the worse it became." Rafe struggled to reach something in his flight suit pocket. "Ahh, here is it."

Suraya watched as he pulled out a a small square, red-velvet box. "Rafe …"

He popped it open, and, for a moment, Suraya was blinded by the light from the instrument panels bouncing off the small, square-shaped diamond.

"I should have done this six months ago. Suraya Shastri, my beautiful Tongue-twister, will you marry me?"

Suraya looked from the ring to Rafe's face.

And saw their future.

What was left of it.

"Yes, she said, nodding. "Yes, I will. I love you, too."

Rafe's face lit up. "Well, then," he said, fumbling with his straps, "only one thing left to do."

"Rafe, stay put. It isn't safe —"

He looked at her, and she saw the determination in his eyes.

"I reserve the right to kiss my fiancé." He bent toward her…

?

When the largest of the alien ships exploded, it caught everyone at Tranquility Base by surprise, despite hoping for that very outcome. The people in the Command Center stared at the screen, watching as the armada of alien ships swiftly turned, as one, and headed away from the earth.

"This … this means that Suraya and the major …" Keith's voice broke.

"It means that O'Connor and Dr. Shastri were successful in their endeavors," Acharya said, his voice shaking so much he barely got the words out.

Keith's face turned ashen. "Maybe … maybe they made it out before —"

"They're gone," Yamada said. "They completed their mission successfully. They'll receive the highest honors anyone can get. They gave their lives. Look, the aliens are already retreating. We're saved."

Keith swung on Yamada. "Saved? Dr. Shastri and the Major are dead. Our world is in shambles. Most of the human population, not to mention wildlife and sea life, are gone. It will take decades to rebuild, and even then, we're not safe. Do you think the aliens are running away in fear?" Keith gave a short laugh. "Think again. They're going to come back, stronger than ever. And, next time, they won't lose."

"You are out of line, son. You don't know what you're talking about. Get out of here," Yamada barked.

"With pleasure, *Sir*." Keith turned and strode out of the room.

"Sir," Acharya said.

"What?" Yamada swung toward him.

"Brodie is correct, Colonel. They'll be back."

"Over my dead body," Yamada snapped, turning toward one of his men. "Get me Doctor Li at the U.N. Security Council. Let's see what the damage is."

"I'm sorry, Colonel," Carmine D'Angelo said, his face slick with sweat, as he turned toward Yamada. "The lines are dead."

END

Lorraine Sharma Nelson

Looking for the Fountain

By: Robert Silverberg

My name is Francisco de Ortega and by the grace of God I am 89 years old and I have seen many a strange thing in my time, but nothing so strange as the Indian folk of the island called Florida, whose great dream it is to free the Holy Land from the Saracen conquerors that profane it.

It was fifty years ago that I encountered these marvelous people, when I sailed with his excellency the illustrious Don Juan Ponce de Leon on his famous and disastrous voyage in quest of what is wrongly called the Fountain of Youth. It was not a Fountain of Youth at all that he sought, but a Fountain of Manly Strength, which is somewhat a different thing. Trust me: I was there, I saw and heard everything, I was by Don Juan Ponce's side when his fate overtook him. I know the complete truth of this endeavor and I mean to set it all down now so there will be no doubt; for I alone survive to tell the tale, and as God is my witness I will tell it truthfully now, here in my ninetieth year, all praises be to Him and to the Mother who bore Him.

The matter of the Fountain, first.

Commonly, I know, it is called the Fountain of Youth. You will read that in many places, such as in the book about the New World which that Italian wrote who lived at Seville, Peter Martyr of Anghiera, where he says, "The governor of the Island of Boriquena, Juan Ponce de Leon, sent forth two caravels to seek the Islands of Boyuca in which the Indians affirmed there to be a fountain or spring whose water is of such marvelous virtue, that when it is drunk it makes old men young again."

This is true, so far as it goes. But when Peter Martyr talks of "making old men young again", his words must be interpreted in a poetic way.

Perhaps long life is truly what that Fountain really provides, along with its other and more special virtue—who knows? For I have tasted of that Fountain's waters myself, and here I am nearly 90 years of age and still full of vigor, I who was born in the year of our Lord 1473, and how many others are still alive today who came into the world then, when Castile and Aragon still were separate kingdoms? But I tell you that what Don Juan Ponce was seeking was not strictly speaking a Fountain of Youth at all, but rather a Fountain that offered a benefit of a very much more intimate kind. For I was there, I saw and heard everything. And they have cowardly tongues, those who say it was a Fountain of Youth, for it would seem that out of shame they choose not to speak honestly of the actual nature of the powers that the Fountain which we sought was supposed to confer.

It was when we were on the island of Hispaniola that we first heard of this wonderful Fountain, Don Juan Ponce and I. This was, I think, in the year 1504. Don Juan Ponce, a true nobleman and a man of high and elegant thoughts, was governor then in the province of Higuey of that island, which was ruled at that time by Don Nicolas de Ovando, successor to the great Admiral Cristobal Colon. There was in Higuey then a certain Indian cacique or chieftain of remarkable strength and force, who was reputed to keep seven wives and to satisfy each and every one of them each night of the week. Don Juan Ponce was curious about the great virility of this cacique, and one day he sent a certain Aurelio Herrera to visit him in his village.

"He does indeed have many wives," said Herrera, "though whether there were five or seven or fifty-nine I could not say, for there were women surrounding me all the time I was there, coming and going in such multitudes that I was unable to make a clear count, and swarms of children also, and from the looks of it the women were his wives and the children were his children."

"And what sort of manner of man is this cacique?" asked Don Juan Ponce.

"Why," said Herrera, "he is a very ordinary man, narrow of shoulders and shallow of chest, whom you would never think capable of such marvels of manhood, and he is past middle age besides. I remarked on this to him, and he said that when he was young he was easily exhausted and found the manly exercises a heavy burden. But then he journeyed to Boyuca, which is an island to the north of Cuba that is also called Bimini, and there he drank of a spring that cures the debility of sex. Since then, he asserts, he has been able to give pleasure to any number of women in a night without the slightest fatigue."

I was there. I saw and heard everything. *El enflaquecimiento del sexo* was the phrase that Aurelio Herrera used, "the debility of sex." The eyes of Don Juan Ponce de Leon opened wide at this tale, and he turned to me and said, "We must go in search of this miraculous fountain some day, Francisco, for there will be great profit in the selling of its waters."

Do you see? Not a word had been spoken about long life, but only about the curing of *el enflaquecimiento del sexo*. Nor was Don Juan Ponce in need of any such cure for himself, I assure you, for in the year 1504 he was just thirty years old, a lusty and aggressive man of fiery and restless spirit, and red-haired as well, and you know what is said about the virility of red-haired men. As for me, I will not boast, but I will say only that since the age of thirteen I have rarely gone a single night without a woman's company, and have been married four times, on the fourth occasion to a woman fifty years younger than myself. And if you find yourself in the province of Valladolid where I live and come to pay a call on me I can show you young Diego Antonio de Ortega whom you would think was my great-grandson, and little Juana Maria de Ortega who could be my great-granddaughter, for the boy is seven and the girl is five, but in truth they are my own children, conceived when I was past eighty years of age; and I have had many other sons and daughters too, some of whom are old people now and some are dead.

So, it was not to heal our own debilities that Don Juan Ponce and I longed to find this wonderful Fountain, for of such shameful debilities we had none at all, he and I. No, we yearned for the Fountain purely for the sake of the riches we might derive from it: for each year saw hundreds or perhaps thousands of men come from Spain to the New World to seek their fortunes, and some of these were older men who no doubt suffered from a certain *enflaquecimiento*. In Spain I understand they use the powdered horn of the unicorn to cure this malady, or the crushed shells of a certain insect, though I have never had need of such things myself. But those commodities are not to be found in the New World, and it was Don Juan Ponce's hope that great profit might be made by taking possession of Bimini and selling the waters of the Fountain to those who had need of such a remedy. This is the truth, whatever others may claim.

But the pursuit of gold comes before everything, even the pursuit of miraculous Fountains of Manly Strength. We did not go at once in search of the Fountain because word came to Don Juan Ponce in Hispaniola that the neighboring island of Borinquen was rich in gold, and thereupon he applied to Governor Ovando for permission to go there and conquer it. Don Juan Ponce already somewhat knew that island, having seen its western coast briefly in 1493 when he was a gentleman volunteer in the fleet of Cristobal Colon, and its beauty had so moved him that he had resolved someday to return and make himself master of the place.

With one hundred men, he sailed over to this Borinquen in a small caravel, landing there on Midsummer Day, 1506, at the same bay he had visited earlier aboard the ship of the great Admiral. Seeing us arrive with such force, the cacique of the region was wise enough to yield to the inevitable and we took possession with very little fighting.

So rich did the island prove to be that we put the marvelous Fountain of which we had previously heard completely out of our minds. Don Juan Ponce was made governor of Borinquen by royal appointment and for several years the natives remained peaceful, and we were able to obtain a great quantity of gold indeed. This is the same island that Cristobal Colon called San Juan Bautista, and which people today call Puerto Rico.

All would have been well for us there but for the stupidity of a certain captain of our forces, Cristobal de Sotomayor, who treated the natives so badly that they rose in rebellion against us. This was in the year of our Lord 1511. So, we found ourselves at war; and Don Juan Ponce fought with all the great valor for which he was renowned, doing tremendous destruction against our pagan enemies. We had among us at that time a certain dog, called Bercerillo, of red pelt and black eyes, who could tell simply by smell alone whether an Indian was friendly to us or hostile, and could understand the native speech as well; and the Indians were more afraid of ten Spaniards with this dog, than of one hundred without him. Don Juan Ponce rewarded Bercerillo's bravery and cleverness by giving the dog a full share of all the gold and slaves we captured, as though he were a crossbowman; but in the end the Indians killed him. I understand that a valiant pup of this Bercerillo, Leoncillo by name, went with Nunez de Balboa when he crossed the Isthmus of Panama and discovered the great ocean beyond.

During this time of our difficulties with the savages of Puerto Rico, Don Diego Colon, the son of the great Admiral, was able to take advantage of the trouble and make himself governor of the island in the place of Don Juan Ponce. Don Juan Ponce thereupon returned to Spain and presented himself before King Ferdinand, and told him the tale of the fabulous Fountain that restores manly power. King Ferdinand, who was greatly impressed by Don Juan Ponce's lordly bearing and noble appearance, at once granted him a royal permit to seek and conquer the isle of Bimini where this Fountain was said to be. Whether this signifies that His Most Catholic Majesty was troubled by debilities of a sexual sort, I would not dare to say. But the king was at that time a man of sixty years and it would not be unimaginable that some difficulty of that kind had begun to perplex him.

Swiftly Don Juan Ponce returned to Puerto Rico with the good news of his royal appointment, and on the third day of March of the year of our Lord 1513 we set forth from the Port of San German in three caravels to search for Bimini and its extraordinary Fountain.

I should say at this point that it was a matter of course that Don Juan Ponce should have asked me to take part in the quest for this Fountain. I am a man of Tervas de San Campos in the province of Valladolid, where Don Juan Ponce de Leon also was born less than one year after I was, and he and I played together as children and were friends all through our youth. As I have said, he first went to the New World in 1493, when he was nineteen years of age, as a gentleman aboard the ship of Admiral Cristobal Colon, and after settling in Hispaniola he wrote to me and told me of the great wealth of the New World and urged me to join him there. Which I did forthwith; and we were rarely separated from then until the day of his death.

Our flagship was the Santiago, with Diego Bermudez as its master—the brother to the man who discovered the isle of Bermuda—and the famous Anton de Alaminos as its pilot. We had two Indian pilots too, who knew the islands of that sea. Our second ship was the Santa Maria de Consolacion, with Juan Bono de Quexo as its captain, and the third was the San Cristobal. All of these vessels were purchased by Don Juan Ponce himself out of the riches he had laid by in the time when he was governor of Puerto Rico.

I have to tell you that there was not one priest in our company, not that we were ungodly men but only that it was not our commander's purpose on this voyage to bring the word of Jesus to the natives of Bimini. We did have some few women among us, including my own wife Beatriz, who had come out from Spain to be with me, and grateful I was to have her by my side; and my wife's young sister Juana was aboard the ship also, that I could better look after her among these rough Spaniards of the New World.

Northward we went. After ten days we halted at the isle of San Salvador to scrape weeds from the bottom of one of our ships. Then we journeyed west-northwest, passing the isle of Ciguateo on Easter Sunday, and, continuing onward into waters that ran ever shallower, we caught sight on the second day of April of a large delightful island of great and surpassing beauty, all blooming and burgeoning with a great host of wildflowers whose delectable odors came wafting to us on the warm gentle breeze. We named this isle La Florida, because Easter is the season when things flower and so we call that time of year in our language Pascua Florida. And we said to one another at once, seeing so beautiful a place, that this island of Florida must surely be the home of the wondrous Fountain that restores men to their fleshly powers and grants all their carnal desires to the fullest.

Of the loveliness of Florida, I could speak for a day and a night and a night and a day, and not exhaust its marvels. The shallowing green waters give way to white crests of foam that fall upon beaches paved hard with tiny shells; and when you look beyond the beach you see dunes and marshes, and beyond those a land altogether level, not so much as a hillock upon it, where glistening sluggish lagoons bordered brilliantly with rushes and sedges show the way to the mysterious forests of the interior.

Those forests! Palms and pines, and gnarled gray trees whose names are known only to God! Trees covered with snowy beards! Trees whose leaves are like swords! Flowers everywhere, dizzying us with their perfume! We were stunned by the fragrance of jasmine and honeyflower. We heard the enchanting songs of a myriad of birds. We stared in wonder at the bright blooms. We doffed our helmets and dropped to our knees to give thanks to God for having led us to this most beautiful of shores.

Don Juan Ponce was the first of us to make his way to land, carrying with him the banner of Castile and Leon. He thrust the royal standard into the soft sandy soil and in the name of God and Spain took possession of the place. This was at the mouth of a river which he named in honor of his patron, the blessed San Juan. Then, since there were no Indians thereabouts who might lead us to the Fountain, we returned to our vessels and continued along the coast of that place.

Though the sea looked gentle we found the currents unexpectedly strong, carrying us northward so swiftly that we feared we would never see Puerto Rico again. Therefore did Don Juan Ponce give orders for us to turn south; but although we had a fair following wind the current was so strong against us that we could make no headway, and at last we were compelled to anchor in a cove. Here we spent some days, with the ships straining against their cables; and during that time the little San Cristobal was swept out to sea, and we lost sight of her altogether, though the day was bright and the weather fair. But within two days by God's grace, she returned to us.

At this time we saw our first Indians, but they were far from friendly. Indeed, they set upon us at once and two of our men were wounded by their little darts and arrows, which were tipped with sharp points made of bone. When night came we were able to withdraw and sail on to another place that we called the Rio de la Cruz, where we collected wood and water; and here we were attacked again, by sixty Indians, but they were driven off. And so we continued for many days, until in latitude 28 degrees 15 minutes we did round a cape, which we called Cabo de los Corrientes on account of the powerful currents, which were stronger than the wind.

Here it was that we had the strangest part of our voyage, indeed the strangest thing I have ever seen in all my ninety years. Which is to say that we encountered at this time in this remote and hitherto unknown land the defenders of the Christian Faith, the sworn foes of the Saracens, the last sons of the Crusades, whose great dream it was, even now, to wrest the Holy Land of our Savior's birth from those infidel followers of Muhammad who seized it long ago and rule it today.

We suspected nothing of any of what awaited us when we dropped our anchors near an Indian town on the far side of Cabo de los Corrientes. Cautiously, for we had received such a hostile reception farther up the coast, we made our landfall a little way below the village and set about the task of filling our water casks and cutting firewood. While this work was being carried out we became aware that the Indians had left their village and had set out down the shore to encounter us, for we heard them singing and chanting even before we could see them; and we halted in our labors and made ourselves ready to deal with another attack.

After a short while the Indians appeared, still singing as they approached. Wonder of wonders, they were clothed, though all the previous natives that we had seen were naked, or nearly so, as these savages usually are. Even more marvelous was the nature of their clothing, which was of a kind not very different from that which Christians wear, jerkins and doublets and tunics, and such things. And—marvel of marvel—every man of them wore upon his chest a white garment that bore the holy cross of Jesus painted brightly in red! We could not believe our eyes. But if we had any doubt that these were Christian men, it was eradicated altogether when we saw that in the midst of the procession came certain men wearing the dark robes of priests, who carried great wooden crosses held high aloft.

Were these indeed Indians? Surely not! Surely they must be Spaniards like ourselves! We might almost have been in Toledo, or Madrid, or Seville, and not on the shore of some strange land of the Indies! But indeed we saw without doubt now that the marchers were men of the sort that is native to the New World, with the ruddy skins and black hair and sharp features of their kind, Christian though they might be in dress, and carrying the cross itself in their midst.

When they were close enough so that we could hear distinctly the words of their song, it sounded to some of us that they might be Latin words, though Latin of a somewhat barbarous kind. Could that be possible? We doubted the evidence of our ears. But then Pedro de Plasencia, who had studied for the priesthood before entering the military, crossed himself most vigorously and said to us in wonder, "Do you hear that? They are singing the Gloria in excelsis Deo!" And in truth we could tell that hymn was what they sang, now that Pedro de Plasencia had picked out the words of it for us. Does that sound strange to you, that Indians of an unknown isle should be singing in Latin? Yes, it is strange indeed. But doubt me at your peril. I was there; I saw and heard everything myself.

"Surely," said Diego Bermudez, "there must have been Spaniards here before us, who have instructed these people in the way of God."

"That cannot be," said our pilot, Anton de Alaminos. "For I was with Cristobal Colon on his second voyage and have been on every voyage since of any note that has been made in these waters, and I can tell you that no white man has set foot on this shore before us."

"Then how came these Indians by their crosses and their holy hymns?" asked Diego Bermudez. "Is it a pure miracle of the saints, do you think?"

"Perhaps it is," said Don Juan Ponce de Leon, with some heat, for it looked as if there might be a quarrel between the master and the pilot. "Who can say? Be thankful that these folk are our Christian friends and not our enemy, and leave off your useless speculations."

And in the courageous way that was his nature, Don Juan Ponce went forward and raised his arms to the Indians, and made the sign of the cross in the air, and called out to them, saying, "I am Don Juan Ponce de Leon of Valladolid in the land of Spain, and I greet you in the name of the Father, and of the Son, and of the Holy Ghost." All of which he said clearly and loudly in his fine and beautiful Castilian, which he spoke with the greatest purity. But the Indians, who by now had halted in a straight line before us, showed no understanding in their eyes. Don Juan Ponce spoke again, once more in Spanish, saying that he greeted them also in the name of His Most Catholic Majesty King Ferdinand of Aragon and Castile. This too produced no sign that it had been understood.

One of the Indians then spoke. He was a man of great presence and bearing, who wore chains of gold about his chest and carried a sword of strange design at his side, the first sword I had ever seen a native of these islands to have. From these indications it was apparent that he was the cacique.

He spoke long and eloquently in a language that I suppose was his own, for none of us had ever heard it before, not even the two Indian pilots we had brought with us. Then he said a few words that had the sound and the ring of French or perhaps Catalan, though we had a few men of Barcelona among us who leaned close toward him and put their hands to their ears and even they could make no sense out of what they heard.

But then finally this grand cacique spoke words which we all could understand plainly, garbled and thick-tongued though his speaking of them was: for what he said was, and there could be no doubt of it however barbarous his accent, "In nomine Patris, et Filii, et Spiritus Sancti," and he made the sign of the cross over his chest as any good Christian man would do. To which Don Juan replied, "Amen. Dominus vobiscum." Whereupon the cacique, exclaiming, "Et cum spiritu tuo," went forthrightly to the side of Don Juan Ponce, and they embraced with great love, likewise as any Christian men might do, here on this remote beach in this strange and lovely land of Florida.

They brought us then to their village and offered a great feast for us, with roasted fish and the meat of tortoises and sweet fruits of many mysterious kinds, and made us presents of the skins of animals. For our part we gave them such trinkets as we had carried with us, beads and bracelets and little copper daggers and the like, but of all the things we gave them they were most eager to receive the simple figurines of Jesus on the cross that we offered them, and passed them around amongst themselves in wonder, showing such love for them as if they were made of the finest gold and studded with emeralds and rubies. And we said privately to each other that we must be dreaming, to have met with Indians in this land who were of such great devotion to the faith.

We tried to speak with them again in Spanish, but it was useless, and so too was speaking in any of the native tongues of Hispaniola or Puerto Rico that we knew. In their turn they addressed us in their own language, which might just as well have been the language of the people of the Moon for all we comprehended it, and also in that tantalizing other tongue which seemed almost to be French or Catalan. We could not make anything of that, try though we did. But Pedro de Plasencia, who was the only one of us who could speak Latin out loud like a priest, sat down with the cacique after the meal and addressed him in that language. I mean not simply saying things like the Pater Noster and the Ave Maria, which any child can say, but speaking to him as if Latin was a real language with words and sentences of common meaning, the way it was long ago. To which the cacique answered, though he seemed to be framing his words with much difficulty; and Pedro answered him again, just as hesitatingly; and so they went on, talking to each other in a slow and halting way, far into the night, nodding and smiling most jubilantly whenever one of them reached some understanding of the other's words, while we looked on in astonishment, unable to fathom a word of what they were saying.

At last Pedro rose, looking pale and exhausted like a man who has carried a bull on his back for half a league, and came over to us where we were sitting in a circle.

"Well?" Don Juan Ponce demanded at once.

Pedro de Plasencia shook his head wearily. "It was all nonsense, what the cacique said. I understood nothing. Nothing at all! It was mere incomprehensible babble and no more than that." And he picked up a leather sack of wine that lay near his feet and drank from it as though he had a thirst that no amount of drinking ever could quench.

"You appeared to comprehend, at times," said Don Juan Ponce. "Or so it seemed to me as I watched you."

"Nothing. Not a word. Let me sleep on it, and perhaps it will come clear to me in the morning."

I thought Don Juan Ponce would pursue him on the matter. But Don Juan Ponce, though he was an impatient and high-tempered man, was also a man of great sagacity, and he knew better than to press Pedro further at a time when he seemed so troubled and fatigued. So, he dismissed the company and we settled down in the huts that the Indians had given us for lodging, all except those of us who were posted as sentries during the night to guard against treachery.

I rose before dawn. But I saw that Don Juan Ponce and Pedro de Plasencia were already awake and had drawn apart from the rest of us and were talking most earnestly. After a time they returned, and Don Juan Ponce beckoned to me.

"Pedro has told me something of his conversation with the cacique," he said.

"And what is it that you have learned?"

"That these Indians are indeed Christians."

"Yes, that seems to be the plain truth, strange though it seems," I said. "For they do carry the cross about, and sing the Gloria, and honor the Father and the Son."

"There is more."

I waited.

He continued, "Unless Pedro much mistook what the cacique told him, the greatest hope in which these people live is that of wresting the Holy Land from the Saracen, and restoring it to good Christian pilgrims."

At that I burst out into such hearty laughter that Don Juan Ponce, for all his love of me, looked at me with eyes flashing with reproof. Yet I could not withhold my mirth, which poured from me like a river.

I said at last, when I had mastered myself, "But tell me, Don Juan, what would these savages know of the Holy Land, or of Saracens, or any such thing? The Holy Land is thousands of leagues away and has never been spoken of so much as once in this New World by any man, I think; nor does anyone speak of the Crusade any longer in this age, neither here nor at home."

"It is very strange, I agree," replied Don Juan Ponce. "Nevertheless, so Pedro swears, the cacique spoke to him of Terra Sancta, Terra Sancta, and of infidels, and the liberation of the city of Jerusalem."

"And how does it come to pass," I asked, "that they can know of such things, in this remote isle, where no white man has ever visited before?"

"Ah," said Don Juan Ponce, "that is the great mystery, is it not?"

In time we came to understand the solution to this mystery, though the tale was muddled and confused, and emerged only after much travail, and long discussions between Pedro de Plasencia and the cacique of the Indians. I will tell you the essence of it, which was this:

Some three hundred years ago, or perhaps it was four hundred, while much of our beloved Spain still lay under the Moorish hand, a shipload of Frankish warriors set sail from the port of Genoa, or perhaps it was Marseilles, or some other city along the coast of Provence. This was in the time when men still went crusading, to make war for Jesus' sake in the Holy Land against the followers of Muhammad who occupied that place.

But the voyage of these Crusaders miscarried; for when they entered the great Mar Mediterraneo, thinking to go east they were forced west by terrible storms and contrary winds, and swept helpless past our Spanish shores, past Almeria and Malaga and Tarifa, and through the narrow waist of the Estrecho de Gibraltar and out into the vastness of the Ocean Sea.

Here, having no sound knowledge as we in our time do of the size and shape of the African continent, they thought to turn south and then east below Egypt and make their voyage yet to the Holy Land. Of course this would be impossible, except by rounding the Buena Fortuna cape and traveling up past Arabia, a journey almost beyond our means to this day. But being unaware of that, these bold but hapless men made the attempt, coasting southerly and southerly and southerly, and the land of course not only not ending but indeed carrying them farther and farther outward into the Ocean Sea, until at last, no doubt weary and half dead of famine, they realized that they had traveled so far to the west that there was no hope of returning eastward again, nor of turning north and making their way back into the Mediterraneo. So, they yielded to the westerly winds that prevail near the Canary Isles, and allowed themselves to be blown clear across the sea to the Indies. And so, after long arduous voyaging they made landfall in this isle we call Florida. Thus, these men of three hundred years ago were the first discoverers of the New World, although I doubt very greatly that they comprehended what it was that they had achieved.

You must understand that we received few of these details from our Indian hosts: only the tale that men bound to Terra Sancta departing from a land in the east were blown off course some hundreds of years previous and were brought after arduous sailing to the isle of Florida and to this very village where our three caravels had made their landfall. All the rest did we conclude for ourselves, that they were Crusaders and so forth, after much discussing of the matter and recourse to the scholarship that the finest men among us possessed.

And what befell these men of the Crusade, when they came to this Florida? Why, they offered themselves to the mercies of the villagers, who greeted them right honorably and took them to dwell amongst them, and married them to their daughters! And for their part the seafarers offered the word of Jesus to the people of the village and thereby gave them hope of Heaven; and taught these kindly savages the Latin tongue so well that it remained with them after a fashion hundreds of years afterward, and also some vestiges of the common speech that the seafaring men had had in their own native land.

But most of all did the strangers from the sea imbue in the villagers the holy desire to rid the birthplace of Jesus of the dread hand of the Mussulman; and ever, in years after, did the Christian Indians of this Florida village long to put to sea, and cross the great ocean, and wield their bows and spears valiantly amidst the paynim enemy in the defense of the True Faith. Truly, how strange are the workings of God Almighty, how far beyond our comprehension, that He should make Crusaders out of the naked Indians in this far-off place!

You may ask what became of those European men who landed there, and whether we saw anyone who plainly might mark his descent from them. And I will tell you that those ancient Crusaders, who intermarried with the native women since they had brought none of their own, were wholly swallowed up by such intermarrying and were engulfed by the fullness of time. For they were only forty or fifty men among hundreds, and the passing centuries so diluted the strain of their race that not the least trace of it remained, and we saw no pale skin or fair hair or blue eyes or other marks of European men here. But the ideas that they had fetched to this place did survive, that is, the practicing of the Catholic faith and the speaking of a debased and corrupt sort of Latin and the wearing of a kind of European clothes, and such. And I tell you it was passing strange to see these red savages in their surplices and cassocks, and in their white tunics bearing the great emblem of our creed, and other such ancient marks of our civilization, and to hear them chanting the Kyrie eleison and the Confiteor and the Sanctus, Sanctus, Sanctus Dominus Deus Sabaoth in that curious garbled way of theirs, like words spoken in a dream.

Nay, I have spoken untruthfully, for the men of that lost voyage did leave other remnants of themselves among the villagers beside our holy faith, which I have neglected to mention here, but which I will tell you of now.

For after we had been in that village several days, the cacique led us through the close humid forest along a tangled trail to a clearing nearby just to the north of the village, and here we saw certain tangible remains of the voyagers: a graveyard with grave markers of white limestone, and the rotting ribs and strakes and some of the keel of a seafaring vessel of an ancient design, and the foundation walls of a little wooden church. All of which things were as sad a sight as could be imagined, for the gravestones were so weathered and worn that although we could see the faint marks of names we could not read the names themselves, and the vessel was but a mere sorry remnant, a few miserable decaying timbers, and the church was only a pitiful fragment of a thing.

We stood amidst these sorry ruins and our hearts were struck into pieces by pity and grief for these brave men, so far from home and lonely, who in this strange place had nevertheless contrived to plant the sacred tree of Christianity. And the noble Don Juan Ponce de Leon went down on his knees before the church and bowed his head and said, "Let us pray, my friends, for the souls of these men, as we hope that someday people will pray for ours."

We spent some days amongst these people in feasting and prayer, and replenishing our stock of firewood and water. And then Don Juan Ponce gave new thought to the primary purpose of our voyage, which was, to find the miraculous Fountain that renews a man's energies. He called Pedro de Plasencia to his side and said, "Ask of the cacique, whether he knows such a Fountain."

"It will not be easy, describing such things in my poor Latin," answered Pedro. "I had my Latin from the Church, Don Juan, and what I learned there is of little use here, and it was all so very long ago."

"You must try, my friend. For only you of all our company has the power to speak with him and be understood."

Whereupon Pedro went to the cacique; but I could see even at a distance that he was having great difficulties. For he would speak a few halting words, and then he would act out his meaning with gestures, like a clown upon a stage, and then he would speak again. There would be silence; and then the cacique would reply, and I would see Pedro leaning forward most intently, trying to catch the meaning of the curious Latin that the cacique spoke. They did draw pictures for each other also in the sand, and point to the sky and sweep their arms to and fro, and do many another thing to convey to each other the sense of their words, and so it went, hour after hour.

At length Pedro de Plasencia returned to where we stood, and said, "There does appear to be a source of precious water that they cherish on this island, which they call the Blue Spring."

"And is this Blue Spring the Fountain for which we search?" Don Juan Ponce asked, all eagerness.

"Ah, of that I am not certain."

"Did you tell him that the water of it would allow a man to take his pleasure with women all day and all night, and never tire of it?"

"So, I attempted to say."

"With many women, one after another?"

"These are Christian folk, Don Juan!"

"Yes, so they are. But they are Indians also. They would understand such a thing, just as any man of Estramadura or Galicia or Andalusia would understand such a thing, Christian though he be."

Pedro de Plasencia nodded. "I told him what I could, about the nature of the Fountain for which we search. And he listened very close, and he said, Yes, yes, you are speaking of the Blue Spring."

"So, he understood you, then?"

"He understood something of what I said, Don Juan, so I do firmly believe. But whether he understood it all, that is only for God to know."

I saw the color rise in Don Juan Ponce's face, and I knew that that restless choleric nature of his was coming to the fore, which had always been his great driving force and also his most perilous failing.

He said to Pedro de Plasencia, "And will he take us to this Blue Spring of his, do you think?"

"I think he will," said Pedro. "But first he wishes to enact a treaty with us, as the price of transporting us thither."

"A treaty."

"A treaty, yes. He wants our aid and assistance."

"Ah," said Don Juan Ponce. "And how can we be of help to these people, do you think?"

"They want us to show them how to build seafaring ships," said Pedro. "So that they can sail across the Ocean Sea, and go to the rescue of the Holy Land, and free it from the paynim hordes."

There was much more of back and forth, and forth and back, in these negotiations, until Pedro de Plasencia grew weary indeed, and there was not enough wine in our sacks to give him the rest he needed, so that we had to send a boat out to fetch more from one of our ships at anchor in the harbor. For it was a great burden upon him to conduct these conversations, he remembering only little patches of Church Latin from his boyhood, and the cacique speaking a language that could be called Latin only by great courtesy. I sat with them as they talked, on several occasions, and not for all my soul could I understand a thing that they said to each other. From time to time Pedro would lose his patience and speak out in

Spanish, or the cacique would begin to speak in his savage tongue or else in that other language, somewhat like Provencal, which must have been what the seafaring Crusaders spoke amongst themselves. But none of that added to the understanding between the two men, which I think was a very poor understanding indeed.

It became apparent after a time that Pedro had misheard the cacique's terms of treaty: what he wished us to do was not to teach them how to build ships but to give them one of ours in which to undertake their Crusade.

"It cannot be," replied Don Juan Ponce, when he had heard. "But tell him this, that I will undertake to purchase ships for him with my own funds, in Spain. Which I will surely do, after we have received the proceeds from the sale of the water from the Fountain."

"He wishes to know how many ships you will provide," said Pedro de Plasencia, after another conference.

"Two," said Don Juan Ponce. "No: three. Three fine caravels."

Which Pedro duly told the cacique; but his way of telling him was to point to our three ships in the harbor, which led the cacique into thinking that Don Juan Ponce meant to give him those three actual ships then and now, and that required more hours of conferring to repair. But at length all was agreed on both sides, and our journey toward the Blue Spring was begun.

The cacique himself accompanied us, and the three priests of the tribe, carrying the heavy wooden crosses that were their staffs of office, and perhaps two dozen of the young men and girls of the village. In our party there were ten men, Don Juan Ponce and Pedro and I, and seven ordinary seamen carrying barrels in which we meant to store the waters of the Fountain. My wife Beatriz and her sister Juana accompanied us also, for I never would let them be far from me.

Some of the ordinary seamen among us were rough men of Estramadura, who spoke jestingly and with great licentiousness of how often they would embrace the girls of the native village after they had drunk of the Fountain. I had to silence them, reminding them that my wife and her sister could overhear their words. Yet I wondered privately what effects the waters would have on my own manhood: not that it had ever been lacking in any aspect, but I could not help asking myself if I would find it enhanced beyond its usual virtue, for such curiosity is but a natural thing to any man, as you must know.

We journeyed for two days, through hot close terrain where insects of great size buzzed among the flowers and birds of a thousand colors astounded our eyes. And at last we came to a place of bare white stone, flat like all other places in this isle of Florida, where clear cool blue water gushed up out of the ground with wondrous force.

The cacique gestured grandly, with a great sweep of his arms.

"It is the Blue Spring," said Pedro de Plasencia.

Our men would have rushed forward at once to lap up its waters like greedy dogs at a pond; but the cacique cried out, and Don Juan Ponce also in that moment ordered them to halt. There would be no unseemly haste here, he said. And it was just as well he did, for we very soon came to see that this spring was a holy place to the people of the village, and it would have been profaned by such an assault on it, to our possible detriment and peril.

The cacique came forward, with his priests beside him, and gestured to Don Juan Ponce to kneel and remove his helmet. Don Juan Ponce obeyed; and the cacique took his helmet from him, and passed it to one of the priests, who filled it with water from the spring and poured it down over Don Juan Ponce's face and neck, so that Don Juan Ponce laughed out loud. The which laughter seemed to offend the Indians, for they showed looks of disapproval, and Don Juan Ponce at once grew silent.

The Indians spoke words which might almost have been Latin words, and there was much elevating of their crosses as the water was poured down over Don Juan Ponce, after which he was given the order to rise.

And then one by one we stepped forth, and the Indians did the same to each of us.

"It is very like a rite of holy baptism, is it not?" said Aurelio Herrera to me.

"Yes, very much like a baptism," I said to him.

And I began to wonder: How well have we been understood here? Is it a new access of manly strength that these Indians are conferring upon us, or rather the embrace of the Church? For surely there is nothing about this rite that speaks of anything else than a religious enterprise. But I kept silent, since it was not my place to speak.

When the villagers were done dousing us with water, and speaking words over us and elevating their crosses, which made me more sure than ever that we were being taken into the congregation of their faith, we were allowed to drink of the spring—they did the same—and to fill our barrels.

Don Juan Ponce turned to me after we had drunk, and winked at me and said, "Well, old friend, this will serve us well in later years, will it not? For though we have no need of such invigoration now, you and I, nevertheless time will have its work with us as it does with all men."

"If it does," I said, "why, then, we are fortified against it now indeed."

But in truth I felt no change within. The water was pure and cool and good, but it had seemed merely to be water to me, with no great magical qualities about it; and when I turned and looked upon my wife Beatriz, she seemed pleasing to me as she always had, but no more than that. Well, so be it, I thought; this may be the true Fountain or maybe it is not, and only time will tell; and we began our return to the village, carrying the casks of water with us; and the day of our return, Pedro de Plasencia drew up a grand treaty on a piece of bark from a tree, in which we pledged our sacred honor and our souls to do all in our power to supply this village with good Spanish ships so that the villagers would be able to fulfill their pledge to liberate the Holy Land.

"Which we will surely do for them," said Don Juan Ponce with great conviction. "For I mean to come back to this place as soon as I am able, with many ships of our own as well as the vessels I have promised them from Spain; and we will fill our holds with cask upon cask of this virtuous water from the Fountain, and replenish our fortunes anew by selling that water to those who need its miraculous power. Moreover, we ourselves will benefit from its use in our declining days. And also, we will bring this cacique some priests, who will correct him in his manner of practicing our faith, and guide him in his journey to Jerusalem. All of which I will swear by a great oath upon the Cross itself, in the presence of the cacique, so that he may have no doubt whatsover of our kindly Christian purposes."

And so, we departed, filled with great joy and no little wonder at all that we had seen and heard.

Well, and none of the brave intentions of Don Juan Ponce were fulfilled, as you surely must know, inasmuch as the valiant Don Juan Ponce de Leon never saw Spain again, nor did he live to enjoy the rejuvenations of his body that he hoped the water of the Fountain would bring him in his later years. For when we left the village of the Indian Crusaders, we continued on our way along the coast of the isle of Florida a little further in a southerly direction, seeking to catch favorable winds and currents that would carry us swiftly back to Puerto Rico; and on the 23rd of May we halted in a pleasing bay to gather wood and water—for we would not touch the water of our casks from the Fountain!—and to careen the San Cristobal, the hull of which was fouled with barnacles. And as we did our work there, a party of Indians came forth out of the woods.

"Hail, brothers in Christ!" Don Juan Ponce called to them with great cheer, for the cacique had told him that his people had done wonderful things in bringing their neighbors into the embrace of Jesus, and he thought now that surely all the Indians of this isle had been converted to the True Faith by those Crusading men of long ago.

But he was wrong in that; for these Indians were no Christians at all, but only pagan savages like most of their kind, and they replied instantly to Don Juan Ponce's halloos with a volley of darts and arrows that struck five of us dead then and there before we were able to drive them off. And among those who took his mortal wound that day was the valiant and noble Don Juan Ponce de Leon of Valladolid, in the thirty-ninth year of his life.

I knelt beside him on the beach in his last moments, and said the last words with him. And he looked up at me and smiled—for death had never been frightening to him—and he said to me, almost with his last breath, "There is only one thing that I regret, Francisco. And that is that I will never know, now, what powers the water of that Fountain would have conferred upon me, when I was old and greatly stricken with the frailty of my years." With that he perished.

What more can I say? We made our doleful way back to Puerto Rico, and told our tale of Crusaders and Indians and cool blue waters. But we were met with laughter, and there were no purchasers for the contents of our casks, and our fortunes were greatly depleted. All praise be to God, I survived that dark time and went on afterward to join the magnificent Hernando Cortes in his conquest of the land of Mexico, which today is called New Spain, and in the fullness of time I returned to my native province of Valladolid with much gold in my possession, and here I live in health and vigor to this day.

Often do I think of the isle of Florida and those Christian Indians we found there. It is fifty years since that time. In those fifty years the cacique and his people have rendered most of Florida into Christians by now, as we now know, and I tell you what is not generally known, that this expansion of their nation was brought about the better to support their Crusade against the Mussulman once the ships that Don Juan Ponce promised them had arrived.

So, there is a great warlike Christian kingdom in Florida today, filling all that land and spreading over into adjacent isles, against which we men of Spain so far have struggled in vain as we attempt to extend our sway to those regions. I think it was poor Don Juan Ponce de Leon, in his innocent quest for a miraculous Fountain, who without intending it caused them to become so fierce, by making them a promise which he could not fulfill, and leaving them thinking that they had been betrayed by false Christians. Better that they had remained forever in the isolation in which they lived when we found them, singing the Gloria and the Credo and the Sanctus, and waiting with Christian patience for the promised ships that are to take them to the reconquest of the Holy Land. But those ships did not come; and they see us now as traitors and enemies.

I often think also of the valiant Don Juan Ponce, and his quest for the wondrous Fountain. Was the Blue Spring indeed the Fountain of legend? I am not sure of that. It may be that those Indians misunderstood what Pedro de Plasencia was requesting of them, and that they were simply offering us baptism—us, good Christians all our lives!—when what we sought was something quite different from that.

But if the Fountain was truly the one we sought, I feel great sorrow and pity for Don Juan Ponce. For though he drank of its waters, he died too soon to know of its effects. Whereas here I am, soon to be ninety years old, and the father of a boy of seven and a girl of five.

Was it the Fountain's virtue that has given me so long and robust a life, or have I simply enjoyed the favor of God? How can I say? Whichever it is, I am grateful; and if ever there is peace between us and the people of the isle of Florida, and you should find yourself in the vicinity of that place, you could do worse, I think, than to drink of that Blue Spring, which will do you no harm and may perhaps bring you great benefit. If by chance you go to that place, seek out the Indians of the village nearby, and tell them that old Francisco de Ortega remembers them, and cherishes the memory, and more than once has said a Mass in their praise despite all the troubles they have caused his countrymen, for he knows that they are the last defenders of the Holy Land against the paynim infidels.

This is my story, and the story of Don Juan Ponce de Leon and the miraculous Fountain, which the ignorant call the Fountain of Youth, and of the Christian Indians of Florida who yearn to free the Holy Land. You may wonder about the veracity of these things, but I beg you, have no doubt on that score. All that I have told you is true. For I was there. I saw and heard everything.

Raising Atlantis

By Jessica Guernsey

I was back in Atlantis.

That hard band wrapped around my heart loosened enough that I worried I'd cry. It had been a little over five years since I'd last stood here.

For as long as I could remember, I saw the remnants of the past, ghostly flickers of colored light left by people whose bones had long ago turned to dust. And this was the only place I had seen those flickers so bright, they outshone the sun.

But not anymore. Not in years.

Dr. Sven Korvis stepped up next to me. His height would normally tower over me, but now he leaned heavily on his cane. His trusty revolver was already tucked in the holster at his hip. "Never gets old, does it? Seeing it again."

I nodded, struggling to get my emotions in check. With only a handful of females on this archaeological dig, I couldn't very well go getting all emotional on the first day. I'd never hear the end. I had three degrees, dammit. Dr. Korvis's presence as the Excavation Director and my job as the Site Manager meant I would be addressed as Dr. Cassandra Chrysopoulis, or at least by Andy, from those who knew me.

As I stood with my mentor on the edge of the camp, another person joined us. I identified Graham Larson first by his musky cologne and then by his nasal voice as he greeted us. I nodded in response, reluctant to tear my eyes from the rock-strewn landscape.

"Wow," the newcomer remarked with a sneer. "What a barren place."

Dr. Korvis and I exchanged a look, small smiles quickly hiding away.

I knew better than anyone what was here, buried beneath the sand, rocks, and centuries of time. Only in recent years had the satellite images shown the truth hidden in the Sahara. They dubbed it the Richat Structure, the Eye of the Sahara. Three concentric rings of stoneworks. Just as Plato had described when revealing the continent of Atlantis.

That was another misconception. Nearly everyone who believed Atlantis had existed once thought it was an island that had sunk into the sea a very long time ago. Or taken away by aliens, if TV shows were to be believed.

But no, Atlantis was an empire, and this was its capital city.

The overly-cologned Lawson would only ever see a group of misguided archaeologists in the middle of the desert instead of the ocean. His specialty wasn't the past but the future. He built lasers. And his financial backers sponsored our dig to test his latest invention. It didn't matter that he looked to use more hair products than I did or that his only facial expression seemed to be leering. He built whatever wonder he'd hauled out here to test in the field, but that didn't put him in charge of my teams.

He'd explained the process to us weeks ago at the briefing meeting, all the time grinning at me like I was his favorite snack. I'd made sure to not encourage him. No smiling. No asking questions. I barely acknowledged him. But that hadn't stopped him from trying to hug me when we met once more at the ancient city of Ouadone before the bumpy four-wheel drive out into the desert. I'd nearly gut-punched him with my outstretched hand, offering a handshake instead.

With no one engaging him in conversation, Lawson left soon enough.

Dr. Korvis glanced after him, then asked in a near whisper, "See them?"

I took in a deep breath before giving a slight shake of my head.

My old mentor was one of only two people who knew about the flickers of life I saw. Dr. Krovis discovered it on my first dig with him, when, as a plucky undergrad, I insisted we were looking in the wrong spot for any sort of structures. I couldn't explain the flickers I frequently saw in that jungle and how they never flashed around our dig site.

Frustrated with the lack of findings and probably my impudence, he'd asked me where I thought we ought to look and I had pointed out an area yards away, covered with heavy growth. There, the flickers frequently concentrated, which told me it had been a doorway or gathering spot of some sort.

Sure enough, we'd found the base of a long-collapsed building, large enough that it may have been more than just a house or domicile. With that new finding, Dr Korvis re-aligned the entire projected dig, and we uncovered several other locations from a pre-Incan civilization.

After I'd had a few too many cups of celebratory mezcal, he'd asked me how I knew. So, I explained the flickers. He listened and never once laughed in my face, especially since he'd seen the proof.

Dr. Korvis wrote several papers on the discovery and even a book, made a bigger name for himself. He casually mentioned my name, praising my connection to the past, but I didn't want the credit. He had taken me under his wing after that. Opened so many doors. Became my thesis advisor for my PhD. And he was still looking out for me, making sure my name made the short list of those considered for this position.

I was the one who suggested he get the gun after a robbery at a previous of our digs where the lone security guy was beaten. Always a fan of cowboy shows, Dr. Korvis took to the idea and never failed to appear at a dig without his revolver.

I didn't see "dead people." I saw flashes of light and color that moved where people had once thrived and were now long gone. Cemeteries didn't have these same sights, except the really old ones I'd found in Europe during my master's research, with stones so worn there were no markings.

Celtic sites. Those held flickers. Even the roots of Vikings were visible. Ancient places.

Ancient places like where we now stood.

But then I'd had my accident here and the injuries I sustained put me in a coma for months.

Nine months. Though to me, it had been three years.

The band on my heart twinged, and I stuffed the memories back down deep inside. Now was not the time.

I turned away from the endless stretches of black rocks in the tannish red sand and helped get camp ready.

I'd taken a silvery blue case off the supply truck and turned to set it down on the ground when Lawson suddenly appeared at my side, making cooing noises as he carefully took the case from my hands. With plenty of contact, I noticed.

"Careful, careful," he cooed. "These are my babies."

I raised my hands and took a step back.

But he turned that grin on me again. "Not saying that you couldn't also be my baby."

I think he winked, though he squinted so much into the blazing sun that it was hard to tell.

"I won't touch the blue cases." I turned away from him and went to a different section of the supplies. He said something behind me that was lost in a gust of wind that flapped everything around us. It was probably another lame attempt at a pickup line, and I wasn't about to guess what innuendo he used this time. I hoped not responding to his casual flirting would put him off enough that he'd cut it out. Really hoped he wasn't the type that needed the more direct approach before he got the point. Those guys turned nasty once rejected. And I wasn't about to lose the money funding this dig. It meant too much to be here again.

After setting up my tent, Dr. Korvis met me, hands stuffed in the pockets of his cargo pants as his stark white hair ruffled in the wind. "Shall we go see what all the hullabaloo is about?"

We'd been instructed to gather with Lawson at his team at sundown on the first day for a demonstration. The sun was halfway down, a blazing ball against the desert sands.

I smiled. "As long as he doesn't flirt with me again."

"Is the flirting bad?" Dr. Korvis looked at me sidelong, his Danish accent a little more pronounced than usual, probably because he rarely got personal. "Graham isn't such a bad guy once you get past the cheese."

I gritted my teeth. "I'm not open to a relationship," I said, focusing on the area everyone gathered instead of looking at my mentor. "You know I prefer to keep the digs nothing but professional. And if Lawson keeps pushing, I'm sure you will have no problems when I make an official complaint in the report of his behavior, Dr. Korvis." I'd known my mentor for over a decade. He knew more about me than anyone else and still, I could not bring myself to tell him about Emas. Definitely could never mention Tala without breaking down completely.

I wasn't open to any sort of personal relationship because several doctors had tried to convince me it wasn't real, that it had all been a hallucination brought on in my coma state.

But it was real. So real. My heart still believed that.

Dr. Korvis gave his customary grunt in response. He did that whenever he didn't like an answer. Well, I couldn't give him a better one. Not now, surrounded by technical staff here for Lawson's wonder project. I could easily tell them apart from the archeology team because most of the tech people wore polos in the same blue color and a few had on jeans. All were American. They'd discover soon enough how poor of a choice their attire was. But it wouldn't be my job to tell them. No, that would be up to Lawson and his Big Bad Corporation that had paid for all of us to be here.

We all signed a stack of NDAs with plenty of privacy stuff. I'd skimmed it, but I didn't care. Who was I going to tell about groundbreaking tech?

"Oh good, you're here!" Lawson had changed his sand-streaked blue polo for a glaringly bright white button-up. "Do me a favor, Cassie, and come up here."

I looked around, waiting for the tech he'd named to step forward. No one did.

That's when I noticed everyone looking at me.

"Are you talking to me?" I asked, refraining from grinding my teeth.

Lawson gave a self-deprecating laugh. "There's only one Cassandra here."

"Not really," I said. "I don't go by Cassandra. I prefer Andy. Or better yet, Dr. Chrysopoulis."

"Oh, come on." He planted his hands on his hips. "That last name is a mouthful. Besides, what's a nickname between friends?"

I didn't budge.

Dr. Korvis nudged me a little, making it look entirely like it was unintentional, but I could read the intention behind it. Play nice with the folks signing our checks.

Fine. I stepped forward.

"There's a good girl," Lawson said, motioning me closer.

I nearly stopped, shooting a brief scowl at Dr. Korvis.

On a folding table were the four hefty blueish cases Lawson hadn't wanted me to touch earlier. He opened one and spun it around for the group to see. Inside was custom black foam lining with a black cube about the size of my air fryer at home. Tucked next to it was probably the tripod to stand it on. Shiny. But what did it do?

"Meet LISA." He gestured like a game show host. "Laser Indicative Senescent Architecture."

Someone muttered "Senescent?"

Lawson honed in on them and sneered as he said, "It means old. How did you get into grad school?"

The tech reddened and dropped his head.

I focused back on Lawson and added "bully" to the list of his traits, right under "douche."

Lawson put back on his broad smile that matched his shirt. "LISA is the reason we are all here today."

He paused. I wasn't sure if it was for applause. And why did he need me up here in front of everyone? I hadn't changed out of my traveling attire. No idea what my hair looked like, but at least my thick black curls were still pulled back in a ponytail. I almost folded my arms, but Lawson over here would probably think I wanted to draw attention to my body. Like my baggy khakis and oversized shirt screamed "sultry."

"Now, with the help of the lovely *Cassie*," he shot me a little wink, "I'll show you what these wonders can do."

Sure enough, he pulled out the item I suspected was a tripod first and spread the feet, planting it squarely on the packed ground around us. Carefully, he nestled the black box on the top, twisting it until it clicked solidly into place. He then motioned for me to carry a case and walked with measured paces about twenty-five feet from the first box, where he repeated the process. We repeated the process with all four devices, forming a square, as the sun finished setting.

In the growing dark, Lawson went back to the table, and I trailed behind.

He removed a remote from his shirt pocket and, pointing it at the first box, pressed a button.

A small green light turned on at the base of the box. A quick check showed the same light on the other devices.

He grinned at the crowd, who were shuffling feet and looking around.

It was so anticlimactic; I wanted to laugh. But one thing a bully can't handle is being laughed at. I brushed at my hair instead, making sure it wasn't a wind-blown mess. It was. No amount of patting would help at this point.

Lawson continued to grin at the group, like this was the most amazing thing we had ever seen, though his smile took on an edge as the shuffling and murmuring increased.

I stifled a yawn. The sun was a faint sliver on the horizon and there had been no discussions of dinner. Hopefully, my stomach wouldn't voice its opinions on the matter.

I was considering which path to take through the crowd to Dr. Korvis when I first noticed the buzzing. Frowning slightly, I looked back at the black-cornered square.

Beams of green light erupted from all four boxes.

My gasp mixed in with those around me.

The lights shimmered down to the ground, leaving behind lines.

Not just lines. *Walls.*

The walls of Atlantis rose before me. And I still couldn't see the flickers of life.

More oohs and ahhs from the group as people unconsciously moved forward.

"Please don't break the lines, folks," Lawson's voice rang out over the group. "We haven't fully tested the laser's abilities, and we'd hate for anyone's clothes to catch fire."

I couldn't see him now in the dark, but so help me, if he directed another wink in my direction…

I brushed away thoughts of Lawson like the annoying gnat he was and gazed back at the walls. From where we were, this should have been the very end of the East Market. The walls weren't very high here. Something wasn't quite right, though.

"What do you think?" Lawson's voice was too loud and too close. I knew he was talking to me.

"The doorways don't look quite right," I mumbled.

"What was that?"

"What I mean is, how do you know the architecture looked like this?" I motioned to the one nearest us, completely rounded and entirely Western in shape. "How do the lasers know there were doorways here instead of a wall?"

I could just make out his grin, teeth radiating slightly green from the laser's light.

"It's all about looking down," he said. "The machines use ground-penetrating radar and sonar to see what is below. Then, they measure the compactness of the dirt and sand along with the arrangement of any remaining stonework. The more tightly packed ground beneath means higher walls above. Slight variations typically indicate an opening, like a doorway. Then they recreate what the city looked like."

I frowned. "What do you *think* it looked like."

Lawson's brief laugh had a little too much of a patronizing tone. "Well, it's not like we have anyone around to prove me wrong."

I snapped my mouth shut before I said more.

"Okay, folks," Lawson addressed the group again like he was the one in charge. "Starting tomorrow, we work in a grid system…"

I tuned him out. Wasn't my job to keep track of the lasers. I was only here for the walls.

And oh, what walls they were. Just seeing them, looking so real, so close, the band around my heart squeezed even tighter.

I tuned back in abruptly when I caught, "Cassie will get our dinner ready soon."

"Uh, what?" I asked, keeping the anger from boiling into my tone.

Lawson only glanced at me. "Just let me know what you need set up before you cook."

"It's Dr. Chrysopoulis," I said, "And I don't cook."

"Oh, I'm sure your cooking isn't that bad." Lawson had the audacity to reach out and pat my shoulder.

"What she means," Dr. Korvis said, stepping between us, "is that Dr Chrysopoulis is the Site Manager. She handles the logistics. We brought Paolo and his assistant to do the cooking. Come, I will introduce you." Dr. Korvis, the sainted man in khakis, then put his hand on Lawson's shoulder and guided him away into the darkness.

As they faded, I turned back to the walls.

So close. And yet thousands of years too far.

That night, I dreamt of Emas, his strong hands, his deep laugh. I woke up with tears cold on my face. He had to be real.

I had barely left my tent when Dr. Korvis waved me over to where he finished a conversation with an intern. The guy nodded to me and departed as I approached.

"Good morning, Andy," Dr. Korvis said. "How did you sleep?"

"First night in the field is always the hardest," I responded.

He hummed, but kept his eyes on my face.

Thinking maybe I had missed some drool, I wiped at my mouth. "What?"

He pursed his lips, then took a breath and said, "I heard you call out in your sleep."

Oh, no. "Did I?"

"I didn't understand the words, but you sounded quite upset."

"Odd. I don't remember having any upsetting dreams." Emas's gray eyes hovered before my face a moment before fading like they had so long ago.

"What is 'eemass?' That is the word you said many times."

I couldn't keep my face from reacting. I could only cover the jolt with a strangled, "Strange."

He hummed again, still watching me. Dr. Korvis was too smart of a man to be fooled, but he also could see I wasn't ready to talk.

"And tell me, my friend." He leaned a little closer, though there was no one around. "Has soaking in the same air helped? Any flickers?"

My shoulders dropped, answering for me.

"Do not worry," he said, running a handkerchief over his forehead. "I have faith that they will return to you."

I nodded, unable to speak. I had gone into archeology expecting that half my class would have the same abilities. Perhaps there would even be a graduate course on just how to make use of this…*skill*…but I was disappointed.

I tightened my ponytail, fingers automatically finding the groove from the emergency surgery that saved my life all those years ago.

The accident happened close to where they set up the cooking tent. I didn't look at the rocks jutting out of the ground, where I'd been standing when lightning struck.

The day of the accident had been a good one. We'd found a wall. A solid, stacked round structure underground. It was the Holy Grail of archaeology finds. And it was here, in the Richat Structure, where so many believed the capital of Atlantis had begun. Still feeling the exuberance from the find, I'd climbed a pile of blackened rocks with my trench team. A storm rolled in while we enjoyed the higher viewpoint, and the others started back down. I waited my turn as I watched the clouds drop on us.

I didn't remember the lighting strike, though the silvery spider web of faded burn scars across my neck and shoulders bore witness to what happened.

I also didn't remember falling.

I remember waking up to strange people in strange tunics, speaking a language that was familiar and foreign at the same time. It took days to figure out that I hadn't somehow crawled to an unknown city here in the middle of the Sahara. When their words started sounding more like the Old Greek my great-grandmother muttered, when I encountered the first set of rings, now filled with flowing, crystal clear water, that's when I knew.

This was Atlantis.

Emas was the local scholar who helped me get a better grip on the language even as he peppered me with questions about where I was from. But even Emas, as smart as he was, could not explain how I had gotten there. Sometimes, strangers wandered into the city in odd clothes and with no understanding of the language. Each had a story of an explosion that knocked them unconscious. And each one had disappeared from the city without notice. Emas assumed they had gone back to wherever they originated from, the pull of Atlantis no longer able to hold them.

When I told Emas about the flickers, he nodded thoughtfully. "Perhaps it is your connection to the past that brought you here." He smiled at me then, and I felt warm to my toes. For the first time, I felt like I was in a place where I truly and completely belonged.

From what I could piece together of their calendar, Emas and I married six months after I arrived. And sweet little Tala arrived less than a year later. Her eyes were pale gray like her father's, though she had my curls.

The day Tala learned to walk was the day I was ripped from Atlantis.

Instead of kneeling on the mosaic floor, arms outstretched to my daughter, smiling as broad as I'd ever done, I opened my eyes to a darkened room, surrounded by strange beeps and sharp smells.

A coma. I had been in a coma for nine months, two weeks, and one day. The only reason they hadn't pulled the plug was because my brain never showed signs of losing activity.

I cried for weeks.

And according to my dreams, I still did.

I stood here again; the walls rendered by lasers not quite right but still very close. And today was the first day we'd start digging.

The sun threatened to rise as I checked through my list. I preferred a tablet to Dr. Korvis's ever-present clipboard. The man was old school. I'd met Jennie, the whip-smart intern he'd assigned to read through his emails. She worked toward a degree in archeology focusing on the tech side of things. Dr. Korvis probably asked her to explain yet again how social media worked. Once, it had been me and I smiled at the memory.

Lawson stepped into my line of vision. "Smiling for me, I see."

My smile immediately dropped. "Nope," I said, looking back at my schedule. "Just at a fond memory of a previous dig." A dig from another life.

"One of these days, I'll make you smile." His hands were in the pockets of his very expensive-looking slacks. Did the man bring a personal valet to take care of his wardrobe?

"Not likely," I said. "Do you need something, Mr. Lawson? I'm due at the first trench."

"Korvis says you are in charge of the teams."

"Yes," I replied, keeping most of my attention on the tablet's screen. "Dr. Korvis is correct."

"Well, someone needs to be there to move LISA's components for me," he said and sidled closer. "You remember how heavy they are? You could help me."

I flicked through my files. "According to the submitted paperwork, you brought three people with you that are specifically assigned as 'handlers.' Shouldn't you talk to them?"

Lawson huffed out a breath. "You are very organized."

"It's my job."

"Yes." He scratched at the back of his head. "So, you're just gonna make me come out and say it?"

I looked up at him and cocked an eyebrow.

He sighed and then grinned, though it looked a little fragile. "I was hoping to spend time with you today."

"Today," I said flatly. "The first day of a dig where I am the Site Manager and have to make sure everyone is where they're supposed to be and knows what they're supposed to be doing? I don't see that happening, Mr. Lawson."

"Call me Graham, Cassie."

"And I'd prefer it if you called me Dr. Chrysopoulis. Mr. Lawson." I didn't smile or blush or simper. Holding his gaze for a beat, I went back to my tablet.

He chuckled and casually strode away. No doubt looking for an easier target.

After he passed out of range, I sighed. It might be a very long dig.

A setting sun meant Lawson's handlers got to work setting up the lasers for that night's section. Although the heat of the sun sapped the strength out of me, I dragged myself to the site, not wanting to miss a glimpse of the city I had loved so much.

Lawson had moved significantly closer to the center of the city, choosing to position his boxes on the edge of the inner canal ring. As the green lights shot into the sky and rained down to reveal the walls, I fought back a strangled cry. The building just on the edge of the square was where the scholars met for lectures.

If I could still see the flickers, would I know which ones were Emas and Tala? My heart said I would, but all the voices in my head from countless medical professionals muttered about hallucinations from my coma state.

I stood within the rings of Atlantis. The city was real. Emas and Tala were real. The only thing wrong was that my feet were on rocky sand instead of their paved streets.

I checked in with the handful of interns assigned to graph the walls, letting the laser walls tell us where to dig. I sat on the edge of the lasers, next to a box. The soft buzzing was rather comforting as I opened my sketch pad and began drawing the walls of my former home.

A huge part of an archaeologist's job was recording findings. I learned to sketch what the ruins could have been long ago and considered it one of my strengths when making my reports. Visuals have a broader appeal than just pages of text. And some people have a hard time seeing ruins as something more than rocks.

Since I knew the buildings so well, I formed the peaked and swooping arches as I remembered, added trellises and balconies, potted plants, and beautiful trees that grew nowhere else. Once the city was on paper, I added in people. Women carrying children, old men chatting together on the corner. Even a young couple sharing a moment. The man might have Emas's broad shoulders and wore his favorite tunic and perhaps the woman featured my curls. Surely that was all a coincidence.

"What's this?"

The nasally voice out of the darkness startled me so much that I jumped up and spun around to face it, but my boot caught on one of the sun-blackened rocks and I tumbled directly in front of the green lasers, my free hand slapping down hard on the top of the shiny box.

The lights flickered, and the buzzing echoed in my head, down my spine, as my vision turned bright green.

Rough hands pulled me upright and out of the lasers.

"Watch out," Lawson nearly snarled, shoving past me and the tech who had helped me up. "These are very delicate."

"I'm fine. Thanks for asking," I spat, taking back my sketchbook from the tech's hand.

Lawson continued to mutter as he fussed over his "baby."

I stomped away to my tent, anger and a little fear making the buzzing feel like it shot out my fingertips.

My bones still hummed the next day as I gave Lawson as wide a berth as one can give on a dig site. When he entered a space, I found a reason to leave it. But I still had my duties, and I wasn't about to avoid those just because the man was odious. That's how he caught up to me shortly before the morning break. Well, snuck up on me, is more like it.

One moment I was making a note of a minor injury one of the hired diggers had sustained when a tool broke and the next, Lawson's distinctly scented shadow covered my tablet screen.

"So, what do you think of my little invention?" Lawson had his hands in his pockets and gave me that too-broad grin. I knew I had to tread carefully.

"It's amazing," I said honestly, but without enthusiasm.

I saw his grin dip. I knew he expected effulgent praise; he wouldn't find that from me. But I imagined Dr. Korvis giving me that little nudge and I offered more.

"Really, it's genius," I said, looking out at the area where my teams worked on trenching the walls shown by the lasers. Already, we'd made tremendous progress on knowing just where to begin. "It's saved us so much trial and error. Finding the right place to dig is never the easy part."

"What is the easy part?"

I shrugged. "Seeing history come alive. Finding the hard proof of the lives that were lived before us."

"Proof." His grin was gone. "So, you really think this is Atlantis? Wasn't that just like Plato's argument for how people were heading in the wrong direction? Like an allegory?"

I stifled a snort. I'd heard this same comment for years, especially once I started saying I'd been there. This argument was one reason I stopped talking about my other life. "Plato wasn't the only one or the first one to talk about Atlantis. And it wasn't just a city. It was a nation. There are similar stories all over the world. Bolivia. The Azores. And even Antarctica. Even if it's not Atlantis, it's still proof that life was here way before anyone else knew. Aren't your walls proof of that?"

Lawson shrugged, obviously not convinced. "There was a city here, sure. Nothing proves it was *Atlantis*."

I continued. "Proof is different to everyone. Some people will take on faith the same thing that others wouldn't believe, even when they've seen it with their own eyes. If your walls could talk, what do you think they would say?" I turned back toward the field and made a note about the trench progress on my tablet. We'd already found the tops of walls in three sections.

Lawson didn't take the question as rhetorical and instead answered, "Pretty sure they would tell me how intelligent, clever, and incredibly handsome I am to have discovered them."

I shot him a sidelong look. "Or they would say 'Look! We were here! We existed! You found us. Now tell our story.'"

Lawson wiped a hand over his large forehead. "I don't understand how anyone would want to make a life out here."

Not looking at him, I answered, "The Sahara wasn't always a desert. There's all kinds of evidence that it was actually quite green until about 10,000 years ago. Surely you must have known that when you picked this site."

He shook his head. "I didn't pick the site. That was all Korvis."

I copied Dr. Korvis's noncommittal sound. Lawson had gone to the foremost authority on ancient architecture and even after seeing the walls rise, he still wasn't buying it.

"So, what's with you and Korvis?" He turned fully toward me.

"Not sure what you mean," I said, still focused on the tablet. "He's my mentor, my friend. We've worked together for over a decade. He was also my PhD advisor."

"So, you're not like…" he made a rolling gesture with his hand.

I gave him my most confused look, which was absolutely genuine. "What?"

"Involved," he said with a weird squeak.

I snorted. "I think his husband of thirty years would tell you no, we were never involved."

"Oh," Lawson said.

I went back to my tablet, moving slightly away from Lawson to get a better look at the far team.

He followed me, standing a little too close, and I held back the sigh for fear of gagging on his cologne. "So, you're saying that you're available." His grin was back. "My tent or yours?"

I thought briefly about grounding one of the many rocks into those too-white teeth. He just was not taking the hint. Maybe back in his flashy science world where money and power make the rules, he was used to being fawned over.

"Mr. Lawson," I said, keeping my words even and calm, though I looked directly at him. "This is a professional environment with a very serious discovery being made. None of us should be so distracted by personal relationships that we can't do our jobs in the very best possible way. This—" I motioned between the two of us. "--will not happen. Not here."

Toward the end of my little speech, one of the team leads jogged up to me and must have heard what I said, because he backed away.

Instead of waiting for Lawson's response, I turned to the new arrival. "What's up?"

"Uh," the team lead looked back and forth before stopping on me. "Need your call on the north trench."

I didn't look back at Lawson before I started after my team member.

After settling the trench issue, I joined the rest of the staff for our early afternoon water and fruit break. Lawson didn't show, so at least I didn't have to avoid him. The blazing sun sent everyone under cover for the next few hours and I had paperwork calling my name.

On the way to my tent, Dr. Korvis intercepted me. His red face wasn't entirely because of the scorching temperature. The way his eyes glinted reminded me of the time he caught a grad student seeding his dig site with artifacts so he could be the one to make the "find."

"Dr. Chrysopoulis." It wasn't a good sign that he used my last name.

I stopped.

"Please come with me."

I followed him to the tent we used for briefings and updates each morning. As soon as he entered, the few interns and diggers hanging out there quickly found a reason to leave. So, they were getting the same vibes I was. This was really not good.

He stopped and sank heavily into a chair, his cane smacking the side of the tent. He slid his holster into a more comfortable position.

I leaned against the table and folded my arms, waiting.

Dr. Korvis took a moment to calm his breathing and mop his forehead before he looked at me. I knew him well enough to know that he was getting his emotions in check so that he could approach our conversation with logic. A cold lump settled in my stomach. I could only wait for calm to prevail. It took several more moments.

He blew out a slow breath and began. "I've had a rather upsetting conversation this morning."

I said nothing.

"Graham came to me with some…interesting claims."

I rolled my eyes. At least he was angry at someone else and not me.

He narrowed his eyes. "Is there anything you'd like to tell me? Any incidents to report?"

"Incidents?" I pulled my head back. "Well, there was a complication with a trench this morning, but that wasn't an issue and easily settled. I didn't think it warranted bringing it to your attention."

He frowned, the wrinkles around his mouth, so used to smiling, growing deeper. "Nothing to tell me? Maybe something happened last night?"

"Last night?" I wracked my brain. "Did I cry out again?"

He shook his head.

"I can't think of…" then I remembered. My sketching. Getting startled. Falling. "Oh."

"Oh?"

"I didn't think it was that big a deal either, but I was out by the lasers, sketching the walls. You know how I like to do that to include it in my reports. Lawson and one of his techs startled me and I tripped. Fell into the path of the lasers, but they got me out quickly and there was no harm done." Except the odd vibrations that rattled my entire frame for the rest of the night. If I concentrated, I could still feel the buzz at the base of my neck.

"You were startled and fell."

"Yes. Tripped over my own feet when Lawson snuck up behind me."

He hummed, but I didn't know what else I could add. Something wasn't adding up.

I narrowed my eyes. "Why? What did Lawson say happened?"

Dr. Korvis blew out heavily through his nose, his lips pursed. "He said he caught you fiddling with the device. He suspected he interrupted a sabotage attempt."

"And what did the assistant say happened?"

Dr. Korvis's eyes hardened. "He is on Mr. Lawson's payroll. Do you think he would not take his boss's side completely?"

My stomach sank. "I would never do that. This dig is far too important to us. To me. Dr. Korvis, you know this. Better than anyone." I hated that tears started to prick my eyes.

His eyes softened. "I know, my friend. Which is why I refused to make an official comment about the incident without an investigation. But you must be careful, dear heart."

"When did he come to you?" I asked.

"Moments before the fruit and water. It is why I have missed it and am overheating." His smile barely lifted the corners of his mouth.

"Moments before." The dots connected. "So, right after I rejected his advances."

Dr. Korvis's eyes widened.

"I told you the man flirted with me." Why did I feel so defensive? "And I've told you I'm not open to any sort of relationship. So, when subtly and never encouraging him didn't work, I had to take a more direct approach."

My sunk stomach soured. Bullies were never good with rejection. I should have known this was coming and prepared for it.

"Did he threaten your position if you did not accept him?"

"No," I said. "But it sounds like he didn't have to. He already had a reason to make me look bad."

Dr. Korvis pursed his lips again. "If I comment on the harassment, then I must also comment on the other claims."

The sourness in my stomach turned to flames. Of course, he would have to. Lawson probably banked on my not reporting him. If this was a game of chess, he'd have me in check. I wondered how many other times this had worked for him.

If I made a formal complaint, how many of my teams would back me up? They were all here because Lawson was paying for the dig. I'd seen the way they fawned over Lawson at every meal. Would they side with him, like so many did when a woman claimed harassment? They knew me, sure. But we all had bills to pay. And reputations to protect. In archeology, reputation was everything.

The only solution was to stay away from Lawson and his lasers.

Which ended up not being as easy as I thought.

Lawson and his group of techs set up the lasers for the night as I met with my team leads for reports. He made us move twice so he could get the positioning right. I avoided looking at him as much as possible and still, he planted himself in my way.

As we wrapped up, I heard him call my name. Well, not the name I preferred, but the name he'd chosen for me.

"Cassie."

I ignored him as I updated my tablet and said good night to the last of the leads.

"Cassie."

I was alone now and there wasn't much point in avoiding him without causing further insult. I made a few more taps on my tablet, closing reports, and opening another app. I turned toward him, keeping my expression flat in the growing dark.

"Can you move the north box about two feet south?"

Really? He was asking me to touch his precious lasers? After accusing me of sabotage.

"I have work to do." I waved my tablet. "Have one of your lackeys help."

"I would, but they are all doing other tasks to get LISA running tonight."

"Wait for one to come back."

He looked up at the quickly darkening sky. "Not a good idea."

I said nothing and went back to my tablet.

He put his hands on his hips and addressed me like I was a petulant child. "This dig is too important to let a single night go without the help of my lasers."

He was right. But I wasn't about to move.

I copied his pose and tone. "Aren't you concerned that I'm trying to *sabotage* you?"

"By refusing to help me right now, you are sabotaging the entire dig."

For such a large team on site, there wasn't another soul in sight that could take my place.

I squeezed my eyes closed hard and prayed that I wasn't setting myself up for a second attack on my reputation. He might be an entire tool bag, but this dig was too important. I sighed heavily, setting my tablet face down on the closed case at his feet. "If you insist, I will help with the lasers. But only because you are insisting."

"I insist," he said, using a patronizing tone, of course.

I shook my head a little. This was such a bad idea. "Do I pick it up by the box or by the tripod?"

"That's my good girl," he said, and I swear I could see his teeth in the dark. "By the tripod is fine. The devices are firmly attached."

I switched on my headlamp and moved toward the position where the northern box should be located. I found it easily enough. A glance back at Lawson showed he'd turned on his own light, but it was small. Probably an energy-efficient one he'd created himself. Gauging the distance, it didn't seem like the box needed to be moved; it lined up perfectly with the others. But Lawson insisted I move it. This dig wouldn't be held up because I didn't like his flirting.

Sighing, I bent over and wrapped a hand around the neck of the tripod, using my other hand to steady the box on top of it. It wobbled slightly, and I stopped. Should that happen? Maybe the box wasn't properly seated.

I looked up to call to Lawson and ask him to come check on his device when his assistant stepped out of the darkness and right in front of me.

"What are you doing?" The man shouted at me.

I nearly dropped the box as it slung sharply forward on the tripod. Grabbing it as best I could, it slammed into my chest, turning my shirt green in its light. I gritted my teeth to keep from screaming. "What the hell, man?"

"Caught you red-handed this time."

"What are you talking about?" I asked, resettling the tripod and making sure the box was steady. "Lawson asked me to move it. He insisted."

"And why would he do that when he has a team of techs here to help with the devices?"

"I don't know, maybe because all of you disappeared?"

"I was right where he told me to be." He motioned to a pile of stacked rocks behind him. "He knew you'd pull something again, so he has all of us on watch. To keep you from messing with the lasers."

"Why would I walk out here with my headlamp on, with Lawson right over there, if I had intended to mess with the lasers?"

He looked back at Lawson and the tiny light.

I dropped my head. "So, you're telling me is that this was a setup. Lawson planned this."

The guy said nothing. Like I could feel the last nail in my coffin, I sat down heavily, not caring about the sharp rocks underneath me. The light I saw was most likely Lawson's phone, recording me the whole time. Talk about "proof."

"Does he always do this?" I asked quietly. "Does he destroy anyone who won't give him what he wants?"

The assistant spoke so quietly, that I almost didn't hear his "Yeah. Just ask all of his previous assistants who were women."

I was sunk. But so help me, I would sink Lawson right with me. I stomped back to Lawson, ignoring the green-reflecting grin, grabbed my tablet, and went to see Dr. Korvis.

On my way to his tent, I saw a flash of blue at my side. I reacted as most people would and turned to look.

Nothing there.

Odd. It looked almost like...

Another one, this one peachy orange and brighter.

Again, empty air.

I slowed to a stop and closed my eyes. The buzzing through my bones revived by the lasers impacting my chest grew to a crescendo.

I opened my eyes slowly and took in the swarms and sparks of color that flowed around me.

The flickers had returned, just as bright and beautiful as they had once been.

They swirled into watercolors as tears filled my eyes.

?

I burst through Dr. Korvis's tent flap. There was a very slim chance that I would catch him before he went to bed, but I had to tell him about the flickers.

Jennie sat at her computer station, wrapping up from the looks of it.

"Jennie, you're good with computers, right?" I asked.

"Sure," she said, flipping her long hair over her shoulder. "I mean, as much as anyone."

"How are you at searches? Finding people? With just a name and maybe the last place they worked."

Jennie's lips quirked up on one side. "Oh, I am very good at that."

"Perfect." I opened my tablet and started tapping. "I'm going to send Dr. Korvis an audio file I made just now. I need you to set up a meeting with him and me first thing in the morning. Shit is about to hit the fan." With any luck, Lawson had made other comments as I walked into his trap, my tablet recording everything as it lay near him in his moment of victory.

Jennie's already wide eyes went even wider. "What?"

"Lawson has been harassing me, and I'm done being his chew toy. One of his techs told me he's treated other women like this, made them suffer the consequences when he didn't get his way."

"Harassing you?" Jennie whispered the next part, "Like *sexually*?"

I met her gaze. "Yes."

I saw her jaw clench. "That…*scumbag*." She muttered a few words under her breath in Cantonese, then held out her hand. "Give me your information. We are bringing this guy down."

I smiled for the first time in what felt like years.

?

The next morning, I headed straight for where the lasers were still up. As the sun rose, the techs would put them away. But for now, green walls shone in the dark. The flickers wove their way through the streets and doorways, like a river and its many streams.

There was a decided murmuring around the camp as people gathered in groups, ignorant of the dashes of color swirling around them. As their eyes followed me through the earliest of morning light, I could guess what the topic was.

Lawson must have started his smear campaign early. He had money and people listened. The only thing I had going for me was that most of the archeology team knew me and knew I would never break even the smallest rule while on a dig. And hopefully, they knew I wasn't the kind of person who would sabotage a dig, no matter what. I wasn't one to lose my cool, which was a big part of how I got this job. Calm under pressure.

Right now, I needed all the calm I could get.

Lawson approached, flanked by all of his tech people.

"Cassie," he said.

I slowed to a stop and kept my back straight.

His chest was so puffed up, I was surprised his tailored shirt didn't bulge at the buttons. "I'm afraid I'm going to have to ask you to remain in your tent until the authorities arrive to escort you back to the city."

I said nothing. Instead, I smirked.

Lawson glanced at his assistant, then back at me. "Look, you did this to yourself. I have you on video messing with the equipment."

A crowd gathered. Lawson was loving the attention from the sparkle in his eyes. He thought he had me in checkmate.

"Sabotage is a crime, Cassie," he said like a lecturing professor. "And you will answer for what you've done."

I said nothing, only folded my arms.

He didn't like my lack of response. Did he expect tears? Begging for a second chance? Yeah, that's probably exactly what he expected, what he was used to from all the other women whose lives he'd attempted to ruin when they rejected him. I was never one for theatrics.

Besides, I had finished my meeting with Dr. Korvis earlier, where Jennie handed him an impressive collection of names, dates, and implied criminal activities that ended careers.

The hammer was falling; Lawson just didn't know I aimed it at him.

A small part of me whispered I should just leave. Atlantis was too important of a discovery to risk the dig shutting down. I'd said my goodbyes to Emas, to Tala. Never being able to see them again didn't change the fact that they were real to me. I would leave here and never return. But I was taking Lawson and his slimy tactics down with me.

"Your career is over." Lawson copied my pose.

I scoffed.

Dropping his arms, he balled his first instead and leaned toward me, perhaps intending to go for intimidation to make me break. "It's over."

I smiled as broadly as he did so often.

It must have shocked him because he blinked and backed down slightly. I'd like to say it was because my smile was that charming. Emas had always loved my smile. But no, I think Lawson finally saw the cracks in his plan.

"Oh, it's over alright," I said. "You just don't know it yet."

Dr. Korvis parted the crowd, holding my tablet. From the speaker came my voice: "If you insist, I will help with the lasers. But only because you are insisting."

Followed closely by what was unmistakably Lawson saying, "I insist."

Murmurs spread through the crowd. Lawson's gaze roamed over the faces that slowly turned against him.

"Now, tell me," Dr. Korvis said, returning the tablet to me. "Why did you record Dr. Chrysopoulis doing only as you insisted?"

Lawson's jaw clenched. His techs, or his posse, sensing the changing mood, took small steps back.

Lawson looked like he would double down. "I don't think you quite understand just who is in charge here. I brought you to this site. I showed you just where to dig in the sand with your little shovels. I am the one with all the power."

"Is that so?" I asked. "Is that the wording you used on Emily Rivers, right before you accused her of embezzlement and had her fired? Because there were no embezzlement charges filed, and I'm guessing it's because the only thing she did wrong was tell you no."

Lawson scoffed. "I don't know any Emily Rivers."

"No?" I said, tapping my tablet to bring up the list of names and information that Jennie had compiled. "How about Ines Espinoza? Do you remember her?"

He sneered but said nothing.

I continued reading. "You told the Board of Directors at your company that she made disparaging and racist remarks about them on social media. But Ines didn't have any social media accounts at the time. I assure you, she does now. And she's not shy about sharing her story. Interestingly enough, she just received a list of contacts for other women who would also want to share their stories."

"Lana Marino?" I said, looking up at Lawson. "Do you remember what you did to her during her first week working as your assistant? It was just six months ago."

The assistant behind him pulled away from Lawson. "That was *you?*"

Lawson perhaps had enough of a conscience left to frown. "I did nothing."

"Or at least that's what you told the police that investigated her attempted assault in the parking garage." I shook my head slowly. "Such a pity that the video footage that could have cleared you was erased. Seems like you're escalating, Lawson. Getting out of control."

Lawson laughed bitterly. "Lady, you have no idea the levels of control I have."

I could feel my smile harden. "One last name on the list. Haruto Kota."

Lawson paled slightly.

I tilted my head to the side. "That's odd. It's not a woman's name, is it? No, Haruto Kota is the vice president of Research & Development at Kota Corp. You might have heard of them. They do a lot of work with lasers."

Lawson swallowed hard, but even from this distance, I could see his nostrils flaring.

Dr. Korvis strolled a little closer to Lawson. "I seem to remember many fancy words about theft, sharing company secrets, and non-disclosure agreements with lots of scary-sounding penalties."

I nodded. "I'm sure your financiers and their lawyers will be very interested in receiving these files. Perhaps even the authorities you called?"

He glared at me. "Never gonna happen."

"And why is that?"

"Because you aren't sending those files."

"I'm not?"

"You're not." Lawson grabbed Dr. Korvis's arm, pulling him close enough that Lawson could remove the revolver before shoving the archeologist away.

I'd never stared down the barrel of a gun. The flickers muted to nothing as my thoughts hyper-focused on the silvery metal pointed at me. Terror seized my lungs and squeezed out all my air. The morning desert air had bordered on cool, but my face felt raging hot.

The crowd reacted immediately, scattering and screaming. If I could have moved a muscle, I would have joined them.

Dr. Korvis shoved his way in front of me, his larger frame easily blocking Lawson from view. "You cannot do this. Graham. Think rationally, man."

Without the gun pointed at me, I could breathe again. I could think. The flickers swarmed back into color.

"Oh, I'm rational," but his voice said he was anything but. "I may be the only rational one here."

"You cannot do this," Dr. Korvis repeated.

I didn't hear what Lawson said in response, but it was probably something just as unhinged as his actions were right now. I had to do something. I couldn't let an ego-crazed man hurt anyone. I had to keep his focus entirely on me.

The buzzing in my bones increased and my attention snapped to the laser box I had been walking toward when Lawson confronted me, still twenty feet away and to my right. Somehow the lasers had reconnected me to the flickers, which meant perhaps that I was reconnected to the past. And if that connection was back, then maybe *I* could go back. Back to Emas. To Tala.

All I needed was an explosion.

Not a cloud in the sky, so lightning was out.

Lightning was electricity. Would electrocution do the same thing?

Only one way to find out.

Lawson was screaming now. "Everyone is going to do exactly as I say! Right now! Exactly!"

If I could have seen him, he probably would have been foaming at the mouth, veins bulging from his neck. He had gone from calm, cool, and collected to a raging control freak with a deadly weapon.

There was no time. He could easily turn on anyone. I had to move.

I spun and raced for the box, shining in the sunrise.

People describe gunshots as a "bang" but that is not exactly right. It's loud, bigger, and far more terrifying when that bullet is coming for you.

Sand erupted about six feet to my left.

More yelling behind and another shot.

This one hit the laser box, cracking the shiny facade and spilling its guts onto the sand.

"No!"

I'm not sure who screamed, but I was pretty sure I joined in.

If the power in the box was dead, so were my chances.

Another shot interrupted my thoughts, and I was shoved in the middle of my back, hard. My arms instinctively wrapped around the shattered box, and I rolled from the impact.

All I could smell was smoke and sand, blue sky filled my vision, though it looked oddly gray around the edges. Maybe a storm was coming.

Too late.

Dr. Korvis was the one screaming now. "Murderer!"

Murderer? Did Lawson shoot someone? Had I failed to save them? But something was wrong with my lungs. I couldn't get air.

Was I already being electrocuted? Was this what it felt like?

That didn't seem right.

Dr. Korvis hadn't stopped shouting. "You killed her! Murderer!"

Sure, he shot LISA, but I was fairly certain she could be rebuilt.

"Andy! Andy, speak to me!"

What? But I couldn't speak.

Oh.

OH.

I was the one being murdered.

That's when the pain started. I would have screamed, but I had no air.

The sky was entirely gray now. And getting darker.

I couldn't die. Not now. Nothing had exploded. It hadn't worked.

The box in my arms shifted as I moved slightly to look, ignoring the spreading wetness that turned my favorite tan shirt a dark red. Inside, the parts were wrecked. Nothing recognizable as useful. Except for an odd shimmery sort of vial, about the size of a thumb and the brightest green I'd ever seen. The lasers. Did this power the lasers? It took everything I had left, but I clasped that tube and pulled, sending up sparks and the scent of burning.

My muscles contracted. All of them. At the same time.

I tasted blood.

Then I sank to the sand.

Everything darkened, faded until only the flickers remained.

The softest blue light hovered near my face, moving in a slow circle until it resolved into a face. A face with gray eyes and bouncing black curls.

"Mama!" the face cried.

Tala.

I was back in Atlantis.

THE END

Bjarni's Last Boat

By: John D. Martin

I told him not to go fishing. Not off the Vínland coast. Not in February, and certainly not on that Moonday morning. But Pa, Bjarni Einarsson, would not be dissuaded. He, with Thorvald and Thormod sons of Víg, and Mashk, Pa's long-time fishing partner from the Ojibwe village up the bay, were determined they would strike out on the whale-walked sea to net their first big catch of the year. They were dressed for the sea in long, black coats that were belted tight, long blue pants, high well-oiled black boots, and tight-fitting gray caps. Pa had his iron-colored hair in a top knot. At his waist, he wore his long knife on his dark leather belt with two other utility knives, along with his small tool pouches. Mashk wore an axe in his girt. They boasted they were going to beat the Kormákssons and everybody else in the district out into that thrashing northwest Atlantic in the year of our Lord 1903. Ma had come with me to speak against this trollishly stupid idea. I can still hear Pa's words now:

"I am Bjarni son of Einar, son of Bjarni, son of Einar, son of Egil, son of Bjarni…", he went on like that when he was angry. He stopped before he got to "Herjolf, the buyer of the last ship of Leif the Lucky" that time, but only because Ma had already started walking back to the big house from the boat launch. We had been arguing with him for perhaps half an hour by then.

"She's right, you know," I said to Pa, as he and our fishing partners set about rigging the boat, that splendid 18-foot longboat, the "Kirsten" (named after Ma, of course), her hand-hewn hull painted green as a May meadow, with brass fore and aft rollocks, the figurehead carved in the likeness of Our Lady, Star of the Ocean. I looked up at sky and pointed to the scudding, scattered clouds the color of mackerel scales. "That sky tells of right changeable weather. You taught me that. Look at it."

Pa looked up from fitting an oar in place and gave a scoffing grunt. "Weather's fine right now. We'll be back with a load of good catch before it goes turdy. Come along with us, Eysteinn. You'll get a share of it as always."

"Nay," I said, "and you four need not put to sea. Wait till later in the week. You'll still beat Thorgard, Kormák, everybody. It´s not so important that you go out today."

Pa finished fixing the oar in its lock and set his eyes on me with a full load of scorn in them. "Your Ma and I didn't raise a coal chewer who's afeared of a little rough water. Now come and help me with the nets."

"And your father didn't raise a cheap shamer either," I paid in response. Then I pointed at the axe scar on my right cheek. "At my age, I don't have to do anything stupid just to prove how brave I am. Neither do you."

"Eyvald would come with me," Pa said with a sharp, accusing look in his eyes.

"No, he's wiser than me, even. He's getting ready to plant. Leave it."

The others had been checking and gathering the nets, Mashk, his long, straight black hair caught in the wind, walked toward Pa and handed him a fishing spear. Mashk said nothing, Pa took the spear, and then he asked, a wry look on his face, "Wiebke ready to make that new bairn with you today, is that it? Love in the afternoon? Your Ma and I sure liked that. I´d understand."

Mashk looked off to the right and laughed. I gave Dad a wry look of my own, probably looking at him like a mirror.

"We'll do that tonight if she gets home in time. I've got to fix the roof on the sauna and the wall of the sheep shed this afternoon," and I looked again at the sky. "If your mood's set on it, there's nothing else to say. I'm going."

"So are we," said Thorvald, joining Pa and Mashk at the boat side. "I'll take your share of the catch, then. Half-owner doesn't come along, his share is forfeit."

"Oh, we'll split it even, like always," Pa said. "And I'd better damn well see a new roof on that shed when I get back tonight."

I nodded, wished them all well, then ran back from the shore on the path toward the great house. Along the way, I caught up with Ma.

"They're going," I huffed, as I slowed to a trot next to her.

Ma spat on the ground. She shook her head disapprovingly and then said, "Sainted Kings! Let them go out and hope they come back before the sun sets. Your father is so stone-headed stubborn."

"Served him well sometimes," I offered in half-hearted defense. Then I asked her, "Can you stay with Kari and Lars this afternoon? I´ve got a lot of outdoor work to do and only little Einar is big enough to help. Wiebke´s gone into the big town and won´t be back till sundown, like as not."

Ma nodded. "Oh, I'll do more than stay with them. I'll play with them and talk to them, even. We could even bake some rye bread. Or cakes." She smiled for the first time in our conversation, and we walked the rest of the way to the great house in silence.

?

I did as I had planned and set to work on the sauna, replaced the missing shingles on the west side of the roof, while my eldest son, Einar, held the ladder and handed me shingles and nails as needed. Then he helped me with the back wall of the sheep shed, holding boards while I nailed them in place. Throughout the afternoon, the weather grew steadily more hostile, and my thoughts turned again toward Pa and his companions in our boat out on the swelling, thrashing waves along Vinland's North Atlantic coast. Around 4 o'clock, Wiebke arrived from her trip to Leifston, turning the older green buggy from the gravel road into our driveway. Einar ran up to her shouting "Mama! How was town?", while I put the tools away and I listened from the tool shed to him interrogate her about her purchases up in the big town. I approached them, told Einar to unhitch and comb the horses, and then offered to carry the baskets into the house for her. As we walked together, I told her about Pa and the boat. She knitted her brow in disapproval. A gust of wind hit us in the back and knocked her cornflower blue felt hat off. I caught it for her and handed it back.

"They're not back yet, then?", she asked.

"And there's not much sun left. I'll turn on the Eidsson lights when we get in. Something more for them to see."

By then we were at the house. We went inside. I remembered to light the Eidsson lamps, indoors and out. Beats lightin' oil lamps. A pair of minutes later in the kitchen, we were set upon by our two youngest. Little Kari asked what Wiebke had brought them from the many stores of Leifston and the two-year-old Lars walked up to us smiling and said, "Mama back". I left Wiebke with the bairn in the front of the house, and went to the bath at the back of the first floor to clean up. A few minutes later, I had the dirt off my hands when the door opened and Wiebke entered the room. She slammed the door behind her and bolted, then leaned against the white-painted oak, slumping in fatigue. She began unbuttoning her dress and asked, "Is there warm water for a bath?"

"Ja, lots," I said, and helped her out of her dress. "Road dirt?"

"Road dirt," she affirmed and finished undressing before putting her arms around my shoulders. "Want to wash my hair?"

Later, still in the bathing room, after we had put on fresher clothes, she noted that the wind was now howling strong enough to shake the house when it blasted hard.

"Do you think your Pa maybe put in at an inlet? Maybe on Karl's Island?"

"I hope. Weather like this, and the dark," I rubbed my chin. "They're all good boatmen, but this sounds like to drive any fishing boat under."

"Ah-ja," she affirmed, as she turned and unbolted the door. "We'll pray for them at evening meal."

We did. Evening meal was great, too. Wiebke served a fish stew…some Breton recipe she read about in the cooking column in one of her magazines. We had some of the rye buns Ma and the bairn had made with the stew. The storm still raged outside there was no sign of Pa, the boat, the men who'd hit the sea with him…and a growing sense that my warnings had been rightly given and wrongly scorned. Ma and the kids took to their bed closets about 8:00, while Wiebke and I disappeared into ours closer to 10:30, after she finished kitchen clean-up, and I stoked the fire for the boiler in the bath and restocked the woodbox next to the hearth in the kitchen.

Falling asleep that night was difficult, for Wiebke and me both, but we did drift into the hazy world behind the eyes, though not without a long, worried talk about the unknown fate of my father and our neighbors. Come the morning, they were still gone, and the weather was still foul. Ma stood outside the house most of the morning, looking down in the direction of the road, where Pa would be coming back if he did. She muttered prayers repeatedly throughout the day, and I made one foray down to the boat slip, where I waited vainly, in the cold, lashing rain, for any sign of them. It was the fading daylight that drove me back home, not the storm.

?

The weather did not improve over the next two days. Pa and the men had left on Moonday. Late on Midweek, Víg came to our farm to ask about his sons. Standing out in the rain under a sky so thick with clouds that noon turned twilight, I had to tell him we´d seen no sign of them. There was a flash of fear and pain in his eyes brighter than lightning before he turned to leave. He asked me to send word when his boys showed up. I told him I would. By Thorsday, when the weather finally cleared up, there was still no sign of them. Einar and I took the good horses over to their farm to tell Víg and Bera that, no, their 3rd and 4th sons had not returned.

"Then," Víg said, looking up at me, the short man´s eyes dewed and taught, "we'll have to ride up to Leifston and tell the pastor to start planning the funerals. Reckon everyone from the quarter will come. Your pa was lawspeaker for three turns, ja?"

"Ja," I answered, and just then, Bera came out of their house, and she was down the front steps before she met Víg´s eyes.

When she saw me, Bera stopped, about two yards from the house. She didn't ask the question and Víg didn't answer it, but she did shout. "Nay!", several times, before she started to weep and scream.

Víg ran to her and embraced her, holding her while she pounded his chest. Then, after she and he said words I could not hear, she shouted at him loud enough for me to hear it: "Wait another day. Just one more day! They'll be back," before pushing her husband away. "Don't you go setting no funeral day for no bodies. They'll be back."

She then spun about and stormed back into the house, still wiping tears from her face.

Víg nodded weakly, and turned a step to look at me. "No harm in that is there, Eysteinn?"

"No harm, no," I said. "We can wait another day. They could have been driven ashore on one of the coast islands."

We talked about chores for a couple of minutes. Sheep to shear, chickens to slaughter, traps to clean, and so forth. Then I bade him a good day and took the longer way home, the one that led me down to our boat launch, where I had last seen my pa, Víg's boys, and Mashk. And our boat. If they were gone, so was it. For a moment standing on the shingle, listening to the waves, looking at the empty shed where we´d kept our tackle, and I thought I heard Bera´s *They´ll be back* whispered by the surf. Then I went home and tended to the farm, almost exactly as I had told Víg.

?

It was in the darkest part of night, that I heard the knocking on our bed closet door. It was insistently loud, but my boy Einar's voice was a shaking whisper.

"Pa, Pa! There´s someone downstairs."

I rustled myself into a sitting position, opened the door, and saw Einar standing there, candle on the brass candle holder held in the right hand, burning wick protected from indoor drafts with the other. Wiebke stirred beside me, murmured something drowsy, then noticed the open door and hastily pulled up the bedcovers over her naked torso.

"Son, what are you…," I only got half the question out before I heard the sound of a chair scraping across the tiled floor of our kitchen. Wiebke heard it too, tensed, and grabbed my arm. Her eyes were wide with fear and surprise.

"Einar," I hissed, "get Kari and Lars and get in here with your ma. Stay quiet." He nodded and walked quickly back to the smaller of the kid´s closets to get his younger siblings. I reached up to the small shelf on my side of the bed closet and retrieved my Larsson .45 – ja, the one with the seven cylinders—from its place right beside the Good Book and Gunnlaugsson´s *History of the Land-Taking*. Wiebke retrieved her nightshirt and pulled it on before reaching for her own Greystone .32. Just in case.

"And your mother?", she asked, as she checked her pistol.

"Seems she's sleeping through it," I answered while I pulled on my own night robe. "Try and keep it that way. I'll go down to see who this is. Maybe a vagrant. There've been some since the last passenger ship arrived."

"But we locked the door," Wiebke reminded me.

Turdweather. She was right. We had. I had that fact firmly in mind as I crept quietly as could be out of our bed closet and trod stealthily toward the staircase. Light from the Eidsson lamps in the kitchen streamed up to meet me. If the unknown intruder was skilled enough with his hands to pick our lock, he´d probably be smart enough to hide around the corner of the stairs to jump me. Great.

I got halfway down the stairs, taking each step carefully before I heard the voices and the sound of– God´s truth– silverware and plates in use. And the voices I knew.

"Pa?", I called from the penultimate step.

"Ja, Eysteinn," came my father´s voice. Yet not his voice. There was something odd about the timbre. My heart raced against my will, and I rushed down into the kitchen to see Pa and his men sitting at the table, eating bread, butter, cold boiled potatoes, and dried herring from our stores. Right there at our kitchen table like it was a regular dinner time. They were all dripping wet, their visible skin a pale green-grey color, and there was seaweed clinging to Mashk's vest and Pa's trousers. Thorvald and Thormod's shirts were fairly covered with it. They had draped their dripping sea coats over their chairbacks and still had their belts and knives. Pa looked up at me and there was an eerie blue-white light burning in his eyes. When the others turned to look at me and say, "Hey, Eysteinn," each in turn, I saw that same unnatural light in their eyes, too, before they turned back to their rapidly emptying plates.

"Pa," I relaxed my gun hand, lowered the pistol, and walked toward the kitchen table slowly. I kept my voice quiet, I hoped, and measured. "You got in with your keys, eh?" He nodded in between bites of herring. Even his teeth had a greenish cast. I held my composure. "What happened with the boat?"

My father– nay, the afterwalker who had been my father– flashed those gleaming eyes at me and said, "It went down. Took us with it. That's why we needed days to get back here. It was hard to see till we reached the shallows."

I nodded and gulped. "You came back why, then?"

"The debt to our family. We took the boat out on my word. My fault it sunk. I owe you, your brother, and my grandsons a replacement. We're here to build you a new one. After that, we leave. We must. Hey, there, Wiebke, Einar. Sorry, we woke you."

And the conversation with the animated corpse of my father had gone so well, seemed so normal up that moment, that I did not notice that my wife and son had crept down the stairs and stopped to stand behind me. Before I could turn to look, though, my boy darted around me, shouting "Pa-Pa!"

Wiebke shouted, "Nay!", and she lunged past me trying to intercept the boy before he reached my father but missed. I missed him as well and in the split of a breath, Einar had crossed the space and thrown his arms around the being that had been his grandfather.

Then, he screamed and let go, stumbling backward and landing in his mother´s arms. The two of them crouched in front of me and I bent down over them protectively. The boy was shivering, muttering. "Cold, sea-cold. Pa-pa´s so cold, Ma."

I looked at the revenants around our kitchen table and they looked at me. There was in all their eyes sadness and surprise. Pa spoke.

"Don't touch us, Einar. Don't anybody touch us," Pa said. There was a nigh-palpable sadness in his voice. Mashk nodded in agreement and the Vígsson boys just closed their eyes and scowled.

"Right," I said, "don't touch any of you." I stood up, holding Einar in my arms. Wiebke moved close and took our still-quaking eldest son from my cradling embrace. I saw then she had tucked her pistol in the waistbelt of her skirt. The terror caged in her eyes shook against its bars for a moment, but they held. I put my hand on her cheek and said, quietly, "They seem to be afterwalkers," and saying it aloud made me almost choke. "If the old tales are true, that they are here for a purpose. Pa says it's replacing the boat. Then they leave." She nodded. I continued. "Go upstairs, wake the other children and mother. Take them to Eyvald's farm. In the green trap."

"What do I tell them when they ask why?", Wiebke asked.

That took a moment´s thought. Then, answered, "Tell them I heard a demon cat out in the woods, and I think it came with company. Tell only Eyvald the truth. I'll follow you to the trap and keep looking at the tree skirt like I´m looking for something."

"Demon-cat. They might believe that. And you?", she asked, looking over my shoulder at our familiar, therefore even more macabre visitors,

"I will stay here and oversee their work, assuming pa is telling the truth," I answered. Then something occurred to me. "And when you get to Eyvald's farm, send for Father Pálsson. He should know what to do with our guests, with …my father and …God's blood." I stopped speaking aloud. What was I going to tell the Vígssons' family? Mashk's wife?

Wiebke just nodded, little Einar had stopped shaking. I looked him in the eyes and told him, "Don't fear. Help your mother with your brother and your sister so she can get mam-ma out of her bed. Understand?"

My son nodded. Then he slid down out of Wiebke's arms and the two of them went upstairs.

Pa and his crew— I had to think of them like that to keep myself from running, screaming, or setting them on fire— stood and, politely enough, gathered their dishes, then put them in the kitchen sink.

"We need to get to work on your boat," Pa said, "the sooner we start, the sooner we´re gone. Eysteinn, could you put on the Eidsson lights outdoors? Leave them on? I mean every night till we're done. We don't need sleep. But we do need light. And food. We need to eat."

The Vígssons and Mashk had already walked from the table to the bootroom heading for the front door. My father and I stood there for a moment staring at each other. I spoke first. "You need to eat. Well. We can feed you. Until you go. How long you reckon it will take?"

He looked away for a moment. It was his "I'm reckonin' a figure" gesture. I´d seen him do it hundreds of times before he died. "We only stay a few weeks. It doesn't need to be finished out. Just seaworthy. Ready to paint. And I know where all your tools are, so we might as well get started." He moved toward the bootroom himself but stopped long enough to turn and say, "Son, I'm sorry. The boat went down. Had I heeded your warning," and again he looked away, "we could all stay longer. I'll say that. And son, don't tell your mother about us. We'll be scarce for a few hours, once I'm out that door. I don't want her to get all scared of us. Of me." Then he left the house through the front door.

I heard Wiebke and Einar getting Kari, Lars, and my mother out of their bed closets and ready to travel. It was still cold, so I heard them rustling around in a clothes-closet for several minutes before they finally came down the stairs, dressed to travel. Ma looked around blearily and the children clustered around Wiebke.

"We're ready," she said. "You'll follow us?"

"Ja. Let me grab my jacket on the way out."

Then we did exactly as I had told my wife we would. The lot of us walked in the light of the outdoor Eidsson lamps to the shed. Wiebke, Einar and I got the buggy ready. Ma seemed too preoccupied with the bairn to notice much, but before she got into the trap, she asked me, "Whose bootprints were those all around the front walk?"

"Ours from earlier," I said, hoping she'd leave the matter.

"Can't be. There's too many of them and some are too big. Kormáksson's causin' trouble again?"

"Maybe," I answered, seizing on the opportunity her surmise provided. "Maybe the Waldmanns. Damn thieves. Either way, it's best if you go."

She looked past me. I turned my head to look where she was staring and for an instant, I saw, at the edge of the trees, four pairs of glowing blue-white eyes watching us. They vanished and I got the barest glimpse of the four silhouettes of our eerie visitors stalking off into the forest beyond our farmyard. I turned back to look Ma in the eyes and her expression was one of comprehension. "I understand, son. We'll talk about this later."

And before I could ask her any questions, she got into the trap with my children. Wiebke lit a lantern, an old oil-and-wick kind, got in the trap and said, "The Lord protect you," before she drove off into the night with Ma and the children.

A moment after I lost sight of them, heading northeast along the big road, I heard heavy steps behind me, turned and saw Pa approaching. He stopped.

"You should get some sleep," he said, "the boys and I can fell the timber. We see fine in this light," and he pointed at the silver-bright moon above us. "You can help us in the morning."

?

It was very difficult to fall asleep that night, with four dead men I had known in life walking about on my family's oldest farm. But the stalking dead man who had been my father, who still sounded and acted like him, assured me they would work and not disturb me. Insane as it sounds, I trusted them enough to sleep…only downstairs. I didn't want to be isolated upstairs in my bed closet where I wouldn't be able to hear the dead coming until they ripped the door off. And they might. I'd heard tell. There are all kinds of tales about afterwalkers, *draugr*, men who didn't know they were dead. Who hated the living. Ate the living. Or just kept acting out the lives they had known but bringing with them a miasma that cursed all the living. But there were some afterwalkers, it was told by old men in dark taverns, around dying fires, some dead who blessed the living by discharging some final debt. That seemed to be Pa and our friends… but undead? Unnatural. Therefore, likely to be treacherous. I had no idea which of these they really were. Not then.

That night I slept in the parlor, on the dark red French divan. Ja, French. It had been an anniversary gift for Wiebke, same year we moved into the main house after three years living on the small farm. It had cost a lot, but she loved it and Kari napped on it often. Like mother, like daughter. That night? The divan wasn´t quite long enough for me to stretch out, but the parlor could only be approached from the front, there were no windows close enough to the ground for anyone, anything, to charge in without warning. The Larsson .45 stayed ready to reach in my jacket pocket. It was not a pleasant night of restful sleep, but enough that I was awake and ready when the morning light did shine in through the high-bayed windows.

?

When I went outside, the morning sky was bright gray with high clouds, and the dead men were nowhere to be seen. Signs of their work were. They had felled an oak, at least 24 feet long and nearly three thick, cut off its branches and left it in the large open sward of the farmyard out west of the house, away from the outbuildings.

"They get another one this size, that's all they´ll need for planks," I said to no one. Then I wondered aloud, "They'll need a whole block, though, a rig to build on if they aim to…." . At the sound of a crash in the woods up west and north of the house, I cut off my rumination. They had already felled another tree, a huge one. That meant that they would be dragging it down to the yard. Soon.

Right then, I began to wonder, how long would it take for Wiebke to get the priest down here? Leifston was a half a day by carriage from even my brother´s place. And it was Lordag. Damned slim chance of catching the priest on Lordag. I had a wait ahead of me, turns out, of two days, at least. Two days, perhaps more, of watching the grey-green skinned walking, talking corpses of my father, two young bachelors whose older brothers had gone to school with me and a man who had been our friend since I was knee high to a mouse do the work of cutting those oaks down, two then three. Once they had them in the yard, they stripped the branches and started barking the trees.

That first day, pa asked me to help, so I did help with the barking for a while, but only until I could no longer stand seeing them there. In daylight. Their blue-white eyes glowed even at noon.

Then there was the way our animals acted around them. They fled. All the cats disappeared, the chickens went to the roost and did not come out into the yard when the afterwalkers were there, and the sheep, penned in, went to the farthest end of their lot, and bleated nervously whenever Pa and our friends were near them. Their fear when the undead were within smelling distance was almost palpable, their near panic making watering and feeding them difficult.

"Pa, I'm taking a walk," I announced. "I'll be back in an hour."

"But you'll miss midday meal," he objected, his inhumanly hued skin almost gleamed in the sunlight. "And someone will need to bake some bread soon. Maybe slaughter a sheep. I saw your larder yesternight, you know. We still need to eat. Like I said."

I thought about that for a moment. The dead needed to eat. At least they ate like living men. That was a relief.

Or was it? They had eaten the most of our larder already. In three days. I considered how much wheat we had stored up. Not much, that time of year. Not much already milled to flour, either. How much ripened cheese stored in the backroom? This early in the year we had hardly any vegetables but roots and canned beans. 24 chickens, 18 sheep on the lot, the rest of the sheep and cattle safely down the road in the big pastures and out of reach. The hungry dead would eat our stores bare if they stayed long enough to cut the timber to planks, plane them, cure them and then they would need nails, pitch, sailcloth, paint...the list of requisites grew rapidly in my head as I walked down the big road. Then what would they eat? Without thinking, I had taken the road headed toward the strand and Leifston.

We lived a fair piece from town, which made the worry of unwanted visitors small. Our nearest neighbor was my brother´s farm, where I´d sent Wiebke. On foot, I could be there in three-quarters of an hour. Faster if I ran. Running would leave those...those former people...alone on my farm. That I would not do. Instead of running off, I walked out a mile and half, then back, thought and prayed on the way, hoping that sooner rather than later, Wiebke would return with Pastor Pálsson. I decided then that I would spend as much time as I could until they returned indoors and away from the dead men.

?

On the fourth day, in the early afternoon, as I came out of the house from my own meager midday meal, just in time to watch Thormod and Thorvald Vígsson catch and start slaughtering our biggest sheep, the one we had called "Curly". I´m not sentimental about livestock, but the sight of dead killing a living thing, slitting its throat, just as I would at butchering time, was frightfully unnerving. Trying to stop them did not occur to me, as I had no idea if I could or should harm them, really. They had to eat, and stores were getting thin.

Thankfully the rattle of a carriage coming up the big road toward our farm kept me from thinking much on it. I dashed toward the road, where I saw my brother Eyvald's red open-topped Phaeton carriage. He and Wiebke were in the front seat, Father Pálsson in his simple but authoritative Sunday regalia in the back. I waved them to a stop and trotted to a halt myself, coming to stand maybe 200 yards from our property. Eyvald braked the carriage and Wiebke jumped down from her seat, then rushed toward me for a quick embrace. We kissed. We held each other at arm´s length, she asked me if I was well.

"Better than many men would be, things being as they are," I answered.

"And how are those things?", Eyvald asked and in that second, I became coldly aware of how closely his voice resembled our father´s. I'd like to hope I didn't shudder, but I can't swear to it. Either way, I told him, Wiebke and the attentively listening Pastor Pálsson how the four days had passed, what Pa had told me of their debt, how the four dead men aimed to settle that debt, and how they were steadily eating their way through our stores.

"They want to build a boat?", Wiebke asked. I nodded. "But that will take months!"

"At least three," said Pálsson, and he stepped down from the carriage less spryly than Wiebke had. "They have not attacked you or threatened you?"

I shook my head. "They've been, mostly, as you'd expect them to be. When alive, I mean. Except for the hunger. They eat prodigiously. They just slaughtered Curly because they wanted fresh mutton."

"Curly?", the Pastor asked.

"A sheep," Wiebke offered, "she gave good wool". Pálsson nodded.

"Should I just pull of the road or drive on into the yard?", Eyvald asked.

"I would not drive into the yard," I advised. "We don't know how the horses will react to them. And Vald?"

"Ja?", my older brother looked me in the eye.

"The being you are about to see looks, sounds and acts like Pa," I explained as I walked up to the carriage, "but he is really, truly dead. Do not touch him. He's cold. Darkest winter cold."

As we walked into the yard, both of the Vígssons were off in a far corner busily gutting Curly, whose carcass they had hung by a rope from the big maple tree nearest the sauna. There was sheep blood all around them on the ground, and they had a fire going in a pit they had dug some yards away.

"They're going to cook the meat. Good," I said quietly to Wiebke. "I had been afraid they wouldn't."

"So, they're the kind that act like they're still alive," she said, loudly enough for the Pastor and Eyvald to hear. "That's a mercy."

"Very much so," said Father Pálsson. "Eysteinn, think about who your father was. I have one test to do first, but I think you have a clear way ahead."

I pondered that pronouncement for a moment, "who your father was", before the afterwalker Pa waved to us and called, "Eysteinn and Eyvald, my boys," put down his axe and walked toward us. "Wiebke, Pastor," he said more softly, now closer.

That was when Pastor Pálsson, the white of his priest´s collar bright in the afternoon sun, drew his hand out from under his overcoat, brandished a gleaming silver crucifix before him, and shouted, in a voice to be heard for a mile in any direction, "In Jesus´s name, I cast you out, I consign you to hell you spawn of perdition. Release the body of Bjarni Einarsson to earthly peace!"

Undead Pa just looked at him, unperturbed. Then, he walked forward to the father, took hold of his crucifix, kissed it, and said, "I know you mean well, parson, but there´s no demon in here," and he thumped his own chest. "My soul may be gone, but it's my spirit talkin' here. We were sent back here to settle a debt. The debt of a boat. We mean to stay till we have done it."

"That we will do," said Mashk, whose approach no one had noticed. The eyes and ears of the living aimed as they were at Pastor Pálsson and my father's revenant.

"And will you also settle the debt of a sheep?", Wiebke asked Mashk and Pa, looking from one to the other and then pointing at the Vígssons, whose work had progressed to the point that Thorvald was quartering Curly while Thormod erected the roasting spit over their fire pit.

"Pa," I asked, cutting off any reply he might have made to Wiebke, "did you tell them where to find the spit?"

"Ja. I want to eat some mutton, too. All this work? Raises hunger."

"You want some mutton, Bjarni?", asked Father Pálsson. The priest had returned his crucifix to its rightful place around his neck. He brushed his coat tight again and asked. "And had you paid your son or his wife for that sheep? The law of God and man demands that."

Pa stared at him for a moment, nonplussed and Mashk opened his mouth to speak, closed it, then said, "We don't have any coin on us. No script, either."

"Well, former lawspeaker?", Father Pálsson pressed. "Now, as a priest, I can only act as an arbiter. I cannot bring charges in these matters of theft, but the rightful owners could."

"Theft?", Pa shouted for the first time since he had returned as an afterwalker. "I've never stolen a thing in my life."

"In your life," Eyvald said quietly, then raised his voice to say, "but you and your crew have taken wood from the forest on Eysteinn's land without asking. Pa, you were lawspeaker. Three times. That is theft, since you did it at night, without telling or asking."

As soon as he said it, a gear in my head turned into place, and I declaimed loudly and directly to my father, "I, Eysteinn Bjarnason, son of Bjarni Einarsson of Leifston, summon you, Bjarni Einarsson, for the crimes of theft of a sheep, theft of forest goods, and trespassing. I call Father Thidrek Pálsson as arbiter and my brother Eyvald and my housewife, Wiebke Thrainsdottir as my witnesses."

"Why you ungrateful, inhospitable," Pa began sputtering at me in a building rage, and his gray-green skin began taking on a darker, deep blue hue when Mashk put his hand on Pa's shoulder and whispered something to him that I could not hear. Pa nodded, then said, calmly, his color returning to lighter shades, "We will discuss a matter of law. Apart." They then walked a few paces away and began a soft-spoken but animated discussion.

"Why discuss a case with him?", Pálsson asked, looking around at us. I wondered why for a moment, then remembered.

"Right. You only came here three years ago," I said. "Mashk was deputy lawspeaker for our district under Odd Thorkellsson, my father's successor in office. Decided he liked fishing better than law, so didn't stand for repeat office at the High Thing."

Pa and Mashk finished their consultation, none of which we heard, and approached the four of us. They looked pleased with themselves.

"We have discussed the question," Pa's tone was chipper, and he addressed the priest without shouting or anger. "If you are an arbiter appointed by the lawspeaker…"

"Which all priests are by dint of office," Pastor Pálsson interrupted. Pa smirked, Mashk glowered, then Pa resumed speaking.

"You do not have the requisite body of three adult men who are neither arbiter nor lawspeaker to hear the case. My daughter-in-law is an adult, but she is assuredly not a man."

I never imagined that a dead man— much less my own dead father— could radiate a smug, self-satisfied air, but that is exactly what happened. Mashk´s glower turned into a ghost of a smile, which under the circumstances…vanished when he saw Pálsson shaking his head.

"Nay, on that point you're wrong," the priest said, "three property owners. And Wiebke Thrainsdottir holds property up on Wandering Hrolf´s Trail, property deeded to her by her grandfather. Is that not true, wife of Eysteinn?"

"Ja, it is," she affirmed. The smugness emanating from Pa evaporated. Mashk spoke up.

"The charges have to be repeated in front of all of the accused," he added.

"Call them," I demanded.

Pa nodded. His face was now flint-hard, unreadable. He shouted at the Vígssons to come to join us, beckoning with his right arm. They came trotting over and when they were standing next to Pa and Mashk, I repeated the charges and the summons, stating the names of all four afterwalking offenders. When done with the recitation, I asked Pastor Pálsson, "Arbiter, is that a sufficient statement of the case?"

"Ja, unless one of you has further charges to bring," he answered. "Does anyone?"

"Housebreaking," Wiebke said, "for entry without permission from the householders five nights past."

"That charge I dispute. We entered that house by my right as first owner," Pa said this loudly and coolly, and I could see the Vígsson´s now had worried looks on their faces. "That was no crime."

"If you were alive, it wouldn't be," Pálsson said, "but the dead have no property rights that are not exercised by the living on their behalf. That is spoken law. Written, too, the last 400 years, give or take."

Pa's hand went to his belt, and I thought for a moment he was going to draw his long knife on the priest, so my hand went to my .45. The afterwalker may have been my father, but an assault on an officer of the law, a priest even, I would not tolerate on my land, and whether a bullet would hurt him or not, Pa noticed my reach and took his hand away from his own weapon.

"We're not welcome here," Pa said. "But we have a debt to discharge. To you, both. My family. I owe you a boat."

His face was suddenly solemn. I thought about his point, then spoke. "You've already cut the timber, sectioned the oak. The rest of the work can't even be done here. Think, Pa. That's all the work you need to do. You hang out the sheep's hide to cure on the back of the hay shed, leave us half of the meat, and I'll count it all as settled."

"So will I," Wiebke added, "and the dead are not welcome in my house, whoever they were in life."

"The terms offered in settlement for your crime are quite generous," Father Pálsson stated, "and the charges are clear. Do you dispute any of them, aside from housebreaking?"

Pa shook his head. "If you'll accept the terms, men, I will as well. What say you?" He turned to look at each of his men in turn and asked each of them for their decision.

Each nodded but was silent, except for Thorvald, who said, "If it must be."

"We are of one mind, then. So, what do you declare, arbiter?", Pa asked.

Pálsson cleared his throat and spoke. "Former lawspeaker Einarsson, Mashk son of Kallik, Thorvald and Thormod, sons of Víg, the wood you felled, the skin, the mutton, are accepted as payment for the loss of the boat held by in common by the living Bjarnarsons. You are released from any debt you owed your living family. You and your crew are banned forthwith from the company of the living."

Pa nodded. "The spoken law. Men, let's roast that mutton and be ready to leave at sundown."

"What will you tell our families?", Mashk asked. I swear there was sorrow and grief in his ice-white eyes, though none in his voice.

"That you died at sea, that's all. No shame, and no word of your walking after," said Eyvald. "That could be a painful disturbance to your families."

"Good," he said. "Vígssons, come with me. Bjarni should settle matters with the arbiter." The three undead men walked away, toward the slaughtered sheep.

"You'll want to bury us," Pa said, and his voice was deep and solemn. "When we leave, we'll walk up into the woods. To the southwest, along the ridge there. Come and find our ends there. In Autumn." He paused and gestured at the priest, Eyvald and Wiebke. "Could you three give me a moment alone with Eysteinn?"

If Eyvald was offended that Pa wanted to speak only to me before leaving he showed no sign of it. "Ja, we'll keep folks if any happen by, from turnin' in here. After five days? It's getting' so people will mark that something's amiss out here."

The three of them turned and left, and I was there alone with Pa. Neither of us spoke until the others were clear of the farmyard and on the road. Then, with a speed that shocked me, he swept forward and locked me in a bear hug.

Cold like I had never felt in my life flooded my body, made my very shirt and jacket stiffen, stopped my breath, and put me to shaking.

"You tried to warn me. I should have listened. If Víg and Bera want to know, tell them it was my fault," he said to me, then let me go. I collapsed to the ground, gasping for air, and he said, "Sorry for that. But I couldn't leave here without that. Go to the living. Watch the road."

Still shivering, I could only nod. He walked away, and I rose a moment later. When I turned toward the road, I saw Wiebke staring at me, tears in her eyes.

The afterwalkers were as good as Pa's word. They left at sundown. Just to be sure, I returned to Eyvald's farm with him and the others that night. Early the next day, Wiebke and I went back to the big house and cleared all traces of the dead we could find from the farm. Only when that was done did we go back to Eyvald's to bring the bairn and Ma back home. It was Lordag by the time we could cart the oaks they had sectioned into town. First, they went to the sawmill, then to Odd Thorkellson, my wife's first cousin, to be turned into a seaworthy craft which we then named "Einar's Debt". I had that boat painted red, though, and left it without a figurehead on the prow.

The funerals, without caskets, without bodies, were held in June. It took that long before Bera gave up waiting on her boys, and all three families had agreed that their ceremony would be held in common. Many said kind words about Pa to us there in the churchyard, but some muttered later that the deaths, the pain, the grief were all come of Bjarni Einarsson's pride. I never argued the point. Neither did Ma. Bera and Víg never asked us what had happened, never reproached us for their loss, either, neither in public nor private. But they never came to the farm again to visit, either. And their other, younger sons avoided us Einarssons from that spring onward. Mashk's wife, Anikashi, did call on us at the farm in March, pregnant as could be. Wiebke alone talked to her, as I was occupied with wagon repairs in the haybarn that day. When I asked what they had talked about, Wiebke said that Anikashi had told us neither she nor Mashk's wider family blamed Pa for the death.

"She understands that boats go under, even with good crews," Wiebke told me after Anikashi had left. "I hope she bears him a boy to take up the name again."

In the Autumn, in the month of yellow leaves, I went with Eyvald and our own oldest boys out into the woods to find the bodies. The hike took three hours, but in the southwest wood we found a crude stone cairn topped with a heavy, flat stone, a yard and a half wide by two long, stacked on top. Opening it, we found them inside. There was a stick, in Pa´s hand. Had he used it to hold the lid open while the others… waited? I did not know how they had ceased. Dead men don't die twice, ja? They just stop.

We left them there. And the last boat of Bjarni Einarsson? She plows the waves like sharp iron.

Warren and Washington

By: Teri Kay Jobe

June 17, 1775: Boston, Massachusetts

Joseph Warren watched the tide of red-coated soldiers rising toward him from behind the dirt barrier of the redoubt on Breed's Hill. The order to retreat had been given by Colonel William Prescott, but he was reluctant to go. There had been plenty of strife with the soldiers King George III had sent to Boston over the last few years, so it was frustrating, no, demeaning, to retreat now. If the people of Boston did not make a stand here when their very way of life was under attack, then when would they get another chance? How could he, a respected doctor turned patriot, fighting for the rights of the citizens of Boston, turn his back to a direct assault on his city?

A year ago, he had dispatched Paul Revere and William Dawes to warn the countryside of the soldier's approach. He had been commissioned as a Major General by the Massachusetts Provincial Congress just three days before. He was expected to protect the citizens of the colony. If he did not act decisively now, then who would? What kind of society would his children grow up in if he did not act?

Someone grabbed his arm and pulled him backward, causing Warren to lose his balance and turn sideways to keep from falling. At the same instant, he felt and heard a musket ball rip through the air where his head had been just a moment before. It suddenly occurred to him that he had avoided death by inches.

What will happen to my children if I die here?

Shaking his head, he allowed himself to be pulled away, his sense of self-preservation finally gaining the upper hand over his mind. He saw the men who had already fallen as he made his way out of the redoubt and followed the rest of Prescott's men north. If the last few years of tyranny and ruthless military tactics used by the King's generals were any indication, there would be more battles to come. More opportunities to avenge the men who had died here. He would be ready when they arrived.

March 20, 1776: Boston Massachusetts

"It is without doubt that we have won a great victory here," Joseph said, raising a glass in a toast to General George Washington.

Washington swirled the wine in his own glass but did not raise it. "The liberation of Boston is only one event in what I fear will be a long march of violence. There is no guarantee that the colonies will emerge victorious at the end of it. As such, I for one am not going to celebrate just yet."

Joseph was silent for a moment before putting his drink back on the table. "I am envious that you will get to see more such events as this war goes on."

Washington raised an eyebrow. "You want to see more destruction and death? I would think that as a Doctor of some repute, you have already seen quite enough hardship in your patients to last a lifetime."

"That is a different situation," Joseph said. "My patients' illnesses are small concerns, important only to them and their immediate families. Whether they live or die is of no consequence to the rest of the city. But what is happening now, with the King firmly against our liberty and independence, is of great consequence to everyone in the city. It's of consequence to everyone in the colonies! If my actions can bring liberation to so many, don't I have an obligation to do so?"

Washington considered Joseph for several seconds before answering. "This road to liberty is likely to be long and arduous. If I am to lead, I will need others who are willing to walk that road. From what I have heard, you have already been deeply involved in the events that have transpired in Massachusetts. Without your timely action, our allies Mr. Adams and Mr. Hancock would be at the mercy of the King's justice. If your passion for helping the people of this country is as strong as you say, then perhaps you are the kind of man who would be willing to stand by my side in this struggle."

"What do you mean, sir?"

"I mean, will you join me as one of the generals in my army?"

Letter from Joseph Warren to Mercy Scollay, April 10, 1776

My dearest Mercy,

I hope that my decision to join General Washington has not caused you too much strife. My obligations to him are likely to keep us apart for some time. There is no way I can express my full gratitude for your patience and your support in caring for my children while I am away. They are quite fond of you, and I trust that they will behave themselves in my absence.

There is not a day that passes that I do not think of all of you, and long to be together in our beloved city of Boston as a family. But for now, I must ensure that this new nation survives its infancy, and such a burden demands our separation. If by any means I can bring liberty to all of us, then by God, I shall see it done.

January 2, 1777, after dark, near Trenton, New Jersey

Joseph lingered after Washington and his officers had concluded their council of war. He couldn't believe what Washington had just convinced his fellow officers to do.

"General…" Joseph said, trying to figure out how to phrase his question without appearing improper. Usually, words came easy to him, but his incredulity was holding back his tongue and all he could say to complete his question was "Why?"

Washington paused as he collected the maps of Trenton and Princeton they had all been looking at. "Why what?"

"What you just said to me and your other officers, what you are asking us to do…it goes against nearly every word of council you have given me in the past year."

Washington raised an eyebrow. "Which council are you referring to?"

"All of it!" Joseph shouted, unable to keep his voice low. "You've been telling me time and again to keep a level head, to not take risks, that we are standing against insurmountable odds and must not allow our passions to overrule our senses. Since we left Massachusetts, you've been constantly scolding me as one would a child to not repeat my actions in Boston.

"But during these last nine days, we have taken one risk after another. Many of our militia were unable to cross the Delaware River because of the weather, and yet we moved onward to Trenton with reduced forces. Barely a day ago we returned and thrice repelled Lord Cornwallis's attempts to cross Assunpink Creek. He has not left the far shore and will undoubtedly come at us yet again tomorrow. Just now, instead of outlining a plan of retreat, you proposed a plan as reckless as any action I ever took, if not more so! It is hypocritical, sir!"

Washington waited for Joseph to finish his tirade. "General Warren," he said calmly "I will not argue the point of hypocrisy. However, I would ask you to consider what is different between your actions in Boston, and mine now."

"I see no difference!"

"The difference is in the hopes and perceptions of the people. In Boston, what was the feeling of the citizens before General Howe attacked Breed's Hill?"

Joseph recognized Washington's tone. It was the one he used whenever he was trying to teach a lesson. Joseph gritted his teeth but kept his voice level as he answered. "Anger and determination, sir."

"Exactly. And what of their perceptions now? We have been hard-pressed to achieve even the smallest victory against the King's generals in New York. The term of enlistment for the men in this army is over. In these circumstances, would you describe the current feelings of American citizens the same way you would have two years ago?"

Joseph was well aware of the situation, and it was dire. He had no intention of giving up the fight regardless of the circumstances, but he had spent many nights wondering how he could continue to resist the will of England if the Continental Army disintegrated now, as it was close to doing. Reluctantly, he shook his head. "No."

"And therein lies the difference. In Boston, there were many who were willing to take up the cause for liberty and independence. Now there are many who are likely starting to come to terms with the idea of this new country failing before it is even fully established. There is more at stake now than the people of one city, it is an entire country we must concern ourselves with. I have taken risks these last few days because there are few options left. If we fail here, then this war has been for nothing, and the people will continue to live under the thumb and tyranny of the King. It is important to understand the appropriate time to take risks. Now is that time. Do you understand? Are you prepared?"

"Yes, sir."

January 10, 1777: Morristown, New Jersey

My dearest Mercy,

I apologize for the delay between my writings. We have made our winter encampment in Morristown and though I dislike being idle, the rest is welcome. I am sure news has probably reached you by now of our exploits on the borders of New Jersey and Pennsylvania. I shall not bore you with all of the minutiae of our planning but suffice to say that within the span of ten days, our situation has taken a turn for the better. Most of the men who enlisted in the army early last year had left by the time we reached the Delaware River and the morale of those who remained was almost non-existent. General Washington has shown both nerve, and I dare say hypocrisy, in the face of such challenges. His actions could be described as entirely reckless, something both he and you have warned me against many times. But for now, it seems he has made the right choices, as recent events have restored some hope for victory in this war.

We crossed the Delaware River during the night of Christmas and took an entire force of Hessian soldiers by surprise, with very few casualties for our efforts. On the heels of this victory, the opportunity to thwart a counterattack from Lord Cornwallis became another victory in capturing the town of Princeton.

These victories have not come without loss. Brigadier General Hugo Mercer fell while defending our flanks. There have been rumors that when he was cornered by the red coats, they mistook him for General Washington himself. I dare not describe the injuries those rascals inflicted upon Mercer, for I do not wish to cause you undue distress, but for him to have held death at bay for several days after suffering such atrocities as were perpetrated upon him is nothing short of miraculous. I don't care to contemplate what state the army would be in now had it truly been Washington in Mercer's place.

But Mercer's sacrifice, and that of all the other men who have fallen, still carry meaning. Already there is talk among the men and officers of renewed hope in this war for liberty. To be able to embarrass the King's army three times in so short a time is proof that victory in the war as a whole is possible.

September 14, 1777: Brandywine Creek, Pennsylvania

My dearest Mercy,
I must apologize for the unsteadiness of my hand as I write, for I am deeply shaken by the events that have transpired in recent days. It is said that ill news travels faster than any other tidings, and word of what has happened may have already reached your ears. There is no easy or gentle way to say what needs to be said…General Washington is dead.

The redcoats under General Howe approached us more quickly than expected on their march toward Philadelphia. We took up position on the Brandywine River to prevent their advance, but there were several fords along that course, and we had no reliable news of where Howe's forces would advance from. General Washington was riding from one position to the next to gather what news he could. Before we fully knew what was happening, General Pulaski rode into our headquarters leading Washington's horse with its rider mortally wounded and unconscious in the saddle. On the heels of this blow,

Generals Cornwallis and Howe appeared on our right flank. The next few hours were chaos. Only good fortune and the fortitude of our officers kept us from being overwhelmed. Darkness was thankfully quick in coming and we were able to retreat.

In the days since, the situation has not improved. I fear that Philadelphia will fall into the hands of the King's generals within the week. Already, the members of Congress are in the process of evacuating the city. General Washington never awoke and passed from this life the day after our flight from the Brandywine. The remaining officers have nominated me to lead the army until the Congress formally appoints Washington's successor. I confess that up until now, I have thought about the glories and prestige of such a posting, but to be so suddenly thrust into this position, even as a temporary measure, is more of a shock than I ever thought it would be. My anger and grief at the loss of such a commander as Washington chase each other in my head, and above it all looms the heavy burden of responsibility. The men of the Continental Army are now under my command, and regardless of however long or short a time it may last, that truth is terrifying.

One small bit of comfort to me has been the opportunity to converse with a new officer whom General Washington invited to his retinue shortly before the disaster on the Brandywine. He is known as Lafayette, and although he is young, he acquitted himself honorably in our recent retreat. This Frenchman's enthusiasm for the American cause is equal to that of any other officer born and raised on this side of the Atlantic. I can only hope that his enthusiasm is not quelled by the tide of misfortune that seems to follow us of late.

February 1, 1778: Valley Forge, Pennsylvania

Joseph sat in an old chair, a thin blanket wrapped around his shoulders. It was very late, but he couldn't sleep. He stared at the low fire in the hearth, barely large enough to give off any perceptible heat. His thoughts wouldn't let him relax. He had led the army here just over a month ago, and the situation was getting worse by the day. The people encamped with him needed a lot of things: food, blankets, medicine, shoes, and other clothing. The list was almost never-ending, and it was getting harder to acquire the supplies they needed. He could feel a headache coming on and put a hand to his temple.

The door opened and the resulting draft made the fire flicker as someone entered.

What new trouble is there? Joseph thought, half hoping the newcomer would think he was asleep and leave him alone a little longer.

"You're going to freeze if you keep the fire that low." The accent of the new voice was unmistakable, and Joseph relaxed a little.

"Lafayette," He said, straightening up in his chair, "people usually knock before just opening someone's door."

"I saw you through the window and knew you wouldn't come to open the door even if I did knock," Lafayette said, pulling a second chair close to the hearth and adding another piece of wood to the fire. "You've had that look of being lost in a forest of worries all day. It's not good for your constitution."

Joseph couldn't help but smile. "The fact that your well of youthful optimism never seems to run dry is astounding. But you are correct. My concerns have been growing recently. I don't know how Washington did it. The army faces much the same hardships as they have in previous winter encampments, but it feels as though I'm the captain of a sinking ship with no hope of rescue. Not to mention the further hardships that are sure to come as the weather turns."

Lafayette looked at him with a quizzical expression. "What other hardships? If you are so hopeless that you are reduced to predicting the situation will only get worse, then perhaps you have not been talking with the right people."

"You know I was a doctor before I took up the cause for liberty," Joseph said. "Without fail, diseases appear much more frequently as the temperature rises in spring. What will I do when people begin to get sick? Will medicine prove as hard to acquire as everything else we have had to go without these past weeks?"

Lafayette was quiet for a minute. It occurred to Joseph that Washington had expressed similar woes to him before on the rare occasions that they conversed in private. *Did I sound as young and optimistic to him as Lafayette does to me now?* He thought. It also made him wonder how much of the past political strife Washington had actually shared with him. He knew Lafayette was aware of the criticism Joseph had received since Washington's death, even though they rarely spoke of it. But the lack of confidence in his capabilities as a leader weighed on Joseph's mind far more than they should have. He had never concerned himself with how his words and opinions were perceived in Boston before the war, so why were they overtaking his thoughts now?

There is more at stake than the people of one city now, it is an entire country we must concern ourselves with. The thought came to Joseph in Washington's voice, and he remembered the brief conversation he had had with the former commander the previous winter. Much had happened since then, and Warren better understood that beneath the scrutiny of an entire country, he needed to carefully weigh the risks and rewards of his words and actions. It was tiring.

Finally, Lafayette broke the silence. "I'm sure your Congress believes you can overcome whatever obstacles are presented to you. Otherwise, they would have selected someone else to lead the army."

"I suppose that's true," Joseph said, though he couldn't muster much conviction into his words. "If only everyone else saw the situation the same way you did."

"I will accept your admission of the possibility of your own competence. It will have to suffice for tonight. Nothing else will be accomplished until we have both enjoyed the tender caress of sleep." Lafayette stood up and walked to the door. Before leaving, he paused. "For what peace of mind it may be worth, as a fellow officer hand-picked by Washington, I will stand by your side. You have my support as long as I breathe."

June 10, 1778: Valley Forge, Pennsylvania

My Dearest Mercy,

The dark and formidable grip of this past winter and spring have finally loosened and with the change in the weather, I feel that the fortunes of the Continental Army may be changing as well. Our ranks were joined by Baron Friedrich Wilhelm von Steuben, and he almost single-handedly transformed the army into a more disciplined and functional military force. He has brought much-needed training to the soldiers, and order to the administrative records of supplies and other necessities.

We are also grateful for the recent return of Major General Charles Lee. His release from captivity under General Howe was secured in exchange for some Hessian officers, and he has rejoined the army. But I cannot hide my thoughts from you, and I admit I have misgivings. General Washington often spoke very highly of the man, and Lee himself expressed his regrets upon hearing of Washington's death. Yet Lee has seen fit to criticize the improvements made by Baron von Steuben, believing our forces should be operated as a militia, rather than a professional army. Even my own efforts to ready our forces to face the redcoats once again have been subject to Lee's harsh opinions. I can only hope that when the time comes for action, he comports himself in a manner befitting his station.

The time is fast approaching when we will be tested against General Henry Clinton. With the promise of support for our cause from France, General Clinton has made preparations to withdraw from Philadelphia. While the temptation is great to attempt to destroy Clinton's forces on the road, nearly all the officers under my command have advised caution. I am loath to let such an opportunity pass by, but I cannot deny the wisdom of caution here. If I am to lead this army to victory, I cannot allow it to fall apart upon its first encounter with the enemy after so much effort has been put into its betterment.

June 28, 1778: Monmouth Courthouse

Joseph had never experienced nervousness before a battle before, but there was some element of anxiety that rolled through the back of his mind like a harbor fog and would not leave. The Continental Army was within striking distance of General Clinton's forces as they retreated from Philadelphia. He had given Major General Lee command of the vanguard, and he could already hear the sounds of intermittent musket and artillery fire ahead of him.

As Joseph approached the bridge, he saw a soldier crossing from the other direction. They appeared unhurt, if perhaps overheated, and were using their musket as a walking stick. Certain the man was attempting to desert his post in the army, Joseph urged his horse forward, his anxiety forgotten.

"Halt! What unit are you from and where are you going?"

The man was pale but looked up at him without concern. It wasn't the face of a man trying to flee his duties. "I'm with General Scott's brigade. Couldn't keep up in the retreat and got separated."

"Retreat?" Joseph asked, the anxiety in the back of his mind returning instantly. "What happened to Lee's vanguard? What position is Scott retreating to?"

"If I knew, that's where I would be."

Before Joseph could reprimand the insulant reply, he noticed a large group of soldiers approaching the far side of the bridge in a similar condition to the man he was talking to. He turned to one of his aids. "Give this man some water until he gets a civil tongue back in his head."

He rode swiftly across the bridge, spotting more units from the vanguard in retreat as he went. He had been hearing the sounds of battle from this direction for some time now, but not enough to warrant such a mass exodus from the front. There were officers in these groups, and none of them could tell him where they were supposed to be, or what action their units should have been taking. Seeing no immediate threat to their current position, Joseph ordered every unit he came across to halt their retreat and await further orders. He had to figure out what was going on. He had to find Lee. Now.

Thankfully, it wasn't long before Joseph found the man in question. He was also thankful he arrived when he did, because Lee was in a heated argument with Lafayette that looked like it was about to come to blows.

"I have never seen such amateur commanding in my life!" Lafayette shouted. "A farmer could have done a better job!"

"I did what was necessary to keep from being overrun. It's not my fault that all the other commanders ignored my orders!"

"Enough!" Joseph bellowed, dismounting from his horse and striding up to his two officers. "I have just ridden past several units from the vanguard, and none of them were able to tell me what their orders are, or where they are meant to be posted. I wish to know the reason for this confusion and disorder."

Lee stood a little straighter and turned away from Lafayette so he faced Joseph directly. "Sir, none of my scouts could give me precise information on where the enemy forces were except that they were approaching. When I tried to respond to what little intelligence the scouts had gleaned and issue orders to my fellow officers in the vanguard, I found that they had abandoned their previously assigned positions. In order to save the men I still had any command over, I retreated further than I had initially intended."

"Sir!" Lafayette interjected. "We had no clear orders to begin with! If Lee had sent us clear communications about his intentions, we would have followed his orders. Instead, we hear nothing as the enemy approaches. We were in danger of being cut off by our foes, with no sign of help or directions, and so we moved."

Lee laughed, sounding more than a little unhinged. "All of this is lunacy! Need I remind you, General, that I was opposed to engaging the enemy at all in their retreat from Philadelphia. It is useless and will only result in more casualties. You are trying to fight the greatest army in the world using their own methods! To try to stand and fight face-to-face against England's army is to invite annihilation! You must come at them from unexpected directions, as a strong militia would do. That is the only path to victory!"

"You damned poltroon!" Lafayette spat. "This army has changed while you were languishing in captivity!"

Joseph had had enough. "Silence, both of you!" Both of his officers and many of the soldiers nearby looked toward him in surprise. It was rare for him to raise his voice within earshot of so many people. But there was no time to smooth over the hostilities between his officers with mere words. They were all close enough to the enemy that wasting time now would see them all killed or captured. The only available option was to try to save the situation. "Lafayette, take your unit and move west to Perrine's hill to organize the artillery. Take all the men I bid wait on my way here with you. I will send more units to that position presently."

His tone left no room for questions. With a brief "Sir!" Lafayette hurried away.

The Commander in Chief of the Continental Army turned his attention to Lee. "I gave you this command because you asked for it. While your words may be true, if you had no intention of following through with the responsibilities of the vanguard in this engagement, you should not have undertaken them. Now collect yourself while I organize a rearguard to cover your lack of judgment."

Within minutes, Joseph had gathered the other officers of the vanguard and issued them new orders. It was nothing more than a rearguard action to buy time to deploy the main force of the army. He hoped it would be enough.

He turned his attention back to Lee, who was watching him with a stunned expression on his face. Joseph motioned for him to approach.

"General Lee, I cannot be in two places at one time, so I give you a choice: Either command the rearguard or go back and deploy the rest of our forces to Perrine's Hill."

Almost without hesitation, Lee answered. "I will command the rearguard, sir."

"Fine," Joseph said. He mounted his horse, turning to address Lee once more. "See that I have not misplaced my trust in you."

Lee stood as straight as he could. "I shall be the last soldier on the field, sir."

Joseph nodded and galloped back the way he had come, hoping he had made the right decision.

August 10, 1778: White Plains, New York

My Dearest Mercy,

These past few weeks have been very trying, and while it seems as though I have been writing one correspondence after another, there has been little time to pen one to you.

Our engagement with General Clinton's forces at Monmouth proved to ultimately be a success. Despite having open hostilities between Generals Lee and Lafayette, reason won the day and we were able to hold our ground. It is a testament to the discipline and training undertaken by Baron von Steuben that once we gained a solid position, we did not leave the field, even after the sun had set. Had Clinton not withdrawn from the battlefield during the night, we would have given them another round the following day. I gave a full account of the day to Congress and they accepted it with enthusiasm. There are now fewer voices raised in criticism of my actions as commander of this army. Nearly all the officers present at Monmouth have spoken out in praise of that victory, which has helped to elevate confidence in this war for liberty.

I say 'nearly all the officers present at Monmouth,' for there are still those who insist on confrontation regarding my conduct. I speak of course of Lee, who has proven to be more insolant than I could have ever anticipated. His repeated affronts and antagonism in letters we exchanged left me no choice but to organize a court martial for disobeying orders, conducting a disorderly retreat, and disrespect towards the commander-in-chief. I take no pleasure in this whole affair. Lee is a good commander, and I believe that if he could have swallowed his pride and let the matter alone, it would have been forgotten. I have heard stories of his prowess on the battlefield in the past, and I sometimes wonder if he came under the sway of General Howe during his captivity in New York. Perhaps his actions since rejoining the army have been with the insidious intentions of undermining the war effort, the Congress, or my own command. But this thought is only my own private speculation and will never appear in any official report unless evidence appears that makes it plausible.

I wish I had more exciting news to write about, but the events I have described are those which have been most on my mind and therefore the first to spring from my pen. If I had known the full extent of tedious minutia the commander of an army must endure, I confess I am not sure I would have been so eager to become one. It is easy to carry out battles of words in newspapers or to rally the support of friends, acquaintances, and neighbors against tyranny in your home city when there are others above you to orchestrate the fight. But it is not so simple to be the orchestrator. In recent weeks, I have been in awe at the actions of men like Adams, Franklin, and even Washington. What nerve it must have taken to be at the forefront of the struggles before the actual war commenced. I know you will argue that I was at the front of the struggles in Boston as well, but I still had others above me who made the gears of revolution turn. Now I find myself in that same position, with scant few I can look up to for guidance.

But despite all the trials and tribulations, there is still renewed hope for victory in this war for liberty. General Clinton has returned to New York, and I have followed. We need only wait for him or some other of the King's generals to make a mistake, then we shall strike the blow that will end this war. I look forward to the day when I can return to Boston and remain there with you and the children in peace.

With fondest love, General Joseph Warren

The End

Men (almost always) in Black

A Joe Ledger Adventure

By Jonathan Maberry

-1-

His name was Jonas Humblecut, and he was the least happy person I think I've ever met.

Certainly the most put-upon.

Sometimes it's guys like him that are the axles that turn the whole goddamn world.

-2-

The first time I met Humblecut he was working in an office nine floors below the Pentagon. A cheerless, windowless, nearly airless box of a room that was crammed with so many groaning file cabinets and overstuffed bankers boxes that there was only enough room for a desk, his chair, one guest chair, and a small table on which was—I believe—the most overused coffeemaker in the free world.

This was shortly after I started working for the Department of Military Sciences as a recent hire by Mr. Church. When I knocked on the door, the response was somewhere between a cry for help and a moan of despair. I opened the door very carefully and peered in. First thing I saw was all the paper. It's odd to see so much of it in this digital age, but the place was like where file folders go to die. Maybe hope and optimism, too.

There was a sign on the wall behind the desk that read:

I WANT TO BELIEVE

Someone—presumable Humblecut—had used a Sharpie to add:

IN ANYTHING.

The man himself was exactly the kind of half-maniacal individual you'd expect. He wore a crumpled white shirt that was probably four or five wearings past dry-cleaning time. His tie was a novelty thing with UFOs and little green men on it that was probably the coolest piece of clothing he owned, but it was cheap. The kind of thing Spencer's sells in bad malls.

His skin was the color of mushrooms grown in wormy soil, and his hair stood up in all directions. Hard to tell if the hair thing was evidence of someone who had simply given up, or if it had just been that kind of day. Both, I suspected.

He looked at me with weak, bleary red eyes and before I could say a word, he said, "No."

I said, "What?"

"Whatever it is," said Humblecut, "the answer is no."

I waved a piece of paper at him. "I have a couple of questions and even brought the right form."

I could see a vein on his forehead throb.

"Just please…no."

"Sorry, brother," I said, coming into the office. "Kind of have to."

He sighed in the way people do who have lost every reasonable argument and flapped his hand vaguely in the direction of the guest chair. I removed a stack of dusty file folders and set them carefully on the floor. The chair was an old wooden one that had likely first seen use during the Lincoln-Douglas debates. It creaked as I sat.

Humblecut stared at me. He was somewhere between forty and two hundred. One of those faces that probably always looked middle-aged even when he was in the third grade. I tried not to look at a dried crumb of mustard by the corner of his mouth.

"I'm Captain Joe Ledger," I said. "I'm with the DMS."

His initial reply was a slow blink of his eyes. A lot like a disinterested iguana. "And…?" He drew the word out to three times its length.

"And I'm doing some after-action follow up. Trying to tidy up loose ends, make sure we didn't miss anything."

"How does that involve me or my office?" asked Humblecut.

"The case was a bit…odd."

"Really? How interesting," he said with a total lack of interest. But then, realizing that my comment had been a leading one, he sighed and asked, "Odd *how?*"

"Well it crossed over with a few different conspiracy theories," I said. "Some of what we came across was pretty absurd. Our computer guy, Bug, said that your office collects and keeps track of those kinds of things, but because of budget shortfalls, the bulk of your information is not yet on a searchable database."

He leaned back in his chair in the way one does when inviting the other person to take a good, hard look at who they were, what they were, what they did, and the resources provided to do their job in the most efficient way possible. It was eloquent.

Humblecut asked, "Tell me, Captain Ledger, which absurd theory in particular?" he asked in a tone so dry I needed moisturizer. "The one that insists you should swallow one piece of gum every seven years because gum is the only real thing inside the shared simulation that is our reality? Or the flat-earth variant that a natural disaster destroyed all real trees and that even the tallest redwood is a sapling that is still growing and will eventually be twenty miles tall? Or that both the Hollow Earth and the Flat Earth are possible at the same time? Maybe you'd like to discuss the hypothesis that the entire Royal Family of England are cannibal vampires. Or that the various personal challenges Britney Spears had to face were orchestrated by the government because she was outing political missteps by George W. Bush. Or that traffic barrels are left up for so long because the department of transportation bought too many and has no place to store them. How about the theory that all rocks are soft until touched? Or that Gisele Bündchen is an actual witch and she hexed Leonardo DiCaprio after they broke up so that he would never be able to date anyone older than she was when they broke up? Or, that Putin is at war with the Ukraine because Ukraine is kidnapping babies to provide and supply the United States, who in turn uses baby parts from abortions to make yogurt? Or— here's a personal favorite—the push for green lawns in the US is a plot by big Pharma because to get green grass, you need pesticides, pesticides cause cancer, cancer is good business for drug companies."

"Actually," I said, "wouldn't surprise me if that last one was true."

Another slow blink.

I said, "What I need is more in the tin-foil hat UFO line."

"And I'm who? Fox Mulder?"

I tried so hard not to glance ironically at his poster. "No, Mr. Humblecut, and I'm not James Bond. I need information so I won't be lying to my boss when I tell him I've dotted all the I's and crossed each T."

He sniffed, then sighed again, this time with a mix of resolution and a show of professional courtesy. "What, specifically, are you looking for?"

"I can't go into all the details of the case, of course," I began. He waved that away and I continued. "On a recent case we encountered several men dressed in—"

"Men in Black?" he said, cutting me off. "Seriously. That again?"

"They were men," I agreed. "They wore black. Black suits, white shirts, black ties. Dark sunglasses. And they carried weird guns that go *TOK!* when they're fired."

I expected more sullen snark, but his eyebrows lifted.

"*Tok*, you say," he mused. "Now that's interesting. Tell, me, did you see the effect of those guns?"

"From way too close an angle. We're calling them MPPs—microwave pulse pistols."

"Appropriate."

"Then you know what I'm talking about?"

"Let me see your ID, please, and clearance rating card."

The Department of Military Sciences does not issue badges or ID cards in all operational scenarios, but for navigating the waters of red tape bureaucracy we have temporary ones. Mine identified me as Joseph Edwin Ledger, Captain, Senior Field-Team Leader. The clearance was TS/SCI, meaning that it was not only Top Secret, but a sub-set level that allowed me unrestricted access to Sensitive Compartmental Information.

He paused for so long I thought he had fallen asleep with his eyes open. Eventually he got up and began opening file drawers. It took him nearly five full minutes to find what he wanted and placed a very old file folder on the desk in front of me. It was about three inches thick and held closed with a dozen oversized rubber bands, all of which looked so desiccated that I expected them to break. Which they did when I picked up the folder. Papers began to spill but I darted a hand out and caught them in time and tapped them neatly back into place. I caught Humblecut watching and even saw a tiny nod of approval. Apparently I had scored a minor point with him.

"Good reflexes," he said.

"Don't want to make a mess," I said.

Another slow blink. They really were strange. I did not even once see him blink at the usual speed of a bit over one hundred milliseconds. His always took a full second. We're not used to that as a normal human action, and it creates an uneasiness. Even I felt it, and I deal with uneasy stuff on a regular basis. If it was natural to him, I wondered if he had some muscle disorder. If it was deliberate, I wondered why.

The folder was labeled ADD/MAJ-PRO/EO. I placed a finger on the letters and gave him an inquiring look.

"Additional materials related to the Majestic Program that is Eyes Only," he said. "You may not remove the files from this office or make copies."

I glanced over my shoulder at the door. The lock had looked normal from outside, but from the inside I saw that the door itself was not a standard hollow-core or even solid wood but a steel panel more than an inch thick. The lock was some complex arrangement welded directly onto the door, with a compatible socket and strike-plate in a steel frame. The hinges were heavy metal and encased in some kind of ceramic shells. There were wire leads rising from the door to a high-end alarm system. Made me wonder if the walls were steel-sheathing behind the plasterboard and old mint green paint. When I turned back, Humblecut wore a faint, smug little smile.

Nothing needed to be said about the security, so I focused on the contents of the material he'd provided. Within the outer cover were a number of thinner file folders. I thumbed through the headings. Weapons. Equipment. Clothing. Sightings. Protective Undergarments. Eyewear. Shoes. Vehicles. The top folder was Non-official Photos.

I flipped that last one open and saw an 8x10 black-and-white glossy printed on heavy stock that was so old the edges of the print were yellowed. I picked it up and stared at a man of about thirty wearing the suit I'd described.

"Man," said Humblecut. "In black."

"A Closer," I said, using the nickname that some of the bad guys we'd just dealt with had for them.

"Closers," said Humblecut. "Yes."

I turned the photo over to read some information typed onto a label affixed to the back.

Civilian Photo 0HH3Y4198/1958/393_NNQ
Taken 02-22-1958
Camera type: Kodak Brownie Bullet Camera 1957 Bakelite Film Camera
Film Type: Rerapan127 / ISO 100 B&W
Photographer: Mrs. Alan (Doris) Kemmer
Location: Brownsville, Texas
Obtained by Project: Blue Book 05-18-1958

In the photo, the man was holding a small pistol that looked like a cross between a Taser and a ray gun from an old 1940s cheap sci-fi flick. It was a smooth curve from handle to a slightly elongated square barrel. At each of the four corners of the barrel were curved metal prongs. There was no opening to the barrel, so whatever this gun did, firing bullets was not part of its function. It looked like a toy but was not. Those pistols fired a compressed and intense burst of microwave energy that caused such intense molecular energy that the target simply exploded from internal heat and pressure. One shot would probably blow that steel door to Humbelcut's office completely off its hinges. A shot to human flesh leaves a messy stew of singed blood and burned meat. I've seen it and do not ever want to see it again.

"Is there an official name for the weapon?" I asked.

"No. MPP is a useful shortcut," he said. "I'll add a post-it to the file."

I browsed the rest of the photos. There were at least three hundred pictures in there, ranging from old black-and-whites to fairly crisp color stuff. The most recent was from mid-2000. When I asked why there was nothing newer, he shrugged.

"In 2000 they added digital cameras to cell phones. Since then the number of prints made has dropped."

"Are there more recent photos stored in your computers?"

He nodded, took a yellow pencil, licked the graphite point, and scribbled a URL. It was a very complex web address, with a wild mix of letters, numbers, and symbols.

"Give this to your computer person. What did you say his name was? Bug?"

"Yes."

"Odd name," said Mr. Humblecut.

I went through the photos all the way to the end and leafed backward through them. There were men *and* women in black. The suits were all era-appropriate. Classic rather than stylish. The sunglasses were always opaque. None of them looked like either Tommy Lee Jones or Will Smith. There were maybe seventy different people in the photos, with some of them in multiple pics.

Then I moved on to reports.

There were a lot of accounts. Lots of theories. Plenty of evidence that Project Blue Book conducted an investigation. But by the time I reached the end of the last folder, I felt that it was like eating cotton candy—plenty of calories but no real sustenance.

I closed the folder and looked at him. Throughout the entire time I was reading the file, Humblecut sat there watching me. I was aware of his stare, and even peripherally caught a few of those slow blinks. He hadn't otherwise moved or interrupted me. It was becoming evident why they squirreled this guy away in the Pentagon's dungeon.

"Where's the rest?"

"Rest…?"

"Full reports from field investigators," I suggested. "Theories, conclusions. Whatever."

"That," he said, "is all of it."

I leaned back in my chair. "Calling bullshit on that. There has to be more."

"Not in this office."

"Where then?"

"*If* more exists, Captain Ledger," he said, "it is kept elsewhere."

"Why not here?"

"Considering that this office—my office—deals with unproven conspiracy theories, I think the question answers itself." He paused for a moment. Blinked. Then added, "The main Majestic Program files are in the DoD databases, and you likely already have access to those."

"Sure, all the UFO stuff is there, but I'm looking for something more concrete about these Closers. The ones we encountered were not working for the Majestic Program or the splinter group, Majestic Three. The M3 group were afraid of these Closers. That suggests they understood who and what they were, and none of that is in the main Majestic files on any computer. Trust me when I say, we've looked."

"Yes, I expect so," he said slowly. "You have that fancy computer system. MindReader, as I recall."

"That's a name you shouldn't even know," I said, my tone cooling.

"Of course I would know about MindReader," he replied without flinching. "There are many rumors about it. Theories as to whether it exists. Theories that it might be an extension of the Pangaea or some other, older super-intrusion system. Yes, Captain, I know about that because it is itself a conspiracy theory. A computer system so powerful that no security software can stop it. A system that can intrude anywhere and rewrite the target computer's security software to remove all traces of its presence. There are some who believe that your boss, Mr. Church, uses it to collect blackmail material on members of Congress, the intelligence communities, the military, and the executive branch to keep them from interfering with his machinations."

"Machinations," I said, smiling at the word. He wasn't entirely wrong, though. Church had some kind of leverage and wasn't afraid of using it. Luckily he's one of the true good guys. I'd hate like hell to see MindReader in the hands of someone with a less accurate moral compass.

It surprised me, though, that there were active conspiracy theories about MindReader. I'd have to talk that over with Bug.

"If you could be more specific, Captain," said Humblecut, "then perhaps I might find something closer to what you're looking for."

"Theories on who or what these Closers are," I said.

A slow blink. "There are a lot of theories."

I tapped the folder. "They're not in here. Nor are they on any Department of Defense computer. And, yes, we looked. How's that even possible?"

"The simplest answer is that nearly every encounter with a so-called Man in Black, or Closer, or Operative is merely bad reportage by witnesses who observed agents from various rather ordinary agencies doing routine field work. The style of dress is in keeping with the dress codes in the Secret Service, FBI, and so on. A dress code that was enforced more rigidly in previous decades but which has slackened a bit since. Federal agents going about their work are not particularly chatty, they wear quiet clothes, they don't share information about their cases, and—I think—they enjoy the mystique of being tall, dark, and mysterious."

"Fair enough. But that doesn't cover the Closers I met. And it doesn't explain some of the things that happened during my recent case. There are elements that cannot be explained away by feds doing what feds do. Along the way, my team and I got the impression that others have seen the same *type* of Closer."

He nodded.

"Maybe I should come at this a different way," I said.

"There are many theories," said Humblecut, "but most are parts of other files attached to different investigations."

"Such as?"

He began ticking items off on his fingers. "International espionage with a bias toward information gathering of secret aircraft testing. Surveillance drones. Certain kinds of abductions of important individuals. Assassinations of key people. Off-book operations. And many unusual cases handled by special agents within the FBI."

I whistled the opening notes of the X-Files theme music. He just looked at me like I was a side-dish he hadn't ordered.

"Tell me, sir," I said, hoisting my best deferential and hopeful smile, "can you recommend the best way for me to find what I'm looking for?"

"Can you rephrase *exactly* what it is you really want to know?"

"I take it you're conversant with this kind of stuff. Not just conspiracy theories in general but Men in Black and UFO stuff?"

I saw his mouth silently repeat, *UFO stuff.* "It's my job to be conversant with most of these sorts of things."

"Sure, that makes sense." I was kissing ass. Sort of apologizing for being a smart-ass around someone who wasn't on that wavelength. Like telling dirty jokes at a church social. So, instead I was trying to be nice, even pleasant. "Would it help if I asked some questions? Maybe that'll help shape this quest of mine."

"That's worth a try," he said, warming just a little.

"Are all Men in Black reports tied with aliens?"

"Too general," he said. "Try it again."

Dick, I thought. Aloud I said, "Are all Men in Black reports related to reports of UFOs, sightings of aliens, or claims of alien abductions?"

"No," he said.

"Okay. What percentage of MiB sightings are related to those themes?"

He considered. "Probably sixty percent."

"To which kinds of cases are the remaining forty percent linked?"

Humblecut nodded. "A high percentage of that balance of reports are linked directly or tangentially to incidents of testing of experimental aircraft."

"The stealth fighters and bombers," I suggested.

"Yes."

"In such cases, is it likely the MiBs were government agents trying to manage spin control and limit exposure of classified materials from accidental eyewitnesses?"

He gave me one of those slow blinks, but also another nod. At this rate I was going to get a gold star on my homework.

"You must understand, Captain, that the great majority of cases of *all* kinds that involved sightings of these so-called men in black overlap with nearly *all* incidents of field testing of stealth aircraft, drones, new weapons systems, and so on. Any eyewitness account is investigated by whichever agency has jurisdiction. In many cases they are agents of military intelligence. The clothing is as close to government standard as it gets."

"That would extend to random traffic stops, at-home interviews, and other encounters? Should I assume a lot of that is just feds or military intelligence cats in plainclothes doing routine follow-up? Checking for leaks, managing any story then shared online, whatever?"

"It is safe to make such an assumption."

"And accounts of these MiB's making threats, sometimes even death threats against them or their families?"

"Threats are occasionally a better option than arrest. A threat that is taken seriously may upset someone, but it doesn't destroy the actual lives of those people. I can show you policy papers and established protocols that bear this out."

"True. I've done that myself."

"That's hardly surprising."

It was not meant as a dig nor did I take it that way. Like the saying goes, being a good guy doesn't always go with being nice.

"Wht percentage of these Men in Black incidents are unexplained?"

"One in five hundred," he said.

"Is that a guess?"

"An informed one, yes."

"Which would make the actual percentage number what…?"

"Going how far back?"

"How far do the files go?"

"You would be surprised."

"Try me," I said.

"The first recorded case of a man in black clothes in a case related to national security predates this country by eight years. Summer of 1768."

-3-

"You're shitting me," I said.

He gave a disapproving sniff. "It is possible the incident is bad reportage from experiments with hot air balloons." He studied my face. "You don't believe that?"

"I used to go hot air ballooning when I was a cop in Baltimore. Woman I was dating had a business taking tourists up over Chesapeake Bay. She wrote a book on it. According to that book, the first untethered hot air balloon test was in 1783."

"Correct. That was the first test recorded by the newspapers of the time, and that's what went into the history books. However, the British military was experimenting with them in what is now Cape May, New Jersey as early as 1762 for possible use in the Seven Years War. I should not have to tell a soldier that military R and D runs years ahead of when the public becomes aware of it. Many of the UFO sightings in the late 1990s and early 2000s were because civilians saw prototype drones. It's the same thing."

I grunted. "And the man in black in that instance?"

"An intelligence agent working for the Crown. He wore dark clothes and a dark cloak. Not, as I understand it, actually black, but dark and nondescript. He was also a polyglot—you know what that is?"

"*Ya znayu, chto eto,*" I said in Russian and then again in Spanish. "*Sé lo que es.*"

He looked mildly impressed. Gold star for sure. "So, when you dig into this kind of an investigation, you have to pause to appreciate the *scope* of it. Men—and in many cases women—dressed appropriately for discrete investigations, have been used by governments as long as there *have* been governments. There were likely corollaries in Mesopotamia, among the Aztecs, and on the payroll of Alexander the Great."

"So, basically spies and cops?"

"Of one kind or another."

"Makes sense," I said. "But what explains those cases where no agency is known to have been involved?"

He spread his hands. "Could be anything. Foreign agents. Investigators following a case outside of their jurisdiction and therefore not including mention of a specific incident on their field reports. And there are times when people see what they want to see. A paranoid person will see threats and enigmatic phenomenon everywhere they look."

"How does any of that explain the MPPs?" I asked. "The technology of those handguns does not align with anything we know about."

"Depends on who 'we' are," said Humblecut.

"People like me," I said. "People who work for groups like the DMS. Mr. Church has a clearance level that doesn't even have a name. He knows where to look. He has MindReader. There is nothing about those guns in any database attached to the United States government, the many intelligence agencies, or the military. You are, in fact, the very first person to now about them outside of our group and what *used* to be Majestic Three before we burned it to the ground."

Humblecut blinked. Paused for a long time. Blinked again. "And yet, as you say, I know about them.

"How exactly did that come about? You have a file folder full of photos of them. How is that possible?"

"The photos are sent to my office precisely because no one knows anything about them, Captain," he said. "There is nowhere else to put such things."

"Odd that there is no reference to your folder in any agency's database."

"Yes," he said, "that is odd."

"And you have no opinion beyond that?"

"I do not."'

"Do you have a theory?"

"I have fifty," he said. "None of them worth much because even my own attempts to do further research hit the same dead ends as yours."

"Try me."

"Well, alien technology is the low-hanging fruit," he said.

"Still not convinced of aliens," I said. "It's a distance thing. My high school science teacher beat us over the head with Relativity. Einstein's thing about not being able to go faster than light is a ticking point. And there's the whole 'space is big' thing."

"There are competing theories. Folded space, warp drive, transposition—what you would call teleportation. Also, it is not inconceivable that a more advanced and significantly older species used generational colony ships to reach Earth. Such ships could take hundreds or even thousands of years to cross the distance."

"Maybe. That theory doesn't hold water because if they took that long, why come here? Telescopes would let them see an older Earth, right? Images travel at or lower than the speed of light. They'd see a planet way before the rise of technology. At *most* they'd see the pyramids, if they knew where to look." I shook my head. "No, I'm not in the camp that believes in little green men."

"Gray is more common to conspiracy theorists," he said. "And the green aliens aren't small. The reptilians—and, again, this is according to theories—are human-sized predatory creatures who would not have come here for any peaceful purpose."

"I know, I know," I said, laughing. "I got the full account of all of that when our recent case got started. My girlfriend thinks they're not so much from *out there* but from next door."

"Ah," he said, "inter-dimensional rather than interstellar travel. Yes. It relies upon the concept of a multiverse or an omniverse."

"Yes."

Humblecut blinked. "Your lady friend is clever. As theories go, it's harder to shoot down using Einstein."

"Junie also thinks that she has some alien DNA, but that's another story."

"Is she gray skinned or green and scaly?" he said, smiling.

"Pale Irish skin with freckles."

"Mm, not sure which planet or dimension that would be from."

"She's out of this world regardless."

"Ah, a man in love," he said, nodding. Then he gave me an appraising look. "Good at your job. Excellent record and you have the trust of Mr. Church, and he is a notoriously hard sell. And the love of an intelligent and complex woman capable of broad thinking. You're a lucky man."

"I'm a frustrated man, Mr. Humblecut," I said. "I don't know where else to go with this. You joked about the reptilians, and we had a moment in our case where a couple of those Closers were injured. Their blood looked green."

"Which is, of course, impossible," he said.

"Since coming to work for Church my list of 'impossible' things has grown a lot shorter."

"No doubt."

I glanced around. "I expect the same is true with you."

"I have learned to keep an open mind," he said.

We sat with that for a moment. I tried not to count the seconds between his blinks.

"Then where do I go next?" I asked.

Humblecut reached across the desk, took the folder, considered it for a moment, and dropped it onto a stack of equally old and dusty files next to his desk.

"If I may offer advice, Captain…?"

"Oh, please do."

"I'd let it drop."

"Drop?"

"There are no trails left to follow. Your computer expert has come up dry, and if you had any even marginally useful leads you would not have resorted to visiting me down here."

But I shook my head. "I can't drop it."

"Why   not?"

"The Closers might have been working for a group that threatened to destroy the outer wall of the Cumbre Vieja volcano on Isla de La Palma in the Canary Islands. If sufficient explosive force was used at the right point, you'd break off the western half of the volcano, which would dump five hundred cubic kilometers of rock as a gravitational landslide and smash down into the Atlantic Ocean. That would send a six-hundred-meter-tall wave across the ocean at six-hundred-twenty-one miles per hour. You'd lose the whole African coast in the first hour. Southern England a couple of hours later. And then in five, six hours it would hit the eastern seaboard of North America. By then it would be thirty to sixty meters high, but that's more than enough to wipe out Boston, New York, maybe as far inland as Philadelphia…all the way down to Miami. Call it fifty million people wishing that evolution hadn't taken away their gills."

"Yes," he said. "Tell me, did you believe this threat?"

"Yes."

"But they did not act on it."

"It wasn't like that. They wanted something from us. My group wanted to find it for our own reasons. Their goals and ours coincided. But we didn't cave to their attempt at extortion."

He tilted his head to one side and studied me. "This thing that they wanted, would that be the Majestic Black Book?"

"How the fuck…?" I began, then eased off. Even Bug had heard of the book. And it *was* a conspiracy theory going back years. I met Junie Flynn because she'd podcasted about it. So, I nodded. "Yeah."

"And you found it," he said.

I shrugged.

"You found it," Humblecut said more certainly. "And you returned it to these Closers?"

"More or less."

"And nothing was done as a result. No destruction."

"So far."

"Do you think there might be more to come? Some ruse or sneak attack?"

I had to give that a little thought, then began slowly shaking my head. "No."

"Why not?"

"Hard to say."

"Try."

"They played fair. So did we."

Humblecut nodded. "That is not dissimilar to what some of these Men in Black have done throughout history. Trying to prevent a disaster by any means necessary. Even to the point of threatening repercussions."

"I guess…"

"Doesn't sound like these Closers were particularly evil. Harsh, perhaps. Brusk. Possibly even desperate. But not pernicious."

"Maybe."

I stood up. "Still not going to let it drop, though. It's not who I am."

Humblecut did not rise. He merely nodded.

And blinked.

"Please be careful out there, Captain Ledger," he said.

And I left his office.

-4-

The corridor outside was empty and quiet. I shoved my hands down into my trousers pockets and slouched my way dispiritedly toward the elevator. As I waited for the car, I thought about calling Church. Or Bug. Or Junie. Even took my phone out, but there was no reception that far underground. The doors binged and I stepped in, still poking at my phone, and hit the button for the first floor. The doors had almost shut when a hand darted out, caught the black rubber safety gasket in time to make them open.

And a guy in a plain black suit who I had not seen anywhere in the hall stepped into the car. He did not look at the display to see which floor I'd picked. He let the doors close.

He was a little shorter than me, slim, and slightly hunched. His hair was dark, skin pale, and he wore sunglasses.

Inside. Nine floors down.

I shifted my weight to the balls of both feet. I didn't like this at all. Maybe I was wired from what I'd been talking about, but even so. Man in black. Now? Here?

"You were given good advice, Captain Ledger," he said without turning. "I hope you are smart enough to heed it."

The elevator had just begun to rise when he reached out and pressed the sub-nine and sub-seven buttons at the same time and the elevator stopped. I slapped my sportscoat flap back and made a grab for my gun, which— of course—I had checked at the security desk upstairs.

He was fast.

Dear lord he was fast.

He turned around, caught my wrist in one hand, and clamped the other around my throat, slamming me back against the wall.

I am not much for hesitation.

I simultaneously kicked him in the balls and struck him in the throat with a two-knuckle punch just off center of his Adam's apple. He should have collapsed down, cupping his nuts and trying to suck in a breath of air.

Instead…he showed absolutely no pain or even discomfort. With that one hand he raised me to my toes and then off the motherfucking floor. I am over six feet and better than two hundred pounds. A strong man would need a solid two-handed grip to lift me. He did it like I weighed less than a half-grown bunny. His grip was hard as iron, but he was trying to hold me, not kill me. And I think he could have crushed my windpipe if he'd wanted.

I wasn't feeling as passive. I kicked him. Over and over again. Real goddamn hard. I used my free elbow to chop down on the inside of the arm that held me up. It was like hitting iron that was wrapped in vulcanized rubber. Then he released my wrist, darting one hand beneath his suitcoat, and pulled out a microwave pulse pistol. He pressed the four prongs against my cheekbone.

"Let this drop, Captain Ledger," he said.

I used my free hand to hit him in the face. A lot. I smashed the temple piece of his sunglasses, a move that usually shatters the nose. The glasses broke. The skin around his nose tore.

And green blood welled out of the wound. He pulled me forward so that we were almost nose to nose. The torn skin hung open in a flap and beneath it I could see.

Green.

Scales.

"We will not ask again," he said.

Then he slammed me backward into the wall with such shocking force that the world spun, fireworks detonated all around me, and then it all went black.

-5-

I woke in the backseat of my own car.

It was full dark.

I felt like shit. My throat hurt, my neck hurt, my back hurt, and the rest of me ached. It was a weird feeling, too. My hair felt loose, my skin felt wrong, and all my teeth feel crooked.

Took me a couple of minutes to sort myself out.

Then it all came rushing back. Everything. Humblecut, the folder with pictures, our discussion, and…the goddamn man in black.

Two seconds later I was out of my car, running toward the entrance to the Pentagon, my heart thumping wildly. I used credentials and threats to get inside. A guard wanted to come with me down to sub-nine, and I said something to him—I really don't remember what, exactly—and he went pale and decided he had other matters requiring his full attention.

I wished I had a gun or knife. Or anything. The elevator dropped slowly down, down, down. There was a soft *ping* and the doors opened.

The hall was empty.

I crept along it, checking every side door, finding them all locked, the offices behind the window glass darkened. There was one office with a light on. I turned the knob, then kicked the door and rushed in.

Mr. Humblecut was behind his desk. It looked like he was in exactly the same position as when I'd left. He blinked slowly.

"I'm surprised to see you back here, Captain," he said mildly. "Did you forget something?"

"What. The fuck. Is going on?"

"With…?"

"Don't mess with me," I warned. "Not even remotely in the mood for it."

"I am sure I don't know what you're talking about," he said. "And I would appreciate you knocking next time."

"In about three seconds I'm going to be knocking your head against the top of your desk. I'll keep doing that until I get an answer to what the hell just happened."

Humblecut leaned back in his chair. "To what end, Captain? I gave you the information I had available to share. There is nothing else here in my office that will be of value to you."

"Who—or *what*—was that son of a bitch in the elevator?"

He blinked again. "He is exactly who—or what—you think he is."

"I…I cut his face."

"Yes."

"He bled green."

"I expect so."

"The skin was a…a…"

"The word you're fishing for, Captain, is organic artificial skin suit."

I stared at him. "Then you know…?"

"Know what? That there are people on this world who share a different biology? Different physiology? Different place of origin? Of course I know. I manage all of the information on those subjects that requires special handling."

My mouth went dry. "Are you…?"

"We do not need to discuss that, Captain."

Then, before I could act, he reached for something that had been hidden behind one of the stacks of folders on his desk. He raised it and pointed the four curved prongs at me.

"I will only say this once more, Captain Ledger. I like you. I respect you. Certain parties have taken note of you and how you handled things during the Majestic Black Book incident. No one that I personally know bears any animus toward you. But we would like it if you let this matter drop. Now, and completely."

The MPP looked like a toy, but I knew its power.

"How *can* I drop it?"

"How can you *not*? Not everyone you meet is your enemy, Captain Ledger."

With his free hand he touched some fitting on the MPP, changing a setting. He blinked again and then I heard, *TOK!*

-6-

And I woke up again in the back seat of my car.

Dawn's early light was just beginning to paint the horizon. The whole night was gone. Lost to me.

I almost went back inside.

Almost.

How can I drop it?

How can you not?

I got out of the car, opened the driver's door, got behind the wheel and thought about what happened before Humblecut fired that pistol. He had blinked. Same slow speed as before, but different. That time his eyelids had closed the wrong way. Not up and down.

They went side-to-side.

"Jesus H. Christ," I said.

I sat there and watched the sun rise.

No, I didn't go back inside. Instead, I drove back home. Maybe I'd drop this. First, though, I wanted to talk with Bug and Church. And Junie.

Or maybe I wouldn't say a thing to anyone.

Wasn't sure.

I drove in silence as the sun rose over Arlington, Virginia.

We hope that you enjoyed this title and look forward to many more to come. Please, leave us a review! Reviews matter to all of our authors.

And don't forget to check out the latest edition of **Car Wars**

http://www.sjgames.com/car-wars/

Or the other amazing titles from
Steve Jackson Games

http://www.sjgames.com

…or the latest in the Car Warriors: Autoduel Chronicle fiction series.
https://threeravenspublishing.com/car-warriors-autoduel-chronicles/

Take a look at some of our other award-winning series at
https://threeravenspublishing.com/series-universes/

Visit us at https://www.threeravenspublishing.com and sign up for our
newsletter for the latest and greatest news on upcoming titles and events.

Other series and titles you might enjoy.

DECLAN FINN
DECLAN FINN
DECLAN FINN
DECLAN FINN
Demons are Forever
LOVE AT FIRST BITE
Honor at Stake
LOVE AT FIRST BITE ONE
Live and Let Bite
LOVE AT FIRST BITE THREE
Good to the Last Drop
LOVE AT FIRST BITE FOUR
The Dragon Award Nominated Series
FREE on Kindle Unlimited!

AVAILABLE ON
AMAZON
JOINT TASK FORCE
13
INTER CAELUM ET INFERNUM
HOLDING THE LINE
BETWEEN HEAVEN AND HELL
13

MYSTERY,
MAGIC &
MAYHEM
WITH A TWIST
OF ROMANCE
J.F. POSTHUMUS
ON AMAZON
FIND ME
B.E.N.T.
BIOLOGIC
ENHANCED
NASCENT
TALENT

THE RAVEN
AND
THE CROW
MICHAEL K. FALCIANI
FIND ME
ON AMAZON

STARFLIGHT
IT CAME FROM THE
TRAILER PARK

3R
Three Ravens Publishing
Are you looking for fun, new fiction?
The Written Word Will Never Be The Same…
https://www.threeravenspublishing.com
Veteran Owned and Operated

You can also keep up to date with our latest release announcements on Scifi.radio and get some of the best fandom programing on the planet.

Scifi for your Wifi

And don't forget to check out our other Sponsors and Affiliates

A southern Appalachian jewel for craft beer lovers, Buck Bald Brewing offers something for everyone. With delicious, locally brewed beverages from across the spectrum, Buck Bald Brewing offers craft brews that are consistently amazing.

From the dark and smooth Shesquatch Scottish ale, to the intense hops of Hippibilly IPA, to the puckering sour of the blackberry and cinnamon in Berry My Heart at the Trailer Park, and more than 60+ rotating brews, you'll find what you're looking for and more.

With smiling faces behind the bar ready to help you find your next favorite brew, a constantly rotating selection of delicious craft beverages, toe-tapping tunes always playing, and the biggest games on TV, you can kick your feet up in either Copperhill, Tennessee or Murphy, North Carolina and immerse yourself in the Buck Bald Brewing experience. So, come out, fill a pint, fill a growler, and fill your mind at your new favorite family-owned craft brewery.

To discover more visit us at buckbaldbrewing.com or follow us on Facebook @buckbaldbrewing and @buckbaldbrewingmurphy.

Vesper Wren's
TRAILER PARK
PIXIE
PUNCH
· A PEACH STRAWBERRY SELTZER ·
BUCK BALD BREWING

BRAXTON HICKS
MIDNIGHT MOCHA MILK
STOUT
BUCK BALD BREWING